HMP
BlackRock

By
GS Burroughs

Poison Pen Publishing
Independently publishing the crime novels of Mr Gary S
Burroughs

HMP BlackRock
First published February 2023

Acknowledgements

Once again I am eternally grateful to my sisters, Sue and Lynn, for kindly passing a critical eye over my manuscript.

Thank you to everyone who said kind words about my first novel. I have lived with the Lovelace sisters for many years and I'm delighted to be able to share the adventure with you. Stay with me! The journey has only just begun.

I must also thank Katie for her constant encouragement and for not playing her music too loud when I am hiding in my little room. Our adventures together inspire me to carry on when the weight of doubt and lack of money teeter me on the brink of giving it all up.

I hope you enjoy this next step in the Lovelace journey. A word of caution though. As the writer, I will never lie to you. If I say it happened, it did.

My characters may not be so honest...

One

Captain Luke Miller sat on the flight deck of the Sikorsky 92 and watched with growing anxiety as clouds, heavy with winter storms, gathered on the western horizon.

It was the last flight today, and the approaching storms made him nervous. It was only a short trip, barely an hour of his time, but he had a date with the cute young barmaid from the hotel and was keen to get off the island in time for a few gins and a night of unadulterated passion. No one in their right mind wanted to get stuck on Devil Island for too long.

His Majesty's Prison BlackRock was no more than thirty miles off the West Coast of Scotland. It was a bleak and desolate rock in the North Atlantic, and even in the best of summers, it could be a nightmare to navigate. High winds were a serious problem, but by and large, the Sikorsky helicopter handled them with consummate ease. Winter storms, however, were something else.

'Do you have the weather report?' He asked.

Flight Lieutenant Tom Russo looked up from the pre-flight checklist and slipped a piece of paper over to his Captain.

The Met Office weather report made for grim reading. A series of North Atlantic storms were gathering nearly a hundred miles away and were moving towards the island in tandem with each other. It was likely that they would collide right over BlackRock sometime later that day. When they did, all flights would be grounded.

Captain Miller looked at the Breitling that adorned his wrist and breathed an audible sigh. They were cutting it fine. Too fine.

'Everything okay?' Russo asked.

'Keen to get going,' Miller replied. 'Sooner we get there, the sooner we can get back.'

'Date?'

'The barmaid from the hotel.'

'The redhead or the blonde?' Russo asked.

'The red.'

Russo nodded in appreciation. 'Nice.'

She was. Captain Miller glanced across the sky and his anxiety rose. There was a serious risk he wouldn't get back to see her and the thought annoyed him.

***

Liam Swift felt the anxiety too. The Head of Mainland Operations paced his office and ground his teeth till his jaw hurt. He had read the same weather report that Captain Miller had seen, but it wasn't that that raised his blood pressure. He was sure he could safely get the helicopter to the island and return it to the mainland before the storms hit. But it didn't matter if he couldn't get it back. The pilots could bunk up in the accommodation block until the storms passed. No, what bothered him was the passenger list.

Liam stepped into the operations centre and walked to where the office manager was sitting. She looked up as he approached.

He held out his hand and said, 'passenger manifest?'

She paused for barely a second before saying, 'I usually tell my children that requests of any kind are generally followed with a "please."'

'Sorry, Alice. If I may have the manifest, please.'

She passed over a sheet of paper she had written a few minutes ago. She understood his stress. There were some powerful people on the list.

'You worry too much.' Alice said.

'You don't worry enough,' Liam replied. 'Wait till your kids are teenagers. That'll change.' He glanced at the passenger manifest. 'Why is this handwritten?'

Alice gave him a look that explained it all. The computer systems were riddled with bugs. She had spent the last month doing little else than trying to fix them.

'I can't seem to connect to the printer. I've raised a ticket.'

Liam looked around the office. 'Where's Gerry?'

Gerry Holt was the office IT genius. He was also BlackRocks' IT genius. It was his software that ran the systems both on the island and the mainland.

'He's on BlackRock.'

'Why? Who sent him there?' Liam demanded.

'You did.' Alice said.

'Oh. Right. Probably for the best.'

Where Gerry was concerned, it was usually for the best. The Island's Operations Manager would likely send him back in a day or so. There was only so much of Gerry Holt a normal human being could take without wanting to kill him. There were already enough killers on the island as it was.

Liam ran his eyes over the manifest and his heart skipped a beat. At the top of the list Alice had written, "Ethan Mackay."

Ethan Mackay was the darling of the popular press and the nemesis of prison reformers across the globe. He was a Scottish billionaire who lived the most flamboyant lifestyle and was the guest of honour at some of the world's most prestigious dinner tables. He had been wined and dined by royalty and presidency alike and had charmed them both in equal measure. His father had died when he was a young man, and when he was fourteen his mother had been murdered by a man who had just been released from prison. It was a defining moment in his life and one that shaped what was to follow. He studied business at University in Edinburgh and made his first million before he turned eighteen. His star had risen to the top by the time he was twenty-one. Everything he touched turned to gold. By twenty-five, he had opened his first private prison in Kent, soon followed by three more across the country. He bought BlackRock island ten years ago and proposed that he build a prison to house those prisoners that society had deemed too violent and depraved ever to be released. It was the place where Evil was sent to die. It was no wonder the staff called the place 'Devil's Island'.

Liam had met the man more than once and felt he had good reason to be concerned. Ethan Mackay expected perfection in everything and everyone and had a low threshold for tolerating those that didn't perform to his standards. He could fly into the most terrific rages at the drop of a hat, and Liam had borne the brunt of several of those. Liam's anxiety increased knowing that Mackay was flying to the island to inspect the progress that had been made since the first prisoners had started to be transferred there two months ago. There was no margin for error. Everything had to be perfect.

"Grace Mahone." Mackay's assistant was next on the list. He had met her a few times. She was cute and intelligent. Not just academically brilliant, but life smart. He often wondered why she continued to work for Mackay. He had heard how he spoke to her, which bordered on bullying. And yet, she always smiled and carried on. Perhaps she saw a good side to him? There had to be one. Mackay was one of the biggest donors to charities in the country. He was quite the philanthropist. He gave away millions of pounds every year. He couldn't be all bad, surely?

Then there was "Sir Malcolm Zambert."

Liam held the manifest in front of Alice's face. 'Who the fuck is Sir Malcolm Zambert?'

Alice took the sheet of paper from Liam and said, 'You know fine well that's Sir Malcolm Lambert, Member of Parliament for East Mercia. That's an "L", not a "Z." She took her pen, amended the manifest, and handed it back to Liam.

Sir Malcolm Lambert was another reason Liam's anxiety was at an all-time high. He was a hugely respected Member of Parliament and was considered by some to be the de-facto Father of the House. When he spoke, people listened. Ironically, he had campaigned for years to prevent BlackRock from being built. He almost succeeded until one day, he just changed his mind, and the legislation required to construct the prison floated effortlessly through Parliament.

Then there was "Esther Friedman," a continual thorn in Ethan Mackay's side and constant critic. She, too, was hugely respected. She was a journalist for The Times and had a brilliant talent for uncovering secrets that people preferred to be left hidden. She had largely failed with Mackay's private life, but now and then, she found bits of dirt in his business affairs. Liam was surprised to see her on the manifest. She hated Mackay's ideas regarding prisons and prison reform. He was a hard-liner; she most definitely was not. He remembered reading an article she had written about a riot in one of Mackay's Young Offenders' institutions where one of the young prisoners had been beaten to death by a prison guard. She ran a series of articles that exposed some of the shortcomings of Mackay's prisons and, in particular, about some of the people he employed. Esther Friedman was no friend of Ethan Mackay. Perhaps Mackay was trying to change her mind?

'Who's this?' Liam asked as he came upon a name he didn't immediately recognise. 'Miss Lovelace? No, wait a minute. That's not Lucy Lovelace, is it?'

Alice nodded. 'She's the police officer that caught that serial killer. The Night Prowler, I think they called him. He's here, you know. And her father.'

Liam felt a little silly. Of course, that's why he recognised the name. Jack Lovelace was a prisoner at BlackRock. Jack Lovelace, the Cherwell Valley Strangler. He remembered the case. When the police went to arrest him at his secluded farmhouse, he cut his wife's throat and set fire to the house, hoping to kill himself and his children. There were two girls, if he remembered rightly. They couldn't have been very old at the time. Sometimes, when he felt the pressures of work, he remembered people like Jack Lovelace and felt pride that people like him were sent to places like BlackRock, where they could do no more harm.

'What's she doing on the island?' Liam asked. The prison hadn't formally been opened yet, and the prisoner transfer from jails across the UK was a work in progress. As a consequence, visitors to the island had yet to be authorised.

'Special dispensation.' Alice said. 'She has some powerful friends in important places.'

Liam nodded. He remembered the flurry of emails that flew back and forth from Whitehall. It was just a pity she had to fly to the island today, what with everything else he had to worry about.

'She's not staying. She'll be on the flight back.' Alice continued. 'Weather permitting...' She left the words hanging there, a metaphorical Sword of Damocles hanging portentously over Liam's head.

Liam let out a sigh. He didn't need the stress. He walked over to the window that looked out across the helicopter pad and watched as the wind sock lifted and dropped in the wind. It had picked up considerably in the last hour, and the clouds were beginning to look dark and moody. As he stood there, rain began to fall, and droplets gathered on the window pane.

'Ethan's here,' Alice called out as a large black car pulled up at the front gate, and the barrier was lifted. From where she sat, she could see out across the operation's office, the front entrance and the helicopter pad. There was very little that went on in Mainland Operations that Alice didn't see.

'Right. I suppose we'd better get started then!'

***

'Do you have any identification?'

Lovelace handed over her passport to the young man with thick-rimmed spectacles and a spotty face. He looked barely old enough to be out of school, and she suddenly felt very old.

'Thank you. You will be subject to a physical search at the prison, which a female officer will carry out.' The young man passed a sheet of paper over the desk to Lovelace and said, 'this is a list of proscribed items that must not be taken into the prison. If you have any of these items, you should dispose of them now.'

The list was comprehensive. Drugs of any kind, including paracetamol; weapons of any kind or anything that may be used as a weapon, such as pens or pencils; alcohol, cigarettes and vapes; food and drink and so on.

It forbade pretty much everything except the clothes she was wearing.

Lovelace shook her head and said she wasn't carrying anything like that.

'If you are found to have any items on the proscribed list, your entry to the prison will be revoked, and you will be removed back to the mainland on the first available flight.' The young man continued, 'if you have a mobile phone, it will be taken from you at the prison gate and returned to you on your exit. Have you any questions?'

Lovelace shook her head. 'No, I don't think so.'

'Good,' the young man said. 'If you would care to place your belongings on the tray and step into the scanner for me.'

The security at BlackRock departures resembled that of airport security, except shinier and more expensive.

Lovelace dropped her car keys and purse onto a tray which was pushed through an X-Ray device, and she turned and stepped into a tube-like structure that reminded her of a single-person revolving door.

'If you could raise your arms above your head as shown in the picture in front of you.'

Lovelace raised her hands, and a peculiar blue light spun around her.

'Okay, you can step through.'

The young man got off his seat and handed Lovelace a small parcel. 'Ear defenders.' He said by way of explanation. 'The pilot may well have the engine started as you board. You can take them off once inside the aircraft; it's perfectly quiet. If you'd like to grab your belongings and take a seat in the waiting room. There's tea and coffee if you like. We're just waiting on Mr Mackay and his assistant. We'll call for you when we're about to board.'

Lovelace took her belongings and walked into the waiting room. It wasn't exactly as she had imagined. Like everything else she had seen, no expense had been spared. The waiting room was like no other first-class lounge she had ever seen. There were comfortable sofas and recliners, coffee and tea-making machines, a buffet of luxury food laid out on a long oak table, bottles of whiskey and wine, a selection of liqueurs, and a tall glass-fronted fridge filled with Champagne. A floor-to-ceiling window looked out across the helipad at the far end of the room. Raindrops were beginning to gather. An older gentleman in a tweed jacket was talking loudly on his mobile phone and pacing backwards and forwards across the window. He walked and spoke like a man in the latter stages of life, but Lovelace knew full well that he was a crafty old fox merely disguised as a harmless old man. She had seen his photographs in the newspapers and had often heard him speak. The old man was Sir Malcolm Lambert MP, MBE and a host of other initials she knew he had but couldn't remember.

He had a booming, deep voice that carried clearly across the lounge.

'No, no, no!' He bellowed. 'Mackay's got me on one of those bloody fact-finding missions at BlackRock. Yes, the prison. Yes, the island one. They've got some prisoners locked up there at last, and he wants to show them off like some modern-day bloody Barnum. No, that bloody woman from the Times. Yeah, that old hack. That's right. That's the one.' He laughed, and his portly figure jiggled.

Lovelace noticed that the only other person in the room was a well-dressed middle-aged woman holding a glass of champagne. She held her free hand to Lovelace and said, 'Esther Friedman. That bloody woman from the Times.'

'The hack?' Lovelace asked and immediately regretted it.

Esther smiled. 'Indeed! The hack! I've been called worse and by better men. Would you like a drink?'

Without waiting for an answer, she poured Lovelace the remains of the bottle of Champagne and handed it to her.

'And who might you be?'

Lovelace was about to answer when Liam Swift appeared in the doorway.

'Oh, good, you're all here. That helps. Ethan Mackay has just arrived, so I suspect we shall be boarding shortly. I'll get one of the girls to come and get you in a moment. Do we all have coats? I'm afraid it's beginning to pick up a bit out there.' He was about to turn and leave when he noticed Lovelace. 'Oh. You must be Lucy Lovelace.' He held out his hand and shook hers.

'Yes, I suppose I must be.' Lovelace said with no hint of sarcasm.

'Lovelace?' Esther said. 'Lucy Lovelace? Well, that explains why *you're* here! I did a piece on your father a few years ago.'

Lovelace nodded. 'I know. I read it.'

'And you had that thing recently in Oxford. The serial killer thing. The Night Prowler. You caught him, didn't you? Saved some girl's life. You're quite the hero. I think he's here. Isn't that right, Mr Swift? The killer Miss Lovelace caught. He's here, at BlackRock?'

'Adam Sinclair? Yes, that's right. Had him transferred a few days ago. Don't think he'll ever leave.'

'We should arrange a reunion,' Esther declared. 'Now, wouldn't that be interesting! I could do a piece for the paper!'

Lovelace smiled. That would certainly be an interesting reunion!

Sir Malcolm boomed something unintelligible down his phone and dropped the device into his pocket. He looked across at Liam. 'Bloody secretaries. Never a moment's peace! I see Mackay's arrived. Shouldn't we be getting on?'

Liam glanced at his watch and then over his shoulder into the arrival's lounge. Ethan Mackay was chatting to Alice and barking orders at his PA. In a few minutes, he would have poured all his passengers into the belly of the helicopter and transferred his stress and anxiety over to Tony Kellerman, Head of Island Operations for HMP BlackRock.

It couldn't come a moment too soon.

Two

Captain Miller drew back gently on the helicopter's controls and steadily increased power. The machine rose effortlessly from the floor, and he held her there for a few seconds while his eyes scanned the dials in front of him. Satisfied that all was well, he increased the power even more, tilted the nose of the aircraft down slightly and adjusted the pitch of the blades so that he achieved forward momentum. They had soared to five hundred feet in a few minutes, and the dark North Atlantic seas stretched before them. Captain Miller turned to his co-pilot and smiled. In less than twenty minutes, they would be on BlackRock, and an hour later, they would be on their way back. His weekend was beginning to look up.

Lovelace sat opposite Sir Malcolm at the back of the aircraft, who had taken the opportunity to lay his head back and fall asleep. The cabin was spacious, with seating for at least nineteen people in extreme comfort. The interior felt like the cabin of a luxury jet. The seats were white leather with lace cushions and comfortable armrests. It was surprisingly quiet, too. She could barely hear the noise of the rotors as they powered above her head.

Lovelace sat back in her seat and relaxed. She was finally on her way to BlackRock. There was no going back now. She looked out the window and watched as the sea surged beneath her, now inky black and topped with furious crests of white horses. She had no fear of flying and held a rotary licence herself. She understood the dynamics of helicopter flight, and it fascinated her. Despite that, she couldn't help but imagine what would happen if they were suddenly pitched into the sea. She didn't fancy their chances in the swell below. She smiled.

If they did end up in the ocean, her money would be on herself and Mackay's Personal Assistant. Everyone else was getting a bit old and unfit, even Mackay, whose life of luxury and excess was beginning to tell.

At the front of the cabin sat Grace Mahone and Ethan Mackay. Ethan was dictating something to Grace, who was transcribing directly onto her laptop. Lovelace had heard of Mackay, but few people in the world hadn't. She had never met the man before, but she instantly disliked him. She prided herself on being a good judge of character, and Ethan Mackay came across as the sort of man she wouldn't like. On the other hand, Grace Mahone was just the sort of young woman she liked.

'That's Grace Mahone,' Esther Friedman had said as they had made their way across the helipad to the aircraft. She had slipped her arm through Lovelace's in a conspiratorial manner and pulled her firmly to her side. 'Do you think they are fucking one another?'

Lovelace hadn't been shocked by the bluntness. Little shocked her; she knew Esther's talent for muckraking. Besides, if they were fucking she was sure Esther Friedman already knew about it. There was very little she didn't know about people.

Lovelace guessed Grace to be in her early thirties. She had a friendly face and eyes that shone when she smiled. Her blonde hair was neatly tended and hung in an organised fashion about her lightly made-up face. She was a naturally beautiful woman, Lovelace mused, and only a few years older than herself. There was an aura about her, too. She sensed a determined and strong young woman. Yes, if they ended up in the sea, Grace Mahone and Lovelace would come back out.

Lovelace wasn't sure about Esther Friedman. She reserved judgement on her. She had read a lot of her work in the newspapers, and there was no doubt she was a talented woman, but there was something about her she wasn't sure about. Esther had held firmly onto her arm as they boarded the helicopter and only relinquished her grip when they reached their seats. Esther's annoyance was notable as Sir Malcolm barged past her to sit opposite Lovelace. The old man liked to look at a pretty face and enjoyed the company of young women. Suitably annoyed, Esther sat across the aisle and stared moodily out of the window. Sir Malcolm promptly fell asleep.

Lovelace was still pondering over her fellow passengers when she felt the aircraft begin to descend. She sat closer to the window and pressed her nose to the glass.

BlackRock had been uninhabited since the 1930s when the last tenant was relocated to mainland Scotland. It had stayed that way ever since. Lovelace watched as the island came into view. It was a relatively large rock in the North Atlantic, and Lovelace could see the waves crashing into the dark, granite teeth that edged its southern coast. It was an island of two halves, separated by a vast hill that straddled its waist. At the northern end, Lovelace saw the new prison Mackay built come into view. It was a majestic throwback to the Victorian age with tall, dark walls around its edge and a crenellated top. Despite its look, it was the most sophisticated prison of its kind anywhere in the world. Within those walls were now some of the most evil people in Britain's criminal world. One of those people was Lovelace's father, Jack Lovelace.

The pilot manoeuvred the craft so that it cut an arc over the prison and pointed south, towards the helipad. The prison was lit up in the fading afternoon light, and Lovelace could make out the forbidding structure as it sat on the northern coast, barely four hundred yards from the cliff edge and the stormy North Atlantic ocean.

As the prison fell away behind them, Lovelace watched as the hill that divided the island passed less than two hundred feet below. It was an awe-inspiring hill bordering on a small mountain, and she watched as jagged crevices and sheer cliff edges stuck out of the landscape like prehistoric monsters. What struck Lovelace the most was the newly tarmacked road that snaked through its lower passes and connected the two halves of the island. It felt out of place and unreal.

As they flew over the hill, the southern stretches of the island came into view. In the distance, Lovelace saw what looked like a three-story hotel perched neatly on the south coast, and a few hundred yards along from that was a modern-built mansion house that she guessed to be the Governor's residence. Between the two buildings sat a squat "H" with its landing lights blazing. Lovelace felt the thrust of the aircraft change as the pilot came in to land. Despite the wind, he handled the aircraft expertly, and it was a few short minutes before the helicopter was on the ground and the engines set to idle. Moments later, the rotors stopped spinning, and the door to the cabin was flung open.

She felt the cold first. It rushed into the cabin like an unwelcome guest and harangued the passengers as they alighted. The wind came, too, and buffered them all as they stepped onto the helipad one by one.

Mackay was the first out, followed by Grace. They were approached on the runway by three men dressed in waterproof coats and hi-viz jackets. The first two walked up to Mackay while the third lingered behind.

'Where are the cars, Preece?' Mackay barked. 'They should be here!'

'This way Mr Mackay,' Johnathon Preece gestured, and as he spoke, a fleet of brand new Land Rover Defenders came rushing up. He opened the rear door to the lead car, and Mackay stepped inside. The third man had opened the door to the other side, and Grace was about to walk around and get in when she stopped suddenly and clutched her head. With her free hand, she tugged at her stomach and bent over as if she was about to be sick.

'What the bloody hell's the matter with you?'

Even as she stepped out of the cabin and into the wind, Lovelace caught the inflexion in Mackay's voice. He was a vile man.

'I feel sick.' Grace replied.

'Well, hurry up and get over it, will you? I've wasted enough damn time already today. We need to get on.'

Grace didn't look like she was going to get over it soon. Preece said, 'Perhaps Miss Mahone should stay here while we tour the prison. I can get my wife to take care of her….'

Lovelace felt Esther's arm link through hers as they watched the drama unfold.

'That's John Preece. He's the prison Governor.' Esther explained. 'And that,' she added, 'is the enigmatic Mrs Elouise Preece.'

Lovelace watched as a woman, barely forty years old, stepped out from the mansion house's front door and walked over to the huddle of people. She was a woman who walked with purpose and who seemed to have no fear of Ethan Mackay. She immediately took command.

'Are you all right, Grace?'

'No. I think I'm going to be sick. My head…'

'This is bloody inconvenient.' Mackay barked.

'Yes, I'm sure it is,' Elouise Preece said with no hint of irony or sarcasm. 'I shall take Grace indoors while you continue with the tour. Come along, Grace. Let's have a nice cup of tea.'

She took Grace gently by the arm and slowly walked back to the house.

'Well, get in then!' Mackay said sharply.

John Preece turned and smiled at Esther and Lovelace. 'Miss Lovelace, Miss Friedman, if you would care to step into the next car. Sir Malcolm, would you join Mr Kellerman in the third car.'

Lovelace leant into Esther's ear. 'Who's Kellerman?'

'That's Tony Kellerman. Head of Island Operations.'

Esther stepped up to the second car and waited while the driver opened the rear door for her. Lovelace walked to the other side and climbed in. John Preece waited while all the passengers had embarked before climbing into the back seat of the first car next to Mackay. He braced himself for fifteen minutes of earache. The third man, who had hovered inconspicuously in the background, climbed into the front passenger seat.

Lovelace had taken a keen interest in the third man from the first moment she had seen him. The first two had been pretty nondescript men in their forties who wouldn't have looked out of place in the City of London. They had clipped, well-educated accents and looked like men of importance. The third did not. He was a man who wouldn't have looked out of place in some of the most dangerous places on earth. He had dark eyes and a gaunt, lived-in face and yellowing teeth. Lovelace knew the kind. She had met many of them. She was a damn good judge of character, and she judged him to be of the lowest type.

'Who's the other man?' She asked Esther as she climbed into the lead car.

Esther looked across at Lovelace and followed her eyes. 'That is the island's head of security, Wayne Sampson.'

Lovelace detected a hint of something in the way Esther relayed the information. She gave her a quizzical look.

Esther felt Lovelace's gaze upon her. She said. 'There are many things I could tell you about Mr Sampson; suffice to say that Mackay has expensive lawyers who are quite happy to slap injunctions on the likes of me. Mackay keeps the very best of people at his side. The best lawyers, the best business people, the best accountants and the best crooks. Mr Sampson is most certainly of the latter and one of his most devoted servants. He killed a man once, you know.'

'Really?'

'During a prison riot a few years ago. It was in one of Mackay's early prisons. Sampson was just a guard then, and he beat a prisoner to death with his bare hands. He pleaded self-defence and, in fairness, a prison guard had been killed previously, so the judge looked kindly on the argument, but....'

'But?'

'The young man he killed was barely eighteen, unarmed and defenceless. Some witnesses claimed that Sampson attacked the young man entirely unprovoked.'

'Then how come he was let off?'

'Money.' Esther said. 'When you have Mackay's finances, you can buy anything. And anyone.'

***

Captain Miller was frantically trying to call Mainland Ops on his mobile phone in the helicopter's cockpit.

'I've got no signal. Damn it. Do you?'

Russo shook his head. 'Nope. Nothing.'

Miller's weekend was fast becoming a hopeless dream. As they had shut down the aircraft and waited while the passengers alighted, something had gone wrong with the instrument panel. For a long minute, all the electronic equipment failed. There was nothing, not even a single light on the panel. It had come back intermittently, but they had lost their Radar and GPS devices. Miller was frantically trying to call the Mainland, but the mobile phone signal was typically non-existent.

'Fuck!' Miller started to unbuckle himself from the pilot's seat. 'I'll put a call in from the office. You might as well go and make coffee.'

Russo nodded. He watched as Miller stepped out of the cockpit and headed over to the three-story building ahead. The top floor of the building had an office which also doubled as an observation tower for the helipad. The rain had started to fall even harder, and the sky was darkening by the minute. He doubted the mainland could get an engineer out before the storm hit and looked like they would be staying on the island for a bit. Russo chuckled. Miller was going to be pissed!

Three

The small motorcade skirted the mansion house and the staff accommodation block before joining the newly made tarmacked road. The road snaked ahead like a black mamba, its venomous head obscured by a low mist that hugged the mountainside a mile or so ahead. After a few minutes, they were deep into the hillside. Lovelace turned to look behind her. She could no longer see the Mansion House, and low clouds similarly obscured the view on either side of her. She felt the pressure in her ears as they rose higher, and the vehicle twisted and turned as they followed the road over the mountainside and down the other side.

'You have a sister, I understand.' Esther said.

Lovelace felt that the question was loaded with more than just simple curiosity. People like Esther were devious and conniving. Lovelace would need to be careful with her words.

'I do.'

'Zoe, isn't it?'

Before she could answer, Esther went on, 'You were fortunate. Your father nearly killed you both. It must have been such a shock to you two girls, seeing your mother killed in front of you like that. Very traumatic. These things leave scars.'

Lovelace instinctively felt for the scars on her arm. It was an automatic response. The fire had burned fiercely and had caught the sleeve of her blouse during her rescue. And her mother. Her poor, dear mother. He had robbed them of so much. He had robbed so many people of their lives and their loves. He had inflicted so much pain.

'It surprises me to see you here. They haven't authorised visitors to the island yet.'

Carefully, Lovelace said, 'I know some powerful people who owe me a thing or two.'

Esther eyed Lovelace and said, 'yes. I understand your sister knows one or two powerful people.'

Tread carefully, Lovelace told herself. She's a talented and respected investigative journalist who knows the tricks of interrogation. She's mining. Slowly she said, 'I wouldn't know. I haven't seen my sister for years.'

'Oh, dear,' Esther said. 'Are you estranged?'

You know full well we are... Instead, Lovelace said, 'We live in opposing worlds. They aren't compatible.'

'Yes. I've heard some things about your sister. People mention her in whispered breaths. I've come close to finding out a few things about her, but she's elusive. It's almost as though she's a myth, but then we know that is not the case, don't we?'

Lovelace let the question hover in the space between them.

'As soon as one gets a witness, they change their minds. Or,' Esther added mysteriously, 'they disappear.'

Lovelace said nothing. It was better not to feed the low flame of journalistic interest.

'What surprises me,' Lovelace said, 'is seeing you here. You are no fan of Ethan Mackay's. I've read some of your stuff. I'd even go so far as to say you're his number one nemesis.'

Esther nodded. 'I fundamentally disagree with everything that man stands for. This island prison is a dark stain on our country's proud justice system. We're separating people and treating them like animals. I can't help but wonder about the character of a man who believes that treating people like this is the right thing to do. I begin to wonder who's worse. Those he's got imprisoned here or Ethan Mackay.'

'There are some evil people on this island.' Lovelace said.

'Yes,' Esther agreed. 'And not all of them are behind bars.'

***

The lead car crested the brow of a hill and powered out through the low cloud. Ahead of them lay the northern half of the island. In the distance, HMP BlackRock's bright lights shone like a beacon in a sea of darkness. Behind that, and far out into the North Atlantic, storm clouds raced towards them.

Mackay was reading through a report Tony Kellerman had handed him as they set off. He closed the file and sniffed.

'Where are we at with the prisoners?' He asked.

'Thirty male prisoners, all of which have whole life tariffs and five women prisoners.' Kellerman had made sure he had kept up to date with everything that he thought Mackay might ask. Mackay demanded perfection in all his employees. He couldn't tolerate slackness.

'Staff?'

'Not yet fully up to staffing levels. But we have some time before we reach one hundred prisoners.'

Mackay looked at Kellerman and asked, 'Why can't we get the staff? Don't we pay enough?'

The pay wasn't the issue, Kellerman thought. It was an extremely generous remuneration package. The problem lay in the shift patterns that the island demanded. Staff worked five twelve-hour shifts over four weeks and had four weeks off before returning. There were two rotations and two teams in each. The hours and living arrangements didn't always suit the best applicants. They had staffed the two rotations with some of the country's least favourable prison officers who had primarily run out of employment opportunities in Government institutions. Mackay was known to turn a blind eye to some of the worst of them. Kellerman looked up at Sampson. He was a case in point. He didn't like Sampson. He didn't like the man one bit.

'I need you to butter up Sir Malcolm,' Mackay said, interrupting Preece's train of thought. 'Rub his ego a bit. The old fellow's feeling the stress of it all. He's getting old. It'll be better coming from you. It will mean more.'

Sir Malcolm had been a staunch opponent of Mackay's from the very beginning. It surprised Preece that Mackay had managed to turn him around. Sir Malcolm was not poor, so he doubted if money had smoothed his conscience. Knowing Mackay, it was something else. Mackay had a habit of holding things over people's heads to get what he wanted. He was a dangerous man to oppose. So it was an even bigger surprise to see Esther Friedman in the party of VIPs.

Carefully Preece said, 'what about the journalist, Miss Friedman?'

Mackay's mouth morphed into a smile. He rarely smiled unless he was trying to win people over or if a news crew had shoved a camera in his face. He knew how to turn it on when needed. But this smile was different. There was something else. It was pernicious and twisted, and the edges of his mouth curled up and shaped the smile into a scowl.

'Leave her to me,' Mackay snarled. 'I have plans for Miss Friedman..'

'And the Lovelace woman?'

'She's here to see her father. Make sure she gets a good impression of the place before she leaves. Can't hurt to have her on our side.'

Preece nodded. Every one of the VIPs was important in their own small way. Sir Malcolm smoothed the Parliamentary process which brought HMP BlackRock into existence and was rightly the most important. Preece worried about Esther Friedman. He had never met her before, but he knew of her reputation. He thought bringing her onto the island had been a mistake, but Mackay had overruled him.

'No. She needs to be here. I need her on BlackRock.'

Preece had obeyed, but it didn't sit easily with him. The Lovelace woman had been a last-minute adjustment to the VIP list. He had initially blocked her journey to the island, but influential people in the background had manoeuvred around him. He reluctantly relented. She had recently been in the news over the Night Prowler incident and the capture of Adam Sinclair. With him and Jack Lovelace in the prison, he was beginning to appreciate that having Lovelace on the island almost amounted to an endorsement of what they were trying to achieve. He would get onto the Press Office later. There was a photo opportunity here, which he wasn't going to let pass.

As he added that to his mental list of things to do, the driver pulled the large vehicle to a standstill outside the front door of HMP BlackRock. The other two cars pulled up behind.

A reception party of prison staff stood waiting underneath the large canopy that overhung the front door to the prison. They rushed to the car doors wielding heavy umbrellas that shook and flexed in the wind. The rain was driving down hard, and the small party of VIPs were herded into the foyer, where they stood in a small huddle, shaking off the water that had evaded the umbrellas.

John Kellerman stood at the head of the group and said, 'Ladies and Gentlemen, if you wouldn't mind, we will need to pass through security before we can begin the tour. Sir Malcolm, if you would like to come over first.'

The portly Sir Malcolm looked aggrieved to be treated like an ordinary visitor. Still, Sampson, the Head of Security, was not a man that looked like he could be convinced to enter into a negotiation, so he reluctantly allowed himself to be subjected to a thorough search. When it was completed, he stepped through a large metal detector and into the next staging area.

One by one, the VIPs were led through the process until they were all standing on the other side of the security gate.

Preece approached Lovelace and quietly took her to one side. In his soft voice, he said, 'Miss Lovelace, I wonder if you wouldn't mind joining us on a tour of the prison. I've made arrangements to have your father brought to the visitor's suite, and as that's the last building we come to on the tour, I thought you might like to see what we've done here?'

Lovelace smiled. 'Of course. That would be lovely.'

Preece smiled in return, and Lovelace noticed that in that short moment, Preece's face had come alive. It had gone in a flash, but she had seen a friendly face smile back at her. A warm, kind face. It struck her as odd that a man like that would be the Governor of such a dark place, but then it was replaced with the face of a man of steel. It was nothing more than a mask, but she couldn't help but feel that everyone on the island was wearing a mask and hiding their true and honest natures.

Kellerman took command once again. 'Ladies and Gentlemen, welcome to BlackRock. You have just entered one of the most secure environments and technologically advanced maximum security prisons anywhere in the world. This is an island fortress designed to house Britain's most dangerous criminals. Those that come through those doors as prisoners of BlackRock will never leave.'

He paused to allow the statement to sink in.

He went on, 'This is the only way in and out of the prison. Everyone comes through these doors: prisoners, prison officers and visitors.

'If you would care to walk this way....'

He led the tour to a set of automatic double doors to the left of where they had been standing. He had a lanyard secured to his belt by a small elastic band which he pulled out and swiped a credit card-shaped device over a scanner on the wall. The red light turned green, and the doors swung inwards. The small group followed Kellerman through the doors and into a wide, window-less corridor, that led to another door. There was no scanner on the wall for this door, and Kellerman stood by the door and looked up. A small camera looked back.

Kellerman reached to his waist and pulled a small radio from its holder on his belt. He spoke clearly into the receiver. 'This is Kellerman. Open 1A.'

There was a short pause before the faintest sound of an electric lock being released, and the doors opened. Everyone followed Kellerman into the room, where he turned around and addressed them directly.

'This is the prisoner reception suite. You will have noticed that I could enter the prison's outer security perimeter using my identification card. It is the only point at which that card will work. It allows us to see who has entered the security perimeter and who is still within the prison walls. Each card has a unique GPS identification chip, enabling us to monitor prison officers' movements and locations. Once through the outer perimeter, remote staff can only operate doors.

'The prisoner reception suite allows us to receive prisoners away from the general prison population. Here, prisoners are strip searched and given their uniforms.'

'Uniforms?' Esther asked.

'Yes. Just a simple blue shirt and trousers. Prisoners are given their allocated uniforms on arrival and will be expected to clean them themselves. They are given a short induction where they will be told what is expected of them and the general prison rules. They will then be given a medical exam in our hospital suite before being shown to their cells.'

Lovelace was beginning to enjoy that everywhere was called a "suite." 'May we see the hospital suite?' She asked.

'Of course. This way.'

Kellerman led them to another door, where he stopped and spoke into his radio. He waited patiently while the door was remotely unlocked.

The hospital suite lived up to its name. There were facilities for thirty beds, a dispensary, five consulting rooms, an imaging centre, a specialist dental centre, a nurses' suite, an intensive care unit, and every imaginable piece of hospital technology that money could buy.

'Very impressive,' Sir Malcolm enthused. 'Bloody good work Preece.'

'Thank you, sir. We've named it the Lambert suite in your honour. I believe you were a doctor in a former life?'

Sir Malcolm puffed his chest like an old peacock fluffing its feathers and beamed proudly. 'Indeed I was.'

'I bet you could tell a few stories, Sir Malcolm,' Esther remarked.

'I've seen a few things that would make a Russian soldier blush,' Sir Malcolm said.

'Perhaps you could tell us a few of those later, Sir Malcolm,' Kellerman interjected. 'I expect you've been privy to a few family secrets in your time!'

'Well, I couldn't possibly say,' Sir Malcolm said, giving everyone the distinct impression that he was going to anyway. 'I took an oath, you know.'

'I expect most of the people you treated are now dead,' Mackay said bluntly.

Sir Malcolm looked across at Mackay and his eyes momentarily burned with fury. Lovelace saw the look, and she saw that Esther had seen it too. It went almost as quickly as it had come, and Lovelace saw that Sir Malcolm had regained his composure and a broad smile swept across his giant face.

He's annoyed with himself, Lovelace thought as the small party was ushered out of the building through another security door. And Mackay was pleased with himself. He followed the tour from the back, and he wore a cynical smile on his face.

They stepped out of the hospital suite and into the fresh air. Above them, storm clouds raced across the sky, but they felt little wind. The tall walls that surrounded the prison hemmed them in, and although they couldn't feel the wind, they could hear it. It roared overhead like an angry beast carrying thick black clouds in its wake.

'This way.' Kellerman cried above the noise.

He walked up to a wire fence that blocked his way. It was over twenty feet high and was topped with evil-looking razor wire. From where she stood, Lovelace got a good impression of the prison's layout.

Immediately behind her was the prison hospital, surrounded by a tall fence. She guessed that the building next to it was the reception suite for the prisoners and, next to that, the security office at the front gate. Beyond that, she saw more buildings, each one surrounded by a security fence topped with roll upon roll of razor wire. In front of her lay three distinct buildings enclosed within their own security fence. To the side of each was a large area that Lovelace guessed to be some outdoor space for the prisoners. At the very back of all this stood an odd-looking tower with an oddly shaped rotunda that sat on top. It had windows across its entire span, so the occupants commanded a perfect view over the prison and the North Atlantic sea. It also had a massive antenna that poked high into the sky and several strange-looking satellite dishes that hung at odd intervals.

Kellerman strolled purposefully over to the largest of the three buildings and spoke into his radio. The red light on the security fence changed to green, and Kellerman pushed the small door open to allow the party to enter. They followed him through the fence and up to the main building. The entrance to this wasn't locked. Kellerman opened the door, and they followed him into the dry.

'Welcome to A Wing,' he said proudly. 'This is the main wing and will house up to one hundred inmates.'

"How many are here already?' Sir Malcolm asked.

Preece stepped up. It was his job to know the details of the prison. Kellerman ran the nuts and bolts, and Preece ran the prison.

'Thirty male prisoners at the moment. Twenty-five in A Wing, five in the VP Wing and five women in B Wing.'

'What's the VP wing?' Esther asked.

'Vulnerable Persons.' Preece explained. 'Child murderers and rapists mainly. The kind of people who wouldn't survive in General Population.'

'I see.'

Lovelace stepped forward and examined her surroundings. She took it all in quickly and didn't linger long on the detail. She saw three inmates dressed in blue uniforms sitting at a table in the centre of the building. She saw a staircase leading to the first floor at the very far end. At either side of the building were at least forty doors, some open and some closed, that she took to be the cells. She guessed that the staircase led to more cells upstairs. Here and there, she saw prison officers in crisp, black uniforms going about their duties.

Kellerman walked over to one of the closed cell doors and opened it. There was a panel to the side of each door with a digital display that showed a number. This one was cell one. A green light indicated that the cell was open.

'All of our cells contain a bed, a desk, a computer with limited functionality, a toilet and a shower cubicle. At 8 am, the doors are automatically opened remotely, allowing the prisoners the freedom of the building. The cells are locked at 10 pm once all the prisoners are inside. All the cell doors can be opened simultaneously or individually, giving us total control over the facility.'

Kellerman closed the cell door and spoke into his radio. A few seconds later, the green light went red. 'There. All safe and secure.'

'What happens if there is a power cut?' Esther asked. 'Won't the prisoners be able to get out?'

'No.' Preece explained. 'The electricity holds the doors open, not closed. In the event of power failure, the doors can only be opened with a key. We would revert to operating as a normal prison.'

'Besides,' Kellerman interrupted, 'there's a bank of diesel generators outside the prison that can power the facility, and all its technology, for several days. There's no danger of the lights going out here.'

Sir Malcolm nodded enthusiastically.

As they stood by the cell door, an inmate hovered nearby. He had approached quietly, intrigued by the visitors. A prison officer shadowed him.

Sampson, the security head, had seen the prisoner approach. He manoeuvred himself between the inmate and the guests. On seeing Sampson block his way, the prisoner paused. He was a small man with an asinine face, and he knew he was no match for Sampson.

'All right, Sinclair. You've had a good gawp. Now on your way.'

Lovelace was surprised at Sampson's tone. It was authoritative but friendly and non-confrontational. She hadn't expected that. She hadn't expected to see Adam Sinclair either. She looked him straight in the eye, and he smirked. Quietly, he turned and walked away.

'Are we quite safe here?' Esther asked. 'You don't seem to have many officers?'

Preece smiled. 'We're quite safe.' He said and was about to add that it helped to have someone like Sampson by your side but thought better of it. Instead, he said, 'Most inmates want a quiet life. They know they're here for the long haul and want it to be as easy as possible. We have one or two violent types, but they are no match for Sampson's security detail.'

Preece nodded in Sampson's direction. He still didn't like him, but he led a tight ship, and he knew his stuff.

'Right. This way!' Kellerman said, and the small party continued their tour.

It was an impressive prison. A Wing had a refectory, television suite, games room, gymnasium, school, library, launderette and lounge. Kellerman and Preece proudly showed off the world they had created. Mackay followed and said very little. Esther seemed impressed, although she hid her expressions well. Sir Malcolm beamed as Preece laid on the compliments thick and fast. Lovelace watched them all with keen interest. She had felt unnerved by seeing Adam Sinclair. She hoped it wasn't going to be a problem.

They left A Wing and stepped once more into the outside world. It was raining heavily, and the droplets exploded dramatically onto the ground. They followed Kellerman one by one as he negotiated the locked security fences separating the various buildings. They eventually entered the strange-looking rotunda that towered ominously above the prison.

'Welcome to the Citadel.' Kellerman said. 'This is the beating heart of HMP BlackRock.'

There were two lifts on either side of the room they had stepped into, and Kellerman reached over to one and pressed the Call button. The door was immediately swept open, and the six slightly wet people stepped inside.

It opened out a few short moments later into a hive of activity. The room was, by its very nature, circular, and the first thing Lovelace noticed was the 360-degree view the occupants had of the prison, the prison grounds, most of the northern half of the island, and the sea, which crashed furiously onto the rocks a few hundred feet below their line of sight.

A bank of computers and their attendant users sat in a circle looking outwards. A few of the staff looked up as the party entered the room. Lovelace saw some of the most sophisticated computer systems she had ever laid eyes on and wondered what magic they contained.

Kellerman explained that the Citadel controlled, managed and monitored everything that happened on BlackRock. It was the brain of the island.

'Is it very secure?' Esther asked.

'Gerry?' Preece looked over at a large man sitting at a bank of five computers drinking a can of cola.

Gerry Holt looked up. He had been monitoring the tour's activities on one of the screens in front of him. 'Sir?'

'Is the system secure?' Preece asked.

Gerry smiled. 'Is it secure? It's the most secure computer system of its kind anywhere in the world.' He gloated. 'The best that money can buy.'

'It's so secure,' Mackay said, walking over to Gerry and laying his hand on his shoulder, 'that Gerry here assures me that it's impenetrable, isn't that so Gerry?'

Mackay smiled, but Gerry did not. Lovelace thought he looked worried.

'Well,' Gerry began carefully, mindful that he had sold his system to Mackay having said something similar, 'as impenetrable as it can be. We invited GCHQ, the British Government's best code breakers and digital spies, to get in, and they haven't yet. And they won't. They would have to get past me first, and they're not that good!'

Gerry laughed at his joke, but it was a nervous laugh. Mackay patted Gerry hard on the shoulder, and he winced.

The tour continued via the VP Wing and B Wing. They were mainly similar to A Wing except smaller. From the accommodation blocks, they returned to what Lovelace believed to be the main building or front entrance, except they had come full circle and were approaching from the opposite end from where they had begun. She felt slightly disorientated.

'Welcome to the security hub.' Kellerman said. 'Mr Sampson, if you'd like to continue the tour.'

Wayne Sampson stepped forward. Lovelace's first impressions of him remained. His eyes were dark and soulless, his face gaunt and twisted and the way he held her eyes for just a few seconds longer than necessary unnerved her. He was a big man, too, the kind of man women crossed roads to avoid, and other men stayed clear of on a night out. Lovelace reluctantly acknowledged that he was probably the right man for the job. Hard and fearless.

'Every staff member that works on BlackRock comes through me first,' he said in that soft, disarming voice that Lovelace found difficulty reconciling to the animal in front of her. 'We train them to recognise dangers, how to read the signs and the inmates' body language. We train them to understand when to step back and when to go in hard. And we equip them with the tools of the job.'

Sampson opened a door behind him, and the small party followed him into a large room that served as an operations centre.

'In the Citadel, they make everything work. Here, we watch. We watch everyone and everything. We have some of the world's finest security gadgets courtesy of Mr Mackay's generosity.'

Mackay appreciated the nod. He liked Sampson.

Inside the room, a dozen men and a couple of women dressed in black uniforms with Security emblazoned across their shoulders were watching screens and monitoring the data.

'This is Cobra Team. My own hand-picked, specially trained guards. They answer only to me.'

Lovelace watched as one or two of Sampson's guards looked up. They were a disparate bunch of misfits. She didn't like the look of a single one of them.

'From this room, we oversee the island's security. Not just here at the prison, but also the Governor's residence and the accommodation block south of the island.'

Sampson pointed to a screen of CCTV images showing the outside of the properties on the south of the island.

Lovelace leant in. 'Do you have coverage inside the buildings?'

'Not inside the Governor's residence and only in the communal areas in the accommodation block.'

'What about the prison cells?' Esther asked.

'Only in the communal areas, the isolation cells and the suicide watch cells. All the other cells are free of CCTV coverage.'

'What about drugs?' Sir Malcolm asked. 'It's a big problem in mainland prisons. I notice you have no netting over the courtyards?'

'Very observant, Sir Malcolm,' Preece said, rubbing his ego some more. 'Drugs are a problem, and we have strict search policies for staff..'

'Yes, yes.' Sir Malcolm interrupted. 'But what about drones?'

Sampson walked over to a cabinet door and removed what looked like a small hand-held rocket launcher. He held it out proudly for Sir Malcolm to hold.

'What is it?' He asked.

'It's a directional Electro-Magnetic Pulse device. You point it in the general direction of the drone and pull the trigger. A few seconds later, it drops out of the sky. Mr Mackay very kindly funds BlackRock Research into developing non-lethal weaponry.'

Sir Malcolm held the device to his eye and turned towards the bank of computer displays behind him.

'Careful, Sir Malcolm!' Kellerman cried. 'You'll knock out our computers!'

'That's okay, Mr Kellerman,' Sampson laughed, retrieving the launcher from Sir Malcolm. 'It's not even switched on.'

'Do you have many weapons on the island?' Sir Malcolm asked.

'Yes. A large number of non-lethal weaponry designed to incapacitate or slow down an offender.'

'Do you have guns?' Esther asked.

'No.' Kellerman answered firmly. 'There are no guns on the island.'

Sampson agreed. 'We don't need guns,' he said. 'It's not our intention to kill people.'

Lovelace recalled the conversation she had earlier with Esther. *He killed a man once, you know.* She looked at Sampson with renewed interest. He certainly didn't need guns. He was more than capable of killing people without them; she didn't believe his last statement.

They left Sampson's empire, moved through several security doors, and began approaching the point at which they had set off on their tour. Kellerman took Lovelace gently by the arm.

'If you'd like to follow me,' he said. 'The tour's over. The visitors' suite is this way, where we have a private room for you and your father. I'll give the others a quick run around the suite, and we'll meet in a little while.'

Kellerman opened a door and introduced Lovelace to a young prison officer. She could barely have been twenty years old, Lovelace thought. She was pretty in a boyish way. Her hair was held in a tight bun atop her head, and her face was lightly made up. She held out a hand, and it was soft to the touch. She squeezed it gently.

'My name's Georgia,' she said, and an innocent smile crossed her face.

Lovelace smiled back warmly.

'Come this way. Your father's been expecting you.'

Lovelace followed Georgia, who opened a door further along the room. It led to a waiting area with functional tables and chairs. A coffee and tea vending machine sat in one corner and hummed. A small fridge was packed with a selection of chilled fizzy drinks.

Georgia opened another door and beckoned Lovelace through. Jack Lovelace sat at a table in the centre of the room and smiled as Lovelace entered.

'I knew you'd come,' he said softly. Lovelace said nothing. She stood at the edge of the room and, not for the first time, questioned her motives for being there.

'I'll be just out here if you need me. Can I get you a drink, Miss?'

'Coffee, please.' Lovelace said.

'Jack?'

Jack Lovelace nodded.

Lovelace sat at the table opposite her father.

'I knew you'd come.' He said again.

Lovelace waited while Georgia brought their coffee and closed the door behind her. She opened a sugar sachet, poured it into the cup, and stirred it slowly. She was filled with conflicting emotions.

After a few minutes of uneasy silence, Jack said, 'They've got Sinclair here. Did you know?'

'Not until I bumped into him a few minutes ago.'

'Oh.' Jack said. He had so much to say, but the words wouldn't come.

'He murdered girls.' Lovelace said matter of factly. 'Young girls. I'm surprised he isn't in the VP Wing. It would be safer for him. He's likely to get his throat cut in A Wing.'

'Yes.' Jack said, holding his daughter's eye. 'I suppose he is.'

Lovelace drank her coffee, and the two sat silently for a few minutes. The conversation didn't come easily. It came in fits and starts, and they spoke of nothing in particular. An hour came and went, and little of substance passed between them.

There was a gentle tap on the door, and Georgia entered. 'I'm sorry,' she said, 'but your party's ready to leave. Mr Preece has asked if you would like to follow on afterwards?'

Lovelace stood up. 'No. I think we've said enough for now. There'll be more time in the future.'

Jack stood up and smiled. 'Thank you.' He said, and Lovelace turned and left the room.

Lovelace was ushered out of the prison in less time than it took to get in. Preece was waiting for her under the canopy, holding an umbrella aloft as he led her to the second Defender. She got in alongside Esther and breathed a sigh of relief. To her surprise, Preece got in the front passenger seat. As the car pulled away from the prison, he turned and addressed Lovelace directly.

'Awfully sorry,' he said, 'but I'm afraid the helicopter's run into a few issues. What with the storm and all that, there's no getting off the island, I'm afraid. You're stuck here with us till it passes. Might be a couple of days before we can get you off.'

'That's okay,' Lovelace said calmly. 'It's not your fault.'

'Mackay was going to put you up in the staff accommodation block, but my wife has overruled him. You'll be staying with us if that's all right? We're not much, but I think you'll like my wife. She has no fear of Mackay! And we have food and enough alcohol to keep us going through the storms.'

Esther took Lovelace's hand and squeezed it. 'Oh good. We're going to be housemates.'

Lovelace smiled nervously.

Esther glowed. 'It's going to be such fun, I can tell!'

Four

The fleet of Defenders drove back through the deepening storm. Wind and rain lashed them as they passed over the mountain. From where she sat, Lovelace could see the peaks begin to take on a white hue, and behind them, far out to the west, she could see the darkness draw in as the day faded away.

Once off the hillside, the weather drove at them even harder, and their visibility was reduced to little more than a hundred yards. By the time the lights of the cars fell upon the Mansion House, night had fully descended and everywhere was pitched into an inky black.

They were ushered into the house and out of the weather and were greeted by Grace and Elouise Preece. The three Defenders drove away from the house and were lost to the night. In the distance, Lovelace could make out the faint lights of the accommodation block.

'I don't see why she couldn't stay in the accommodation wing.' Mackay roared, slipping off his coat and handing it to Grace.

'Because she isn't staff,' Elouise said bluntly. 'She is my guest and is welcome here for as long as the storm continues,' she added with a smile. She walked over to where Lovelace was standing and slipped her arm through hers.

'It's my bloody house,' Mackay snapped.

'No, Mr Mackay, it's my house,' Elouise said, firmly. To Lovelace, she said, 'come, let me show you to your room.'

Like everything on BlackRock, the Mansion House had been built with no expense spared. Elouise guided Lovelace through the large, well-furnished reception area and up a large sweeping staircase. Stunning modern works of art adorned the walls, and expensive-looking antiques sat in every nook and cranny.

'Take no notice of Ethan,' Elouise said as they climbed the staircase. 'He likes to be in control of everything and everyone.'

'But not you?' Lovelace commented.

'He tries.' Elouise laughed. 'I think it annoys him that I stand up to him while everyone else is busy kissing his feet.'

'I don't mean to be any trouble.' Lovelace said. 'I'm quite happy to stay in the accommodation block.'

'Good god, no!' Elouise said, 'Do you know how dull this place is? I'm desperate for the company! And you intrigue me.'

She was an elegant woman, Lovelace thought. She looked older than her husband, but she walked, talked and dressed with style. She had an engaging smile set back in a soft white face and beautifully enhanced by the bluest eyes. Her hair was blonde but tinged with red and fell across her shoulders in waves.

'I've put you in my daughter's room,' Elouise said. 'She's at university in Edinburgh. She doesn't like it here, and I can't say I blame her. There's a darkness to the place. You'll find some clothes in the wardrobe that should fit you, and you look about her size.'

They walked along a small corridor that was dog-legged at the end. Each room they passed had a plaque fitted to the wall next to the door. Lovelace read them as she walked by.

"Shipman." "Lemon." "Maybrick." "Thompson." "Moriarty."

Elouise stopped at a door that had no plaque. She opened it and stepped inside.

'My daughter's room.' Elouise declared.

'Why doesn't it have a name?' Lovelace asked.

Elouise smiled, but behind that smile, Lovelace saw a crack.

'Mackay plays games with people. They're not very nice games, but it amuses him. He instructed that all the guest rooms for this little event of his be named in a certain way. My room is the "Thompson" one. Sir Malcolm is in "Shipman," Grace is in "Lemon", and Mrs Friedman is in "Maybrick." He wasn't expecting you hence the lack of a name. Don't be deceived; he'll find a way to wind you up. Don't let him get under your skin; if he does, don't let him see. Nothing annoys him more.'

'I suppose Ethan Mackay is in "Moriarty."'

'Of course!' Elouise said with a little chuckle. 'The master manipulator. The mastermind. The legend. I'm afraid our Ethan is a legend in his own mind!'

They laughed, and behind them, they heard approaching voices.

'Let the games begin.' Elouise said quietly, and the two of them watched through the crack in the door as Ethan Mackay led his less-than-merry band to their rooms.

'I've put you in "Shipman,"' Mackay thundered so that everyone could hear.

Sir Malcolm wobbled. He wasn't a man who could easily hide his emotions, and from where she watched, Lovelace saw the rouge rise up his neck and fill his rotund face. He opened the door and went inside, slamming it behind him.

'Grace, you're in "Lemon."' Mackay said.

Grace's expression betrayed no emotion.

'And you're in "Maybrick."' Mackay declared, watching Esther closely.

Esther Friedman looked at the plaque and then directly at Mackay. 'Thank you.' She said. She opened the door and disappeared behind it. Mackay looked annoyed.

Mackay turned on Grace. 'My room. Twenty minutes. We still have work to do.' He opened the door to his room and slammed the door behind him. Grace stood for a moment in the silence before going into her room.

'It's all very odd.' Lovelace remarked.

'Mackay doesn't do anything without reason.' Elouise said. She turned and smiled at Lovelace. 'I daresay we shall find out at dinner.' She took Lovelace's hand and held it firmly. 'Whatever you do, don't get involved. Ethan's a dangerous man, and he'll want to control you. Stay away from him.' She released Lovelace's hand. 'Please make yourself at home. Wear whatever you like. Emma wouldn't mind a bit. There's a TV and some books. All the rooms are en-suite if you want to freshen up.'

'Thank you,' Lovelace said. 'I will.'

'Dinner's at eight. By all means, tour the house. There's a lot to see. We'll probably all gather for drinks at the bar at around seven.'

'There's a bar?' Lovelace asked.

'Yes. Fully stocked too. I defy you to find a drink we don't have.' She said proudly. 'We also have a swimming pool, sauna and gym room. There's a huge library, a lounge and a twenty-five-seat cinema.'

'Wow.' Lovelace remarked. 'I think I may go on that tour!'

'Do.' Elouise said. 'Emma may have left a swimming costume if you feel inclined.' She turned and went to leave. 'I'll see you for drinks later.'

She closed the door behind her.

Now that, Lovelace said to herself, was interesting.

***

Lovelace showered quickly and helped herself to some of the clothes that Elouise's daughter had left behind. Elouise had been right in her estimation of Lovelace's size. Most of the dresses she tried on fitted perfectly. She admired Emma Preece's taste, too. There was nothing in her wardrobe that Lovelace wouldn't be seen in. She settled on loose-fitting black trousers and a simple white blouse. It was understated but elegant.

Lovelace spent a minute addressing the issue that was her hair. Ever since she was a child, it had done pretty much what it wanted and had resisted many years of futile intervention. Her sister had suffered in the same way. It was an inherited trait from their mother, and all three of them had thrown their hands up in frustration and given up trying to control its whims. By and large, they had settled on the dragged-through-a-hedge backward look, with some semblance of control thrown in for good measure. Today, Lovelace tied it back in a ponytail, wrapped a hairband tightly to the base of her scalp and watched as strands of wispy auburn hair began to escape and launch themselves across her head in abandon.

She sighed. It would have to do.

She opened her bedroom door and looked out. The corridor had dog-legged where Lovelace's door opened. Directly ahead of her was the staircase from where she and Elouise had walked up not an hour previously. On each side of the corridor were the oddly named rooms that had been given to the other guests by Mackay. As she closed her door, she could hear Mackay's voice bellow from behind "Moriarty". He had an unpleasant voice, Lovelace thought, which seemed to go hand in hand with his character. He always appeared to be barking at someone, usually his PA, Grace. Not for the first time, she wondered why the sweet-looking young Grace Mahone put up with it. It couldn't just be the money. No amount of money was worth the abuse she was getting from behind that door.

Lovelace turned and followed the corridor along the dogleg. There was another door without a name, and a quick peek told her nothing more than where to find the cleaning products should she require them. As she walked along the corridor, the ceiling lights came on, and as she passed each one, they went out. At the end of the hall, another staircase welcomed her. This one was much smaller and spiralled downwards. There was only enough room on the stairs for one person at a time, and it would have been quite a squeeze to meet someone coming the other way.

Lovelace took in her surroundings as she rounded the bottom of the stairs.

She had stumbled on the swimming pool. It was a large room, about the size of a small ballroom, and the pool lay in the middle, lit up from within the water by purple and blue strip lights. Around the edge of the pool sat several loungers and tables lit up by cleverly situated LED lights that threw a subtle purple and blue glaze over everything. Lovelace's eyes followed the pool's edge to the other side, where a hot tub had been sunk into the floor. It, too, glowed in purple and blue. Behind that was a door that said "Sauna".

Lovelace walked around and took a look. It was a simple sauna of Scandinavian design, fully wood panelled. Next door to the sauna was a gym. It was a small room filled almost to capacity with every form of gym equipment that sadistic designers could imagine. A massive television hung on the wall at the room's far end. Lovelace was impressed.

Next door to the gym was an even smaller room with no door. Behind it sat a classic barber's chair, a small shelf full of grooming implements and a large mirror. It also glowed under a faint purple and blue hue.

Lovelace wandered through the next door and out of the pool area. A staircase to her left led up a level and into what she took to be the lounge. It was lavishly furnished with a huge U-shaped sofa that could comfortably seat a dozen people. Windows looked down over the pool and out into the night. The storm that raged outside battered against the glass, but the glazing heavily dulled the noise.

Around the edge of the room were more comfortable-looking chairs and tables. Bookcases were scattered here and there and were accompanied in places by cabinets full of strange-looking curios and antiques. Despite being heavily influenced by a male hand, the room had the strong allure of a female mind. Lovelace felt Elouise's presence in every corner.

A fire burned in a stocky-looking log burner that stood proudly in front of the U-shaped sofa. From where she stood, Lovelace could feel the heat emanating from it. There was no fireplace to speak of. The log burner sat on its squat-looking legs on a black granite base, and a single black flue struck out from behind and up into the ceiling.

Next door to the lounge Lovelace found the bar that Elouise had spoken about. She had barely believed Elouise's statement that challenged Lovelace to ask for a drink she didn't stock, but now, looking across the bar, she wondered if it wasn't true.

Ahead of her, and across the entire room, was shelf upon shelf of every known brand of alcohol she knew of, and even some she didn't. The shelves were lit lightly in the same purple and blues that had been such a part of the pool area. Beneath the shelves sat three integrated glass fridges with contents that ranged from fizzy drinks and tonics to expensive-looking champagne. Lovelace felt her taste buds tingle.

Between that and the bar was enough room for two people to mill about making drinks. The bar was a colossal piece of furniture made from the finest wood and topped with black marble. Several pumps serving ale, lager and Guinness took pride of place at the centre. At the bar sat six comfortable-looking bar stools. Lovelace sat on one and turned to look at the rest of the room.

The room had been designed to look like an authentic English pub. It was softly carpeted and wood-panelled. Several cocktail chairs of varying sizes, and small mahogany tables, were scattered here and there in a moderately organised fashion. Paintings on the walls depicted a vision of a long-lost England, with quiet villages, peaceful streams and the perfect country idyll. On closer inspection, however, Lovelace adjusted her assumption of the vision of a long-lost England. The landscape was decidedly Scottish, with sweeping vistas of ancient lochs and mediaeval forests.

From the bar, Lovelace walked across an open plan floor space with windows looking out over the pool to another door. Behind this was the cinema that Elouise had spoken about. It was a small room with a huge white canopy at the far end. Between that and where Lovelace stood were a selection of luxurious-looking cream leather sofas, in varying sizes, that all looked forward at the canopy.

Lovelace raised an eyebrow. Even though the room was relatively small, it occurred to her that she had lived in bedsits that were smaller. The whole house felt like a grotesque and obscene waste of money, but it wasn't lost on her that Mackay was one of the wealthiest men in

Britain. The house had probably felt like small change to him.

She left the cinema room and followed the corridor to where the main staircase reached the landing. Earlier she and Elouise had climbed those stairs and walked down the corridor that dog-legged next to her room. Lovelace smiled. A picture of the complex building formed in her mind. She had just completed a circuit of the upper level, with a brief drop-down into the pool area. It was a clever design that allowed those that lived in the house to reach any of the rooms without necessarily walking through the others. It allowed a certain level of anonymity and privacy.

Lovelace walked down the grand, sweeping staircase and back into the reception area where she had first arrived. Several doors led off from the reception, and Lovelace started at the door furthest away from her.

It was a large room, much like the lounge upstairs, but less formal. It had the feel of an average living room, which existed in many forms up and down the country, where ordinary people lived and relaxed. Lovelace guessed that this was where Johnathon Preece liked spending most of his free time. An LCD television sat in one corner beneath closed curtains, and a heavily worn sofa sat in front of it. There was a log burner here, too, with the remnants of glowing embers within its chest. On the couch lay a heavily thumbed book and an ashtray. Lovelace could smell the faint aroma of tobacco. It was interesting, she thought. The room felt distinctly like a bachelor's room, not the room of a married man.

Next to this room was the library. Lovelace opened the door and strolled in. Johnathon was sitting at a desk in front of a large computer screen. He turned when Lovelace entered.

'I'm sorry,' Lovelace said, 'Elouise said I should look around the house. I didn't mean to disturb you.'

Johnathon smiled, but Lovelace couldn't help but notice the strain his eyes tried to hide.

'That's perfectly okay,' he said. 'Come in. Have a look around. Take a book if you like. They're a bit dull in here, I'm afraid. Legal tomes, Hansard and the like. A few classics, if that's your thing?'

'I don't mind the odd Dickens,' Lovelace admitted, 'although I'm more partial to a Wodehouse or two.'

Jonathon was wearing reading glasses which slipped to the edge of his nose as he looked over the rim. 'Really? I didn't think young people liked that sort of thing anymore. Thought you'd be more into the Fifty shades stuff.' As he said it, he realised how it sounded. 'I'm sorry, that sounded pretentious and superior. I didn't mean it to.'

This time Lovelace smiled. People consistently underestimated her. She liked it. It worked better that way. They never saw her coming.

Johnathon got up from where he was sitting and walked over to a bookshelf. He was busy running his eyes over several books. Lovelace looked at the computer screen and Johnathon's desk. He seemed like a very busy man.

'Here,' Johnathon said, pulling a book from the shelf and handing it to Lovelace. '"Pigs Have Wings", it's one of my favourites. People over-rate the Jeeves stuff, in my opinion. I much prefer the Blandings books.'

Lovelace took the book and held it gently in her hands. It was an old copy, in orange and white, the classic Penguin cover for general fiction from the fifties and sixties.

'Thank you.' She said.

'You'll get plenty of time to read it, I'm afraid. The weather forecast has us at the storm's mercy for at least forty-eight hours—no chance of a relief flight before then. You'd better make the most of it. Have you visited the bar yet? Help yourself to anything you want. There'll be no surprise bills at the end. We're a fully inclusive hotel!' As he said it, he chuckled, and Lovelace warmed to him a bit. She got the impression from him that he was a cautious man, not one to reveal himself too readily. He also felt shy, and she noticed how he failed to hold her eye for longer than a second. In some people, she would hold that as an example of someone she couldn't trust, but coming from Johnathon Preece, it felt different. It felt like he was trying to prevent people from looking into his soul and getting too close. He was a man that kept people at arm's length, but she couldn't work out if that were to protect them or himself.

She thanked him again and turned to leave. As she passed through the door, she saw something she had missed as she entered. There was another plaque on the door, similar to the ones that adorned the upstairs rooms. This one said "Ireland". It was odd, she thought, that this room was named after a country while all the others had been named after people.

She closed the door tightly behind her and continued her tour. The next room she fell into was a hive of activity. Elouise was in a heated conversation with a woman Lovelace hadn't seen before who was stirring something in a large pot. They were bent over one of the most extensive cooking ranges Lovelace had ever seen. Lovelace doubted if a more extensive kitchen existed outside of a professional kitchen.

Elouise turned to greet her as she walked in.

'Oh, hello. Taking in the house?'

'Yes,' Lovelace said, 'I hope I'm not intruding?'

'Not at all,' Elouise said, and the woman behind her grumbled something unintelligible. 'We're debating whether or not tonight's curry requires more heat. Mrs Brent suggests not. I believe it does. Here, what do you think?'

Elouise dipped a clean spoon into the pot and held its contents aloft for Lovelace to try. Mrs Brent stepped to one side to allow Lovelace to pass and threw her a warning look that would have melted weaker people. Lovelace was undeterred.

The aroma of the sauce came to her first, and her saliva glands reacted positively. That was always a good sign. Lovelace held the spoon and swallowed the food. She had spent much time in Asia and was well-versed in the multitudes of various flavours the east could produce. She thought Mrs Brent had done a sublime job, correctly assuming that she was the cook. The flavours were well-balanced and subtle and lingered on the tongue long after the food had gone.

'I'd have to say I agree with Mrs Brent,' Lovelace said after a moment's consideration. 'If you add more heat, you will be in danger of upsetting the balance. More heat does not always equate to more flavour.'

Mrs Brent beamed. Elouise gave a little nod in the cook's direction and conceded defeat.

'Let me show you the dining room,' Elouise said, taking Lovelace's arm and leading her away from the glowing Mrs Brent.

The dining room was everything Lovelace expected. No expense had been spared. A large oak dining table took centre place, surrounded by eight antique-looking chairs. Each place was already set for dinner, and the silverware glowed in the light.

'There are eight places,' Lovelace noted out loud. She never missed a thing. She knew all too well that there were only seven house guests, including the Preeces. 'Who's the eighth?'

'That would be Tony Kellerman, Head of Island Operations. You must have met him today?'

Lovelace nodded. 'Yes. He seemed like a nice man.'

'Don't rely too heavily on appearances,' she said mysteriously. 'People are well-versed at hiding their true selves on this island.' Then, realising that she may have spoken out of place to a stranger, 'dinner will be another hour. Perhaps you would like to have a drink at the bar? The others will be gathering there shortly.'

Without saying anything else, Elouise disappeared back into the kitchen.

Lovelace smiled to herself. She found people interesting, and the characters she had flown out to the island with earlier that day were definitely that. She was looking forward to finding out more about them.

'There you are, my dear!' Esther cried out as Lovelace entered the bar. 'I took the liberty of opening a bottle of champers. You look like a champers kind of girl? Here, come and sit down.'

Esther Friedman had acquired one of the comfortable-looking cocktail chairs and was holding a half-full flute of champagne. A very expensive-looking bottle of champagne sat on the table in front of her. An empty flute was placed in front of a cocktail chair on which Lovelace sat in. Esther filled her glass to the rim.

'Bottom's up!' Esther cheered, and Lovelace took a sip of the drink.

'Now,' Esther said, tapping Lovelace on the knee, 'tell me about your sister.'

'There's not much to tell.' Lovelace lied.

'Now, we both know that's not true.' Esther stated. 'There's a great deal to tell. The question is, why won't anyone talk about her?'

'Why would they?' Lovelace asked.

'Because Zoe Lovelace is a mystery. I'm an investigative journalist, my dear, and it's my job to know things about people. For the last couple of years, your sister's name has cropped up several times in the mouths of some of the world's most feared crime bosses. She's spoken of in hushed tones. Quietly, as if to say her name aloud would cause terrible harm to those who spoke it. Some of the most fearsome men in the world are scared of your sister, and I want to know why.'

Esther swallowed her glass of champagne and poured another. Lovelace sipped hers slowly.

'I really can't help you,' Lovelace said. 'I haven't seen my sister for years. I told you, we're estranged. We don't talk.'

Esther cocked her head to one side and watched Lovelace carefully. For a moment, Lovelace feared that she could read her thoughts.

'You're a cautious little thing, aren't you?' Esther said, and Lovelace, flinching at the patronising statement, saw the dangerous side of the journalist come to the fore. 'I'll find out your secrets, you know, I always do.'

'Why don't you leave the girl alone?'

Lovelace turned and was surprised to see Sir Malcolm behind the bar, pouring himself a huge glass of whisky. For a large man, he moved quietly, Lovelace thought.

'Why?' Esther asked. 'What is it to do with you?'

Sir Malcolm held Esther's eyes for a long minute. It was clear that there was no love lost between the two.

'You talk about secrets like they're yours to know. They're not. Keep your bloody nose out.'

'What about your secrets, Sir Malcolm?' Esther probed. 'Who knows them? Should I go digging? Do you have skeletons in your closet, or have you had them all cremated?'

Sir Malcolm puffed his chest out, and Lovelace saw the anger rise up his face. 'Be careful, woman. Everyone has secrets. Even you. Even *Maybrick*.'

Lovelace watched Esther's expression carefully. She had wondered what Maybrick had meant and why Mackay had had Esther's room named that way. She had an idea who Maybrick was, but it didn't make sense. Esther gave nothing away. Her face was ice cold and devoid of expression. She wasn't letting anyone see whatever turmoil was going on behind those eyes.

'Touche, Doctor Lambert.' Esther said, using Sir Malcolm's original title.

Sir Malcolm almost took the bait. Lovelace could see the conflict in his eyes and his body language. Then, in a masterful show of self-control, he said, 'To hell with you, woman. You're just a salacious hack.'

Sir Malcolm took his drink and sat at the table furthest away from Esther, turning his back to her.

Grace came into the bar and smiled at Lovelace. To Esther, she said, 'you've not been upsetting the good doctor, have you, Mrs Friedman? You do know he's Ethan's guest of honour?'

'Ethan's puppet, more like,' Esther snarled. 'What does he have on him?' She asked.

Grace picked up a champagne flute from the bar and sat opposite Lovelace. She was dressed in a white T-shirt and blue denim dungarees. Despite no longer being a teenager, she carried the look nicely. She was still slim enough to pull it off but curvy enough not to look too young or immature. Lovelace guessed that the only person on the island using the gym was Grace.

Grace poured herself a glass from the bottle and topped Lovelace's up.

'Now then, Mrs Friedman. Let's not go down that route, shall we?'

Esther leant forward and said quietly, 'what the bloody hell does he mean by putting me in Maybrick? What's he trying to say?'

'I don't know,' Grace said truthfully. 'Ethan doesn't tell me everything. Sometimes I wonder if he tells me anything at all. He named my room after a fruit, and I have no idea why.'

Lovelace had forgotten that. But was it a fruit? Or did it mean something else? Was Mackay implying something about Grace's sexuality? That didn't seem to fit. She did not doubt that Grace could be gay or straight or anything in between, but it was the twenty-first century, and it was hardly blackmail material anymore. It meant something, Lovelace was sure, but she couldn't quite put her finger on it.

'I trust your room is comfortable?' Grace said to Lovelace. 'I apologise if Ethan says anything out of order to you. He can be quite nasty sometimes and gets particularly annoyed when he can't control his environment.' Grace looked at Lovelace and smiled. 'He doesn't know you and hasn't had a chance to plan for you. You're the element he can't control, and that worries him.'

'He needn't worry.' Lovelace said. 'I'm nobody. Certainly nobody Mackay should worry about.'

That wasn't entirely true, but the lie came easily.

'Even so,' Grace said cautiously. 'Be careful around him. He can turn on a sixpence.'

They were interrupted by Tony Kellerman, who entered the room with a flourish. He looked like a man who had just come in from the storm. He wandered over to the bar and poured himself a lager.

'Storm's not getting any better.' He said moments after sinking half his drink. 'The rain water's running off the mountain in floods.'

He dropped his glass on the table in front of the women and said, 'May I?'

He pulled up the spare chair and sat down. 'Mackay not here yet?'

'Conference call.' Grace said. 'He'll be along shortly.'

Elouise came into the bar. Lovelace noted that she had made a quick change of dress. She looked stunning in a low-cut dress that hung close to her figure. She was a woman that was ageing gracefully, Lovelace thought, and there was still much about her to admire. Lovelace doubted if there would ever be a time when she wasn't attractive.

'Oh good,' Elousie said, 'you've opened the champagne.' She found a flute from behind the bar and poured what was left of the champagne into it. She sank it in one go. 'Dinner's almost ready,' she said, and Lovelace noted an edge to her voice. 'When you're all ready, of course. Where's Ethan?' She asked, directing the question at Grace.

Before she could answer, Mackay appeared at the doorway behind her.

It was a perfectly timed entrance. His presence brought with it a chill that everyone felt.

'Did I hear dinner mentioned?' Mackay asked. 'I'm famished.'

One by one, the guests followed as Elouise led Mackay out of the bar and down the staircase to the dining room. Lovelace stepped in behind Grace at the back of the line. The solemn line of well-dressed people reminded her of a funeral procession, and the thought raised the hairs on her arm.

Lovelace felt the tension in the air. It was palpable. A strange phrase Elouise had used earlier came back to mind, and it rang loudly in her head.

Let the games begin.

Five

Mackay sat at the head of the dining table and took his seat before anyone else. Sir Malcolm sat to his right and, opposite him and to Mackay's left, sat Esther. Elouise Preece hovered behind her seat next to Sir Malcolm and waved Lovelace onto the seat next to hers. Johnathon Preece sat opposite Elouise, and Grace sat next to him. At the opposite end of the table sat Kellerman. Elouise waited until everyone had taken their places before dropping gracefully into her seat. As she did so, she nodded at Mrs Brent, who lingered expectantly by the kitchen door. Mrs Brent turned and disappeared behind the door, soon replaced by three waiters, and an older man that Lovelace guessed was probably Mr Brent. They were dressed impeccably in black suits, crisp white shirts and purple and blue bow ties. Slowly and with much formality, the waiters passed around the table pouring wine.

Lovelace raised her glass and took a sip. She still had the book Jonathon had given her, and she had placed it on the table in front of her.

Kellerman leant over and said, 'been in old Jonathon's library, I see?'

'Yes. He was kind enough to lend me one of his books.'

Elouise smiled. 'He does that. He firmly believes that books shouldn't just be collecting dust on shelves. I wouldn't be surprised if you end up with a handful of personally picked books before you leave.'

'What book is it?' Grace asked, tilting her head and trying to read the title upside down.

'Pigs have Wings.' Lovelace said and was about to name the author when she was cut short by Grace.

'I adore PG Wodehouse,' she declared enthusiastically. 'He was a big fan of Agatha Christie back in the day. He was addicted to crime fiction in his later years.'

'Grace knows all about that sort of thing, don't you, Grace.' Mackay said. 'Always got your head in one of those cosy crime books. A load of stuff and nonsense. Bloody waste of paper, in my opinion.'

Grace looked crestfallen.

'I'm rather partial to Agatha Christie,' Elouise said, ignoring Mackay. 'And there's nothing cosy about her books. Certainly nothing cosy about murder.'

'I'd agree,' Lovelace said, coming to Grace's defence. 'The idea that murder can be committed by ordinary people living ordinary lives is far from cosy. Quite the opposite, in fact.' She looked directly at Grace. 'I love the Miss Marple books, although my favourite is a Poirot story. Do you have a favourite?'

'I do like Miss Marple.' Grace admitted, cautiously glancing in Mackay's direction. 'But Poirot is my favourite. I think his best case is the ABC Murders.'

'Just stories. It's not real life,' Mackay spat.

He paused as a young waitress placed his starter in front of him.

'Real crime,' Mackay continued, raising his fork and plunging it into a juicy prawn. 'Now that's interesting. Real people committing real crimes that's what interests me. Not fiction. No one has time for fiction anymore.'

'Is that why you build prisons, Mr Mackay?' Esther asked.

The table fell quiet, and everyone waited for Mackay to explode.

'My mother was murdered,' he said softly. 'It changes a boy. It makes them hard-nosed. I haven't got time for this namby-pamby left-wing, rehabilitation rubbish the do-gooders constantly throw at me.'

'Do you not believe in rehabilitation?' Lovelace asked.

'It has its place. Not all criminals are beyond redemption.'

'And yet you built a prison where the prisoners are beyond redemption?' Esther noted.

Mackay finished his starter and pushed his plate away. 'The people in this prison, on this island, have been judged to be beyond redemption by others, not by me. Our prisons are overcrowded and at breaking point. All I have done is taken the worst ones out of the general prison population and brought them here, where they can wait to die.'

'It feels like a slow execution,' Lovelace added. She watched as a ripple of uncertainty did a circuit of the table.

'That's rather well put.' Mackay said. 'I sense you may get it.' He held Lovelace's eyes for a long time. Lovelace looked away and then at Elouise. She remembered what she had said earlier. *Don't let him get under your skin.*

The conversation drifted in that vein for some time while they waited for the plates to be cleared. The waiters took another turn at the wine glasses; soon, everyone was two glasses into the meal.

Lovelace felt the warmth of the alcohol course through her. As the alcohol began to take its toll on the other guests, she noticed that the conversation got louder and people got braver. Mackay, she noticed, was drinking slower. He was staying in control.

'What sort of prisoners do you have in BlackRock?' Esther asked, directing her question at Kellerman, who, up until that point, had remained remarkably quiet.

Kellerman had already sunk his second glass of wine. His lips looked rosy.

'We're gradually picking up every convict given a whole life tariff and one or two given minimum terms of over twenty-five years.' Kellerman said, and his delivery sounded like something he had been practising for the newspapers.

'Yes, I know that,' Esther said, 'I meant specifically. Who? Can you tell us?'

Kellerman looked at Mackay. He said, 'it's a matter of public record, so I suppose no harm can come from telling you.'

'There's Miss Lovelace's father, of course,' he said, looking at Lovelace for forgiveness for reminding everyone of that fact.

'The Cherwell Valley Strangler,' Esther said gleefully. 'We do need to chat, my dear,' and she directed the reply at Lovelace.

'He's a model prisoner,' Johnathon interjected. 'He's never given us a moment's problem.'

'And then there's Adam Sinclair.' Kellerman added.

'Another one of yours?' Esther said, firing the question at Lovelace with a wicked smile.

'Nothing to do with me,' Lovelace remarked.

'But you caught him, though, eh?' Sir Malcolm piped up. He was looking at Lovelace directly while draining his glass of wine.

'Saved a girl's life, too, didn't you?' Elouise asked. 'I read about the case in the papers.'

Lovelace smiled nervously.

'I think we have three more serial killers,' Kellerman went on.

'How do you define a serial killer, exactly?' Sir Malcolm asked.

Jonathon leant forward. 'Well, it's an American term. We have no official way of determining exactly when a killer becomes a serial killer, but we would loosely describe one after three murders.'

'And there are five in the prison?' Esther asked.

63

'That's right,' Johnathon admitted.

'Possibly even six, on the island.' Mackay said, laughing.

'No, I'm pretty sure it's five, Ethan,' Johnathon said, correcting his boss.

'Well, you can't possibly know for sure,' Mackay said, 'there may be more. You never know. One of us around this table could be a serial killer. What do you think, Sir Malcolm?'

Lovelace watched as Sir Malcolm battled with the rouge that began to climb up his face. Everyone else noticed it, too.

'I mean, you must have slipped an old dear or two an extra dose of morphine to ease their pain in their final moments? Or prescribed a fatal dose of penicillin to someone with an allergy?'

Mackay's smile twisted his face. 'Tell me, John, how many doctors have been convicted of murdering their patients in the United Kingdom?'

Johnathon looked at Mackay and then at Sir Malcolm. He felt Sir Malcolm's pain and discomfort. He'd been there himself, too, many times. Mackay could be very cruel. He sighed and said, 'I believe only one doctor has ever been convicted of murdering their patients in this country.'

'One?' Esther cried. 'That can't be true!'

Johnathon nodded. 'I'm afraid it is.'

'What about Dr Crippen?' Lovelace asked.

Johnathon shook his head. 'He murdered his wife. She wasn't a patient.'

'That seems to be a remarkable fact,' Kellerman said. 'But there are no doctors in our prison.'

'Not yet, eh, Sir Malcolm.' Mackay smirked as he tapped him on the hand.

Sir Malcolm looked distinctly uncomfortable. His discomfort was relieved as the main course was brought in and placed in front of the guests. More wine was poured, and the waiters and waitresses disappeared.

The table fell quiet as the guests dived into their food. Lovelace finished first and washed down her meal with a large glass of wine. She looked around the table and watched as the other diners avoided eye contact.

Mackay placed his knife and fork onto his plate and sat back in his chair. He looked smug, Lovelace thought. She was beginning to feel grateful that Mackay hadn't had the time to dig too much into her past. Even so, she was wary. He was a man who liked to play games. They were dangerous games, too, she couldn't help but feel. Who, exactly, was he going to wind up next?

'This reminds me of a dinner party Winston Churchill went to,' Mackay began, as everyone else continued with their meals. 'back when he was an MP.'

Everyone turned and looked at Sir Malcolm. Sir Malcolm fidgeted.

'I believe,' Mackay went on, 'that he had a particular dislike for Nancy Astor, who said to him, "Sir, if you were my husband, I'd poison your tea!" to which Sir Winston replied, "And if I were your husband I'd drink it!"'

Mackay laughed.

'I don't suppose there are any poisoners in the prison, John?' He asked.

Johnathon shook his head. 'No. I don't believe there are.'

'More of a woman's crime.' Mackay went on, not looking at anyone in particular. 'Although not so much these days. Criminals aren't what they used to be. They have no style, sense of class, or imagination—a quick slap over the back of the head with a frying pan. Or stabbed. So very boring and mundane. So very modern. I suppose that's why you like those Agatha Christie books, Grace. I understand she used poisons to great effect in her plots.'

Grace smiled, and Lovelace noted a nervousness to it. 'Yes. Yes, she did. But I suppose poisons were easier to get hold of in those early days.'

'Indeed they were!' Mackay agreed. 'One could acquire strychnine by buying rat poison and arsenic by buying fly paper. I believe it was possible to extract the arsenic from the flypaper by soaking the sheets in water and then administering it to one's intended victim by placing it in their food. I wonder how many people have successfully offed a loved one that way? What do you think, Mrs Friedman?'

Esther, stoic and unflappable by nature, flapped. Lovelace watched her expression with interest.

'I'm not married, Ethan, as you well know. I'm a spinster.'

Esther's face was strained with the effort it took not to give herself away too much. "It's Miss Friedman, Ms Friedman or Esther.'

Mackay grinned. 'My apologies. It wasn't my intention to offend you,' he lied. 'Have you never been married?'

'No.' Esther said firmly.

'I see. It's unlikely you've ever been tempted to poison your old man, then? If you've never had one, that is?'

'Quite.' Esther said.

'I suppose it's not just poisoning you could use to off your partner,' Mackay continued. 'I understand glass was once used in a case. Isn't that so, John?'

Johnathon shook his head in a disinterested fashion. 'I can't say I've ever heard of that.'

'Yes, yes, I'm sure of it. Back in the early twentieth century, I think. Some middle-aged woman fell in love with a younger man and plotted her husband's death. I'm sure she tried glass in his food. It wasn't successful, and in the end, the lover got bored and stabbed the husband to death in the street. They were both hanged for it.'

Lovelace watched as Johnathon stole a glance at his wife, Elouise. He looked scared, she thought. He was searching his wife's face for help.

Lovelace felt Elouise move in the chair beside her.

'You're thinking of Thompson and Bywaters,' Elouise said matter-of-factly. 'You named my room after Mrs Thompson. Very subtle of you. And they were hanged, and for his part, Bywaters accepted his guilt, although many people argue that Edith Thompson was entirely blameless. A fantasist, but not a murderer.'

Lovelace admired how Elouise disarmed Mackay by laying out his game in front of everyone before he could play his hand. Very clever.

Mackay looked momentarily perplexed. Honesty was a strategy that confused him. You couldn't play games with an honest person. Still, he was going to try.

'But you were married once?' Mackay went on. 'Before John?'

'I was.' Elouise admitted freely.

'And you met John while you were married?'

'I did. And he prefers to be called Johnathon. To call anyone but the name they like to be called by is just rude.'

Lovelace smiled. She was beginning to like Elouise even more.

'Your husband died.' Mackay said bluntly.

'He did. And then I married Johnathon, and we had a baby. We've been married ever since. All of this is public knowledge.'

'And yet you spend most of your time in your home on the mainland? Away from your husband?'

'I do,' Elouise said. 'I don't like this island. I find it claustrophobic. I prefer town life. I have friends and associates there and a life I enjoy.'

'While your husband is here?' Mackay probed.

'That's enough, Ethan,' Johnathon said firmly. 'Our private life is not your business or how we lead our lives.'

'Oh, no, please go on,' Esther drooled. 'It's beginning to get interesting.'

Johnathon turned to Esther and said, 'How about we just talk some more about poisoning husbands?'

Esther's smile disintegrated.

'No, you're quite right, Johnathon,' Mackay said pointedly. He turned to Elouise. 'Please accept my apologies.'

Elouise nodded, but Lovelace could see the insincerity writ large across Mackay's face.

'Tell me,' Mackay continued. 'Did you bury or cremate your first husband?'

Elouise said, 'Cremated.'

'Shame.' Mackay said. 'That destroys the evidence, wouldn't you say, Sir Malcolm?'

Lovelace remembered what Esther had said to Sir Malcolm at the bar. *Do you have skeletons in your closet, or have you had them all cremated?*

Sir Malcolm nearly choked on his wine. He was saved again by the waiting staff, who cleared the plates and opened more bottles of wine. Lovelace watched as Mackay skilfully avoided topping up his drink. He was staying perfectly sober. Lovelace drained her glass and accepted another. She didn't need to avoid the drink. Alcohol had almost no effect on her.

The puddings came and were laid out in front of the guests. Elouise called over Mrs Brent, who had constantly hovered near the kitchen door.

'Once they've loaded the dishwashers, you may let the waiters go. The weather must be pretty awful out there. If you make sure the breakfast things are ready for the morning, you may go too.'

'We can stay to pour brandy?' Mrs Brent said keenly. She had caught most of the conversations that had entertained Mackay and was keen to hear more.

'That's quite all right, Mrs Brent. Mr Preece and I will take care of the rest. I'll see you in the morning at seven.'

Mrs Brent struggled to hide her disappointment. 'Very well. I'll see that the kitchen is tidied up, and we'll be on our way.'

Mackay finished his chocolate pudding and stood as if to leave. 'I think a quick snifter at the bar is in order. Sir Malcolm?'

Sir Malcolm fidgeted. 'Well, time is getting on, you know. I'm not a young man anymore. I think I might retire.'

'Nonsense,' Mackay insisted. 'Come on. We'll take it up to the lounge. Much more comfortable.'

Mackay grabbed his glass of wine and a bottle from the table. 'Come on then.'

Reluctantly the guests stepped in behind Mackay and left the dining room. Lovelace followed Elouise out of the room and into the reception area. As she did so, she noticed a door she had missed earlier.

'What's in there?' Lovelace asked.

Elouise followed Lovelace's line of sight. 'Oh. That. Come, I'll show you.'

Elouise strolled across the floor to the door and opened it. There was a simple handle on the door but no lock. Above the door, Lovelace noticed a camera looking back at her.

'I thought there were no cameras in the house?' She asked.

'It's the only one and links to a screen inside the room. It can't be remotely accessed, and it doesn't record anything. Sir Malcolm?' Elouise shouted to get the old man's attention. He and Mackay stopped in the middle of the reception area. 'Would you like to see the panic room, Sir Malcolm?'

One by one, the guests stepped inside the large room. It was equipped with toilets, sinks, stoves, kettles, refrigerators, televisions, sofas, armchairs and a huge pantry that stored just about every type of long shelf-life product you could imagine.

'What makes you think you'll need a panic room?' Esther asked as she admired the room.

'One can never tell what is likely to happen given the right opportunities,' Johnathon explained. 'It was considered a necessary addition to the house as we developed our emergency plans. There's a panic room in the main accommodation block and one at the prison. Should anything go drastically wrong on the island, staff and visitors can stay safe here for as long as it takes for the mainland to send force over to sort the problem out.'

'The camera's just for us inside to see who is outside,' Elouise explained to Lovelace. 'The door cannot be opened from outside. It can only be opened from inside.'

'Very secure.' Lovelace admitted.

'Well, I shouldn't think it will ever be needed.' Mackay said. 'The prison's one of the most secure facilities in the world. This was just a waste of money.'

'But you can never be sure,' Elouise said. 'That's why we built it. Better to be happy that you wasted money than be in a position to regret not building it. Right. Shall we have more drinks?'

***

There was an atmosphere in the lounge that reminded Lovelace of a scene in a classic whodunnit. The room was lit by a few table lamps that cast shadows upon the walls, and they were joined by the flickering light from the log burner that Sir Malcolm had just stoked.

They were all strangers to Lovelace, although she knew some of them by reputation. Mackay had been the biggest surprise to her. Everyone knew of the great billionaire Scottish philanthropist and prison reformer Ethan Mackay, but Lovelace wondered how many knew what an absolute shit he was in person. She prided herself on being a good judge of character, and her judgement of Mackay was poor.

And then there was Sir Malcolm. He was a Member of Parliament and a well-respected diplomat. He was an old man, Lovelace mused and he seemed to be tiring of life. She felt sorry for him. Mackay had prodded and teased him like a school bully, and Sir Malcolm was entirely defenceless against him.

And then there was Esther Friedman, scurrilous hack and investigative journalist. She was an intelligent woman with a long and illustrious career behind her, but she worried Lovelace. It seemed to her that Esther was the sort of woman you couldn't trust, but then, what journalist could you trust? Lovelace was cautious. Esther was a nosey, prying old woman with a knack for sniffing out a juicy story.

Lovelace liked Elouise Preece, but she seemed lonely. Mackay's sniping at the dinner table had hinted at problems between her and her husband, Johnathon, but

Elouise had dealt with them with consummate ease. She was certainly not a woman to be easily intimidated, and certainly not by Mackay, but Lovelace couldn't help but sense a pain behind those green eyes.

Johnathon Preece was a bit of a mystery. He said very little, preferring to listen to what others had to say and only interjecting a comment if one was solicited from him. He was a private man, Lovelace mused. Or was he secretive? He had stood up to Mackay when his wife had been threatened, and Lovelace admired that. Lovelace thought there was more to Johnathon, but she couldn't quite place her finger on what that might be.

Kellerman had followed the small party to the lounge, and while Esther had grabbed another bottle of champagne from the bar, he had made his excuses and left. Lovelace made no judgement on Kellerman. He was little more than a suit, who had earned his place at the dinner table by his position on the island, but Mackay took almost no interest in him. He hadn't objected as Kellerman took his leave.

And then there was Grace. Lovelace admired how she held herself and the deftly professional way she anticipated every one of Mackay's whims. She was pretty, too, and her cute little dungaree outfit emphasised the beautiful figure of the young woman who wore it. Lovelace nodded in appreciation. There was an edge to Grace, and she couldn't figure out why such a talented young woman like that would want to throw her lot in with Mackay. Every time he spoke to her, he was vile. He spat words at her like she was nothing, a mere hindrance to his day. It was passive-aggressive, too, the kind of words that he could claim were without malice but which, spoken in the way that he said them, meant so much more.

Lovelace didn't like Mackay.

Then it came back to her again. The feeling that she was in a scene from a whodunnit. The weather howled with fury outside the room, and rain lashed relentlessly at the glass. And there was Mackay, holding court among his subjects, probing, prodding, and teasing. There was a danger, Lovelace thought, that one day he would say the wrong thing to the wrong person, who would pull out a gun and shoot him in the face, and she wouldn't be entirely upset if that happened.

Yes, Mackay would be the victim. It was classic Golden Age stuff. But who would be the murderer, she wondered?

She was interrupted in her musings by Grace, who handed her a glass of champagne from the bottle that she had managed to wrestle from Esther's iron grip.

'Thank you.'

Grace smiled sweetly. Quietly she said, 'I'm sorry about Ethan.'

'No need to be sorry.' Lovelace looked at Mackay, who was pouring whiskey into Sir Malcolm's glass. Then she looked at Esther, who was sitting on the sizeable U-shaped sofa staring in her direction.

Grace followed her look. 'She's a bit of a dragon, isn't she?' She giggled. 'She's been trying to dig the dirt on Ethan for years. It was quite a surprise that he had invited her to the island. It's like one lion inviting another lion into the lion's den.'

'I wonder who would win?' Lovelace pondered.

'Well, they both growl a lot, and they're keen on baring their teeth, but in the end, I think it would be a case of some intense hair-pulling!'

They laughed, and Lovelace warmed to Grace even more.

Mackay caught the sound of laughter and glared in their direction.

'Something you'd like to share with us?' He growled.

'Girl talk.' Lovelace said curtly. 'Nothing that would interest you.'

Mackay felt the sting. 'You interest me,' he said. 'You interest me because I know almost nothing about you. Well, apart from the obvious, of course. Daughter of the infamous Cherwell Valley Strangler, former police officer, suspected murderer....'

The words hung in the air for some time.

Lovelace smiled. So, Mackay had done a bit of homework after all.

'Yes, of course,' Esther slurred. 'I'd forgotten about that. Are you still a suspect? Or did you manage to convince them that Zoe Lovelace killed him?'

'Killed who?' Grace asked. 'Is Zoe your sister?'

'Two Lovelace sisters.' Mackay continued. 'One a law defender, the other... not so much. Daughters of a psychopath who murdered their mother in front of them and then tried to kill you both, isn't that right?'

'That's right,' Lovelace said.

'It seems one of the Lovelace sisters may have inherited some of their dear daddy's criminal tendencies.' Mackay went on. 'She's a bit murderous, I'm told. Certainly, one to steer clear of.'

'I wonder if psychosis is inheritable?' Esther said, throwing Lovelace a look.

'Well,' Sir Malcolm said, relishing the fact that Mackay had turned on someone else. 'It depends on whether you feel that environmental factors play a part in the development of psychosis or whether genetics play a part. Certainly, most criminals in this category share a similar upbringing. Broken families, alcohol abuse, sexual abuse. That sort of thing. But there is some argument that genetics play a part.'

'If genetics were a small part of a larger machine,' Mackay wondered, 'and children were brought up in an environment similar to one in which their psychotic father had grown up, surely the conditions would be right for the production of more psychotic individuals.'

'I suppose so, yes,' Sir Malcolm said. 'But I'm not sure whether that has ever happened.'

'I wonder if the evidence isn't standing right before us.' Mackay said.

'Now look here, Ethan,' Johnathon stood from his seat and confronted Mackay. 'I won't have you being rude to my guests. Not in my house.'

'But it's not your house,' Mackay snarled. 'And she's not a guest. She wasn't supposed to be here. She's an interloper.'

Lovelace stepped towards Mackay. She laid a hand on Johnathon's arm and said, 'thank you, Johnathon, but it's okay.'

Johnathon turned and smiled at Lovelace.

'Chivalrous to the end, eh, John?' Mackay snapped. 'It surprises me that a young woman can still turn your head.'

'Mr Mackay,' Lovelace said, 'may I call you Ethan?'

'No.'

'Very well. Mr Mackay, you are the vilest human being I have ever had the misfortune to spend time with in my life and believe me when I tell you that I have met a few. You play games with people. You bully them and tease them, and I can only imagine what that serves to achieve. You have no redeeming qualities apart from the fact that you are rich, which only serves to make you an even more disgusting human being. You talk to people like they are scum when it is you, sir, that is scum. You have no idea who I am, what I have done, or what I am capable of. You have no respect for anybody or anything.

I will not stay on this island for a minute more than I have to, and it is my dearest wish that you do us all a favour and go fuck yourself.'

Lovelace dropped her glass onto a table, turned and left the room.

Six

'What do you know about her?'

The party had taken Lovelace's rant at Mackay as their cue to depart. Sir Malcolm finished the golden liquid Mackay had recently poured into his glass, begged everyone goodnight, and took his leave.

Esther had stood up from the couch, clutching her bottle of champagne with one hand and her glass in the other, and said, 'well, that was fun. We should do it again,' and stumbled out of the room.

'I think it's time I went to bed, too.' Grace said and looked at Mackay for permission.

Mackay still stood where Lovelace had left him. He wore an expression that warned Grace to approach with caution. Mackay had a reputation among friends and associates for ranting and raving like a banshee, but Grace knew full well that it was when he was quiet and subdued that he was at his most dangerous. He was like that now. He stood gazing at nothing in particular whilst running his finger around the rim of his glass. The drink inside lay untouched.

'Ethan?'

Mackay looked up. 'What?'

'I'm going to bed. Is there anything else you need from me?'

Mackay shook his head. 'No.' He said quietly. 'That's enough for today.'

Grace turned and said goodnight to Elouise and Johnathon and left the room.

'May I get you a top-up?' Elouise asked.

Mackay continued to stare into space.

'Ethan? Can I get you a refill?'

Mackay tipped the glass to his mouth and drained the contents. A smile gathered on the edge of his lips, but it turned into a snarl as it grew.

'I'm going to bed.' He said, and Elouise noted the tension in his words. She doubted he would be sleeping much this evening.

Mackay dropped his glass onto the table and walked out of the room without saying another word. Elouise and Johnathon were tidying the lounge when Johnathon said, 'What do you know about her?'

'Lovelace? Nothing at all,' Elouise admitted. 'Only what I've read about her in the newspapers. Even then, not much.'

'Don't you think it's odd? That she's here? I mean, that she's here now? At the same time as the others?'

'No, I don't think so. Just an odd coincidence.'

'I don't like coincidences.' Johnathon said. He was going to add more, but he wasn't entirely sure he knew what he meant or how to word it.

'Coincidences happen,' Elousie added. 'That's why there's a word for it. She always planned on visiting her father, and her role in catching Sinclair has made her the darling of the legal system and the popular press. It was hardly her fault the helicopter ran into problems.'

'Yes. Another coincidence. Just like the storm….'

Elouise chuckled. 'You can hardly accuse the girl of manipulating the weather! It's just an unfortunate combination of events, that's all.'

Johnathon knew that had to be true, but the doubt lingered in his mind, and he found himself incapable of expressing it. He sighed.

Elouise gathered the last of the glasses, and Johnathon followed her down the staircase to the kitchen. Mrs Brent had done an excellent job at cleaning away the dishes, and one of the machines continued to hum in the background. Elouise washed the remaining glasses by hand, and Johnathon dried them and put them away. When they had finished, Elouise kissed her husband on the cheek.

'I'm going to bed.'

She held her hand on his cheek for a long moment and searched deep into her husband's eyes. 'Don't stay up too late.'

Once she had left the room, Johnathon searched the cabinets for a glass and poured himself a glass of red wine from one of the leftover bottles. He sat at the kitchen table and sipped his drink while his mind tried to work out what it was that felt so wrong.

***

Grace knew that Mackay wouldn't be long behind her. She also knew his mood. She raced out of the lounge and ran softly along the carpeted corridor until she found Lovelace's door. She tapped on it loudly enough for someone behind it to hear but not so loud that the noise carried to the next room. She waited a few seconds before she knocked again. No-one came.

Quietly she opened the door and peeked in.

'Lucy?'

Still, no reply came. She reached for the light switch but then thought better of it. Everyone had sunk quite a lot of alcohol that evening. Perhaps Lovelace was asleep. She didn't want to disturb her. She just wanted to warn her. She liked Lovelace. She felt like a kindred spirit. And Mackay wasn't about to let her off the hook for what she had said. But then, Mackay was a coward. He would never confront her face to face. He manipulated things from behind the scenes. She would have plenty of time to warn her.

She closed the door behind her just as she heard Mackay approach. She nipped lightly across the corridor to her room and closed the door firmly behind her.

***

Johnathon walked across the reception holding his glass of wine, and opened the door to his study. Everyone else had named it the library, but he considered it his office.

'Oh. Hello.'

Lovelace was sitting on an easy chair with her head in a book. She looked up as Johnathon walked in.

'I'm sorry, I came here to hide. I figured this was the last place that Mackay would come looking.'

'Well, you're not wrong there,' Johnathon said. 'But I wouldn't worry too much. Mackay's not the confrontation type. He prefers to wind people up and stir them a bit. And I must say, you don't strike me as the sort of girl to avoid confrontation. You seem more than capable of dealing with Mackay.'

Lovelace smiled. He wasn't wrong there. Mackay was no threat to her. She said, 'you're quite right. I'm more than happy to stand up to bullies, and Mackay is definitely one of those. But your wife was kind enough to offer me a place to stay while this storm passes, and I felt like I had spoken out of turn.'

'Nonsense. You've met Elouise. You remind me of her a bit. Fearless and strong.'

Lovelace watched as a smile swept across his face. There was affection and love there. But something followed in the smile's wake—pain, anguish, and confusion. As Lovelace had walked into the room earlier, she noticed a rolled-up duvet and pillowcase stuffed behind a bookcase. It was beginning to become evident that the two Preeces lived separate lives, although the love and compassion still lingered. She was still trying to work out why Johnathon's room had been named after a country when a thought occurred to her. She smiled inwardly. It would certainly explain a few things.

Lovelace folded her book and laid it on the chair as she stood up. 'Perhaps I should go to bed.'

'I think you'll find the coast is clear,' Johnathon said, 'Mackay went up a little while ago.'

As Lovelace reached the door, he said, 'you should be careful, though. You would have upset Mackay, and he holds grudges. He may not come for you in person or while you're on this island. But he will come for you.'

Lovelace wasn't afraid of Mackay. She had taken on bigger and tougher men and left them wanting. She said, 'thank you. I'll be careful. Goodnight, Johnathon.'

Johnathon sat down at his desk. He leaned over and switched on the monitor, filling the room with a sharp light. There was something about the Lovelace girl he liked. She was very much a younger Elouise. He typed her name into Google and watched as the girl's life story filled the screen.

***

'Mister Mackay!'

Esther spat the words out with as much venom as she could muster. In her head, it sounded perfect, but to Mackay, it sounded like the drunken ramblings of an old woman.

Esther had finished her bottle of champagne, decided the night was yet young and embarked on an ambitious plan to acquire more. She had bumped into Mackay as she stumbled out of her room.

'You,' she slurred, 'are a horrible man, and I don't like you.'

Mackay tried to step past her, but her frame blocked the way. 'And I don't care.' He said.

'But you will,' Esther rambled. 'You will. I'll see to it that you will! You've picked on the wrong woman here, and I'll tell you that for nothing. Maybrick, I ask you! What do you mean by that, I wonder?'

'You know very well what I mean.' Mackay replied. 'Now, if you don't mind, I'd like to go to my room.'

'Stir, stir, stir. Making your nasty little comments to everyone. You,' she exclaimed, pointing a curled finger at Mackay, 'don't know what you're talking about. You don't know what you think you know.'

'I know that I'd like to go to bed.'

'One day,' Esther dribbled. 'I'm going to stab you in the back, you odious little man.'

The door to "Lemon" opened, and Grace stepped out. She had changed out of her dungarees and was draped in a long white bathrobe.

'Miss Friedman? Is everything all right?' Grace asked.

Esther stumbled away from Mackay. 'I'm going for more champers!' She declared. She took a single step and toppled into Grace's arms.

'Perhaps it would be better if I helped you to bed?' Grace suggested.

'Why? Are there champers there?'

'I think, perhaps, you've had enough for tonight.' Grace said, dropping an arm around Esther and guiding her back into her room.

Once she dealt with Esther, she closed her room door. Mackay was waiting for her in the corridor. He was standing in front of "Lemon."

'She's drunk. She didn't mean anything by that.'

'I know.' Mackay said, and Grace felt his eyes tour her body.

Grace tightened the belt to the robe and pulled the collar around her neck. Mackay moved closer to her until she was pinned to the door of "Maybrick."

'Ethan, no!' Grace cried, but he had moved so close she could smell the whiskey on his breath. She wanted to pull her arms away from her clothing to fight off his hand as she felt him lift the hem of her robe around her waist. She did so with her right hand, but it exposed her upper body, and Ethan ripped open the belt and pushed her hard against the door.

She was naked save for the robe that hung off her shoulders.

'Ethan, no. You promised.' She cried and desperately fought off the strong hands that groped her.

'Ethan, leave the girl alone.'

Elouise stood in the doorway to "Thompson." She was still wearing the dress she had worn to dinner.

'Why does every fucker want a piece of me today!' Mackay yelled.

He stood back from Grace, who drew her clothing back around her body. The two women sensed the rage that was burning through Mackay's blood. Someone was going to suffer for his anger.

Elouise stood aside from her door and beckoned Mackay. 'Leave the girl alone, Ethan. Why don't you come and sit with me for a while?'

Mackay looked back at Grace. His eyes burned with darkness. Then he turned and pushed passed Elouise as he walked into her room.

Elouise looked at Grace, and a benevolent smile spread across her face. Grace looked terrified. 'Go to bed. I'll take care of Ethan.' She said and closed the door.

Grace stood for a few minutes, composing herself. Her heart was in her mouth, and she could feel the adrenaline coursing through her veins. Once she had settled herself, she opened the door to "Lemon" and disappeared behind it.

Lovelace crept around the corner to the corridor and waited for Grace to shut the door behind her. She had been halfway up the staircase when she heard Esther cry, 'Mr Mackay!'

Without being heard, Lovelace manoeuvred herself into a position where she could see and hear the exchange between Esther and Mackay. She was still there when Mackay had attempted to assault Grace before Elouise had intervened. The image of Grace's naked body and Mackay's groping hands filled her with fury. She had been moments away from knocking Mackay into next week when Elouise had stepped in.

Quietly, Lovelace stole past the guest rooms to her own. She opened the door and closed it softly behind her.

***

The storm raged unabated outside her bedroom window. Lovelace had changed into some of Elouise's daughter's nightwear, climbed into her large double bed, and lay there listening to the rain as it lashed furiously against the window pane. She was still lying there an hour later when she heard a door open in the corridor. She opened her door a fraction and watched as Mackay left Elouise's room and crossed to his own. A moment later, his door opened again, and Mackay returned and made his way back to the staircase. She lost sight of him as he descended the stairs.

Lovelace climbed back into bed and listened to the storm. It played a fierce melody in the air outside and hummed her slowly to sleep.

The night played its many tricks in her mind as she slept. An image of Grace came to the fore, dressed in a long white robe that fell from her shoulders, and she stood before her with a hand outstretched, beckoning her forward.

Mackay loomed into her mind, a door slammed somewhere in the house, and an evil grin stretched across his face. And then there was Elouise. Beautiful, elegant and graceful. Graceful. Grace. Back full circle in front of the mysterious and stunning Grace Mahone.

But why a lemon? No, not that. She understood that. That wasn't the question. What was the question? She felt she ought to know.

And why was there knocking at her door, and why wouldn't they shut up and go away?

Slowly her eyes opened, and she took a few moments to root herself in the here and now. It was still dark, and the wind continued to howl outside. The knocking continued.

Lovelace rolled out of bed and draped a bathrobe over her shoulders. She made it to the door as the knocking continued.

She didn't know why, but she had expected to see Grace. She was surprised to see Johnathon and

Kellerman, still dressed in last night's clothes, standing at her door.

'Is everything okay?' She asked.

The look on Johnathon's face suggested that everything was not okay.

'I think we may need your help,' Johnathon said slowly.

'You're probably the only one who can,' Kellerman said, trying to explain things.

'Mr Kellerman suggested we ask you,' Johnathon went on, 'as you have some experience in this sort of thing.'

'I'm not sure I understand.' Lovelace said.

'Perhaps if we show you?' Johnathon suggested. 'I think it would become clearer then?'

Lovelace looked at the two men and saw hesitation and confusion engulf them. Whatever had happened had spooked them.

She said, 'wait here. I'll get changed.'

She closed her bedroom door and quickly changed into jeans and a white t-shirt. She was back outside her room and following the two men down the staircase in less than five minutes. They strolled along the reception area without saying a word, and both men hesitated before the kitchen door. Johnathon turned and held an arm outstretched, allowing Lovelace to pass first.

Her first thought was that they should at least have warned her. It was unfair to have let her wander into the kitchen without so much as a "brace yourself" beforehand.

Johnathon said, 'I didn't know what to do, so I called Kellerman, who came right over. He wasn't sure what to do either, and then he remembered that you were a police officer once and that maybe you would know the right thing to do….'

Lovelace looked at the two men, who continued to look confused and stared at Lovelace, hoping she would take control. Then she looked back into the kitchen.

The kitchen had been cleared and cleaned down after last night's dinner. Sat at the kitchen table, slumped over a bowl and with both arms splayed out in front of him, was Mackay, with a large kitchen knife protruding from his back.

Seven

Detective Chief Inspector Latham McBride was never generally in the best of moods, even on a good day. Today was not a good day. He sat in the passenger seat of an old Volvo estate as it was being driven by his long-suffering DS, Aisha Sandhu. He would generally have preferred to drive himself, but the call had come through as he had sunk another glass of single malt and reluctantly accepted DS Sandhu's offer to drive them both.

'Can't it wait until the morning?' He had asked his Chief Constable grumpily.

'No, it can't,' had come the stern reply. The Chief Constable had braced himself to face the fury of McBride, but he had faced little choice. Despite his nature, McBride was the best he had.

'I've just had a drink.' McBride had argued.

'It's four o'clock in the morning!'

'It's my weekend off,' McBride had continued.

'I don't care,' the Chief Constable had countered. 'Sober up. Get your DS to drive, but get there now.'

An hour later, McBride had found himself at the mercy of his DS's erratic driving, a vicious winter storm that promised to blow them into the sea, and a raging headache that had been barely tempered by a gallon of water, three coffees and an array of painkillers.

'How much further?' He asked.

'We're nearly there.' DS Sandhu said quietly.

She had fought McBride's temper and the storm's attempt to kill them both with the calm focus she had become well known for. Nothing fazed or upset her. As a Glaswegian police officer, she had seen everything the city could throw at her and dealt with it with the calm studiousness of a woman twice her age. She even liked McBride, despite his attempts to prove that he was a miserable, unlikeable old git. But then, she had grown up in a large household of miserable, grumpy old gits, and it didn't bother her. Perhaps that was why they worked well together.

She guided her old car through the narrow lanes until the tall security gates of BlackRock's mainland headquarters came into view. It was still early, and no sign of the impending dawn showed in the sky. Large lights cut through the cloud and rain, casting everything in a sharp, unnatural white.

They pulled up at the main entrance, which was blocked by a security barrier. They waited patiently while a guard donned a bright orange waterproof coat and stepped out of his little hut into the storm. He approached DS Sandhu's window.

'DCI McBride and DS Sandhu to see Mr Swift. He's expecting us.' DS Sandhu said as she lowered her window.

The guard nodded and walked back into his guard house. A couple of hours ago, the operations centre had suddenly sprung into life, and he had received notification of some new visitors. The guard had no idea what was happening, but something serious had occurred, and the arrival of the police had only increased his curiosity.

DS Sandhu drove through the barrier as it lifted and continued up to what she considered to be the main entrance. They were greeted inside by Liam Swift. He held out a hand to McBride, who shook it reluctantly. Since the pandemic, he had grown used to not having to touch people. It pained him that people were returning to the old ways.

'Liam Swift, head of Island Operations for HMP BlackRock.'

'DCI McBride. This is DS Sandhu.'

Liam smiled at DS Sandhu and gently shook her hand.

'When can we get on the island?' McBride demanded.

Liam looked confused. 'You can't. I'm afraid the storm has grounded all flights. Even commercial flights are being re-routed to Europe.'

'Well, how long's that going to last?' McBride asked.

'At least another twenty-four hours,' Liam said, noting the grim expression that McBride pulled.

'Can we get a boat to the island?' Sandhu asked.

Liam shook his head. 'Afraid not, no. We are building a dock on the island, but even if that had been finished, there's no way we'd be able to get there in this weather.'

McBride sighed. His day was getting worse. 'So how the bloody hell am I supposed to investigate a murder if I can't see the crime scene?'

'Well,' Liam began and hesitated. 'We do have eyes on the island. Professional eyes. I thought we could do what we can for now and the rest when we can get you there in person?'

Slowly Liam explained about the presence of Lovelace in the house.

Sandhu looked at her DCI. 'She was the one that caught that serial killer in Oxford. Adam Sinclair.'

'That's right,' Liam said. 'He's on the island too. As is her father.'

McBride looked at Liam for clarification. Sandhu said, 'she's Jack Lovelace's daughter. The Cherwell Valley Strangler.'

McBride remembered the case. 'If she's in the house, she's a suspect. It would be wrong to involve her in the investigation.'

'And yet she's likely to be the only one who can preserve the crime scene and any evidence.' Liam added. 'And she's not known to Mackay and has no motive for wanting him dead.'

'Even so,' McBride began.

'And we have Kellerman.' Liam interrupted.

'Kellerman?'

'He's the island's operation's chief. He wasn't in the house at the time of the murder. Could he act as an independent observer? We're setting up comms with the house so that you can control the investigation. You would see and hear everything, almost as if you were there.'

Sandhu said, 'it can't hurt to talk to Lovelace. It's better than nothing.'

McBride reluctantly agreed. The crime scene did need preserving, and it would be easier to explain the process to an experienced hand rather than some fat-fingered idiot in a suit.

'Okay. Let's do it. Can I get a coffee?'

***

Lovelace immediately cleared the kitchen and told Johnathon to call the mainland and inform the police.

From that moment on, everything had taken on a different pace.

Gerry Holt, the island's IT guy, had been woken from his sleep and ordered to pull the security footage from around the house, starting from when Kellerman had left the previous evening to when he had returned in the morning. The cameras had been set to record any movement through the night and ping a specific email address each time that occurred. Due to the nature of the storm, there had been much movement around the house, and Gerry was busy looking through the footage.

Kellerman had returned to the Citadel and gathered several boxes of surveillance equipment and recording devices to help with the investigation. Lovelace and Johnathon returned together to Johnathon's study and drank strong coffee.

'This is not good,' Johnathon said. 'This is not good at all.'

Lovelace agreed. It wasn't good. She couldn't help but remember what Mackay had said over dinner the previous evening. *Criminals aren't what they used to be. They have no style, class, or imagination—a quick slap over the back of the head with a frying pan. Or stabbed. So very dull and mundane.*

Someone had been very dull and mundane indeed. Mackay would not be pleased.

Kellerman returned and laid out the boxes in the study. There were microphones, video cameras, body cameras, and various other complicated-looking devices. Kellerman's face was strained. 'I've just spoken to Gerry. He's reviewed the footage from the CCTV cameras from last night. No one left after me, and no one came into the house before I did this morning.'

'So, whoever killed Mackay came from within the house.' Johnathon said. He'd been afraid of that.

Lovelace hadn't been afraid of that. She saw it coming. At least the field of suspects was small.

'I've spoken to Liam on the mainland,' Kellerman continued. 'The police want us to walk the crime scene, hence the cameras.' He picked up a body camera and handed it to Lovelace. 'You'll be leading the investigation.'

'You're joking?' She exclaimed. 'Surely I'm a suspect?'

'You are. Hence the cameras. Everything you do and say will be recorded. I'm to act as an independent witness. Gerry's setting up comms as we speak. Let's set up this room as the interview room. Once everyone has woken up and had breakfast, we'll have to interview them all. You'll be connected to the police on the mainland through this..'

He handed Lovelace an earpiece. 'They'll guide the interviews. They also want to talk to you first. We'll set up a camera just here....'

It wasn't long before the cameras in Johnathon's study had been installed and connected to the island's mainframe computer. Gerry worked his magic and connected them to the Island's Mainland Operations Centre. Before long, Lovelace was sitting in front of Johnathon's computer, looking at the face of a man she had never seen before.

At the mainland centre, Liam handed a sheet of paper listing everyone on the island to McBride. McBride passed it to Sandhu, who glanced at the list and placed it on the table in front of her. The list was comprehensive. It included the guests at the Mansion House, the staff at HMP BlackRock and all of the incarcerated prisoners within its walls.

'Okay.' Liam said, nodding at McBride. 'We're online.'

McBride looked at the pretty face that looked back at him on the screen. She had scruffy hair, he noted, but then she had been woken up unexpectedly and probably hadn't had a chance to freshen up.

'Miss Lovelace, my name is Detective Chief Inspector McBride. This is Detective Sergeant Sandhu.'

'Hello,' Lovelace said.

'Miss Lovelace, as an experienced police officer I know you'll understand the importance of securing the crime scene as quickly as possible.'

'Of course.'

'Do you have any objection to doing that for us and taking witness statements while the last few hours' events are still fresh in everyone's minds?'

'Not at all. But surely I'm a suspect too?' Lovelace asked.

'You are. That's why we are going to film and record everything that happens. You will be shadowed by Mr Kellerman, who is not a suspect in Ethan Mackay's murder. Do you have any objection to that?'

'No.'

'Good. Perhaps we should start by asking you a few questions. You can help us draw a picture of the circumstances of Ethan Mackay's murder.'

'Of course. Fire away.'

'Why are you on the island, Miss Lovelace?' The question was blunt and to the point. Lovelace admired McBride's style.

'I'm visiting my father, Jack Lovelace. He's a prisoner on the island.'

'And yet there are no visitors allowed on the island?' McBride asked without asking.

'That's correct. I know a few people. I pulled a few strings.'

'Did you know any of the other guests in the house before arriving on the island?'

'No.' Lovelace said. 'I knew of Mackay. And Sir Malcolm Lambert. I also knew Esther Friedman's reputation, but I'd never met any of them before. I'd never heard of or met anyone else.'

'How long were you supposed to be on the island?'

'I was due to leave on the same day, but the helicopter ran into some issues. Elouise Preece kindly offered me the use of her daughter's room while we sat out the storm.'

McBride nodded. He already knew all of that. Liam Swift had run him through the details as they set up the comms. What he needed to know now was what Liam Swift didn't know.

'Talk me through the events of the day.'

Quietly and succinctly, Lovelace drew out the day for McBride. She began in the departures lounge on the mainland and talked him through the various interactions between the guests. She talked through the tour of the prison and her visit to her father. Then came the drive back to the house and the tour of the Mansion House. She spoke briefly and directly and didn't linger on any point for long. She didn't speculate or guess; she just gave McBride the details. She ran through the naming of the guest rooms and the sniping Mackay engaged in throughout dinner and afterwards. She confessed that she had taken a swipe at Mackay and had gone to hide in Johnathon's study later. Johnathon confirmed that that much was true. Lovelace then carefully described the events she had witnessed outside of the rooms when Esther had challenged Mackay and when Mackay had tried to assault Grace sexually. Lovelace left nothing out. By the time she had finished, Mcbride and Sandhu knew everything that Lovelace had seen or heard.

'Thank you, Miss Lovelace. You have excellent recall and respect for brevity. Tell me more about the naming of the rooms. What do you think they mean?'

'I can't be sure. I think Esther's room is named after someone that was a potential suspect in the Jack the Ripper murders. I don't understand why that's relevant?'

Sandhu had been typing away on her iPad as Lovelace had run through the last few hours' events. 'You're right about that. James Maybrick was a Victorian cotton merchant. His diaries came out a few years back, which pointed to him being Jack the Ripper, but they're widely believed to be a hoax. On the other hand, his wife was convicted of murdering him in 1889. She was sentenced to hang but eventually served about fifteen years. She was much younger than her husband.'

'How did Maybrick die?' Lovelace asked.

'Florence Maybrick was convicted of poisoning him with arsenic.'

Lovelace pondered the point. 'During dinner, Mackay made a few mentions about women poisoners. He speculated how many people had managed to poison a loved one in that manner. He aimed it at Esther, specifically. Then he asked her if she had ever been married and been tempted to do in her husband like that.'

'How did Miss Friedman respond?'

'She was very unhappy. She looked rattled. And when they had a row outside the bedrooms, Esther said she would find a way to stab him in the back.'

'I wonder if she meant that literally.' McBride looked at DS Sandhu, 'do some digging into Esther Friedman. See what you can find.' To Lovelace, he said, 'what about Thompson? You said that Mackay had tried to wind Elouise Preece up with that, but she had cleverly countered him? What do you think? Anything there?'

'If there is, Elouise didn't show it. Johnathon wasn't happy about it.'

Johnathon stood in the background, watching Lovelace and McBride's exchange.

'I..I..I... I can explain all that,' he stuttered.

'No need, Mr Preece,' McBride said, 'we'll come to you soon enough.' Aside to Sandhu, he said, 'dig there, too.'

'Sir Malcolm seems the most obvious,' McBride went on. 'Old Dr Death himself, Dr Harold Shipman.'

'That seems most likely.' Lovelace agreed. 'Even Esther was digging at the poor old man.'

Do you have skeletons in your closet, or did you have them all cremated?

'Mackay wasn't very subtle with his digs at the old man,' Lovelace continued. 'And Sir Malcolm opposed BlackRock until fairly recently.'

'Blackmail, you think?' McBride asked.

'It makes sense,' Lovelace agreed. 'Once Sir Malcolm was on board, the prison was a sure thing. Mackay probably had something on him and used it to get him to support BlackRock.'

'What about Grace Mahone's room?' McBride asked. 'What do you make of "Lemon"?'

Lovelace had an idea, but she wasn't sure how it would play out. 'I don't know,' she lied. 'I've been trying to work that out.'

'No problem,' McBride said. 'We'll dig into it a bit more at our end.'

There was a long pause as McBride struggled with a problem. In the end, he said, 'Mr Preece, have any of the guests woken up yet?'

Johnathon stepped up to the screen in front of Lovelace and said, 'no, not yet. I don't think it will be long.'

McBride looked at his watch. 'I'm conscious that Ethan Mackay is still in the kitchen with a knife in his back. I wouldn't want anyone finding him like that.'

Or spoiling the crime scene, he mused.

'I called Wayne Sampson a little while ago.' Johnathon said. 'He's our head of security. There should be a couple of his people outside the kitchen by now.'

'Very good.' McBride said. 'Go and check that out, would you, while we finish up here. And guide the guests somewhere else while we clear the kitchen.'

McBride waited as Johnathon disappeared from view. 'Are we alone?' He asked.

'It's just me and Mr Kellerman.' Lovelace said.

'Good. What do you make of the sign on Johnathon Preece's study door?'

'I wondered about that, too.' Lovelace began. 'At first, I wasn't sure why Mackay would name it after a country, and then he said something earlier which made me re-think my approach.'

'Go on.' McBride prompted.

'It was just before my little rant at Ethan. I'm afraid he rather pissed me off. He was being rude to me when Johnathon stepped in and warned Ethan off. He didn't like that a bit. Then he turned to Johnathon and said, very sarcastically, that it surprised him that a young woman could still turn his head.'

'You think he's dipped his wick in young wax before?'

Lovelace took a second to digest his question. 'No. Not like that, at least. But when you consider all the other rooms are named after people, or more specifically murderers, you have to question if any killers have ever been called Ireland?'

'Colin Ireland.' Sandhu said.

'That was my thinking.' Lovelace agreed.

'You have to forgive me,' McBride said, rubbing his throbbing head. 'My history of sick fucks is somewhat lacking at the moment. And my head hurts. Does anyone care to enlighten me?'

'I met him,' Kellerman said softly. 'They called him the Gay Slayer. He murdered five young men. He died himself a few years ago.'

'Okay. So Mackay thought Johnathon was gay. Hardly blackmail material in this day and age. Certainly, nothing to hold over a man's head.' McBride leant into his screen.

'You must know Johnathon Preece quite well, Mr Kellerman. Is it possible he's gay?'

'Of course, it's possible,' Kellerman replied. 'but it would hardly stop the man from doing his job. And I don't know his sexuality or care for that matter.'

McBride leant back. 'Yeah. It doesn't work. It doesn't fit. It's weak.'

'Unless..' Lovelace began.

'Go on. Don't hold anything back.'

'As I understand it, Johnathon's been a prison governor for a few years. I wonder if they were female prisons or male ones?'

McBride felt a smile gather on his lips. He suppressed it. 'I like the way your mind works, Miss Lovelace. A little twisted, but I like it. So, nothing wrong with a gay prison governor, but everything wrong with one that may have abused his position for his own gratification? That is most certainly blackmail material.'

'There were rumours; now I come to think of it.' Kellerman said. 'Not even rumours. Just the way some people can talk when they want to say something but can't. They imply and insinuate. I don't listen to people like that.'

'But people have hinted?' McBride asked.

Kellerman nodded. 'Yes. they have.'

'Very well. We'll look into that, too. Quite a bit to be getting on with, I think. Perhaps we ought to walk the crime scene?'

Eight

Kellerman clipped the body camera to the strap that Lovelace had woven around her neck. He handed her a small earpiece which she popped into her right ear. McBride's voice came through loud and clear.

'When you're ready, I want you to don a pair of gloves Mr Kellerman has acquired and walk over to the kitchen. Mr Kellerman will follow behind you with a camera that will live stream everything to us here on the mainland. We should be able to see and hear everything that you do. I understand that Gerry Holt is online with us as well. Is that so, Mr Holt?'

Lovelace heard a click, followed by a plastic bag rustling in the background. Gerry's voice came through her ear. He was chewing something, and the noise in her ear irritated her. 'Yeah, I'm here.' Gerry said, between chews.

'Good.' McBride said. 'Let's get on with it then, shall we?'

DS Sandhu placed a large mug of coffee in front of McBride. She sat next to him, and they both looked at a bank of monitors in front of them. They could see Lovelace rise from her seat and watched as her body camera beamed the images back to them. She turned and looked at Kellerman, who was holding a camera in her direction. The screens in front of the two detectives showed Kellerman and Lovelace from each other's perspectives.

Lovelace took a pair of gloves from a box that Kellerman had found lying around Johnathon's study. Along with a dozen new masks and testing kits, they were the last remaining indications that a global pandemic had swept past them all.

That was now forgotten as their current situation held their focus. It wasn't lost on anyone that not only had a high-profile and extremely wealthy man been murdered in their midst, but it was almost certain that another high-profile person had committed the murder. It was an inescapable truth that someone who had stayed in the Mansion House overnight had stabbed Mackay in the back. And, despite McBride's assurances to the contrary, Lovelace knew she must be a suspect. He was an intelligent copper, and she could tell that. She may have had no motive, but she had to be a suspect. She needed to tread carefully.

Kellerman followed Lovelace out of the study and into the reception area. They had little idea what time of day it was, but the light that came through the front doors suggested that the morning was in full swing. Despite the light of day, the storm still raged outside, and Lovelace could see the rain driving at the front doors.

'I demand to know what is going on!'

Lovelace turned towards the kitchen door and found her way blocked by Esther Friedman. She stood barely an inch from Wayne Sampson, the island's Head of Security, who was flanked on either side by two uniformed security guards.

'I'm afraid I'm not at liberty to say.' Sampson snarled. Lovelace's impression of the man didn't change. She didn't like him.

'Well, who is?' Esther demanded. She looked across at Johnathon, who had appeared by her side. He looked at Lovelace as she approached. Lovelace felt sorry for him. He was clearly out of his depth.

'Well? Why won't this gorilla let me pass?' Esther said, waving a dismissive hand at Sampson.

'That must be Esther Friedman.' Lovelace heard McBride's voice in her ear.

'Jonathon? What's going on?'

Elouise Preece glided off the last step as she came down the staircase, followed by Grace. Sir Malcolm followed a few paces behind.

'What is all this?' Sir Malcolm demanded.

On the mainland, DCI McBride started to put names to faces. He pointed at the screens as each face showed. 'Esther Friedman. Elouise Preece. Grace Mahone and Sir Malcolm Lombard. Who's the gorilla?'

Lovelace followed McBride's rundown of the guests and looked at each one as he said their names. She looked at Sampson as McBride asked his last question. She said, 'That's Wayne Sampson, head of security. I don't know the other guards.'

'I wouldn't trust him as far as I could throw him,' McBride commented. 'He looks dodgy.'

Lovelace nodded. McBride was a good judge of character.

'Okay, Lovelace,' McBride said in her ear. 'You'd better tell them what's going on.'

Lovelace stepped forward.

'Perhaps if we could all move somewhere else,' Lovelace began, 'I can explain it to you all.'

'I'm perfectly fine here.' Esther said, with a haughty air.

'Very well.' Lovelace continued. 'I have some bad news. I'm afraid Ethan Mackay died last night.'

Esther took a step back. Elouise looked shocked. Grace held a hand over her mouth, and Sir Malcolm grumbled something incoherent.

'Good god.' Sir Malcolm said, pulling himself together. 'What was it? His heart? He was a young fellow, but these things can happen. I knew a chap in my twenties….'

Lovelace cut him off. 'No. It wasn't his heart. Ethan Mackay was stabbed to death. He was murdered.'

This time there was silence. Esther noticed that Kellerman was recording their every move. 'Why is he filming us?'

'Everyone who stayed in this house overnight is a suspect in Mackay's murder.' Lovelace said. 'Mr Kellerman is filming me as I undertake the initial investigation. You are currently all being watched by two detectives on the mainland.'

'You can't possibly think one of us killed the man, do you?' Esther asked. 'Someone must have come in from outside.'

'No.' Lovelace said. 'No one left the house after Mr Kellerman left last night, and no one came into the house before Mr Kellerman was summoned here this morning after Mackay's body had been found. The only people who could have murdered Mackay stayed in this house overnight.'

Lovelace watched as the realisation dawned on their faces.

'But surely that includes you?' Elouise asked.

'It does, to a degree.' Lovelace admitted. 'I wasn't supposed to be here, I didn't know Mackay, and I have no motive for wanting him dead. Like all of you, I had the opportunity, but I am largely excluded from the list of suspects. I'm also being recorded.'

Esther looked across at Sampson, who stood in front of the kitchen door, flanked by two other guards. 'He's in there, isn't he?'

'He is. He was stabbed while he sat at the kitchen table.'

'Perhaps we should all go upstairs to the lounge?' Johnathon suggested. 'Elouise, could you arrange for Mrs Brent to prepare breakfast in the staff accommodation block kitchens and bring them to us here? Sir Malcolm, would you care to come to the lounge while Miss Lovelace takes care of the formalities? Miss Friedman? Some coffee, perhaps. Or something a little stronger?'

'Well, it has come as quite a shock.' Esther admitted.

With the deft hand of a man well-versed in dealing with awkward people, Johnathon gently corralled everyone away from the crime scene. Lovelace thought he may have been out of his depth a few minutes ago, but Johnathon Preece had suddenly found his footing.

Grace stepped up to where Lovelace was standing. 'Is there anything I can do?' She asked. 'As Ethan's PA, I probably know more about his affairs than anyone.'

'No.' Lovelace said. 'We'll just take care of the formalities for now. As soon as we get off the island, the police can take over. They'll probably need to speak to you more then.'

'Okay.' Grace smiled. She looked at where Sampson was standing and shuddered. 'I'll go and sit with the others.'

Lovelace waited while Grace turned and climbed back up the staircase. Lovelace watched her as she went. She pondered a minor detail when McBride's voice came to her through the earpiece.

'Right. Let's do this, shall we, before I die of old age.'

***

Lovelace stood within the kitchen and waited while Kellerman closed the door. They both stood for a long moment, transfixed by the grisly sight that met them.

'Show me the room from where you're stood.' McBride asked.

Kellerman held his video camera aloft and swept from one side of the room to the other.

'That's a big fucking kitchen.' McBride said. Kellerman smiled. He had placed an earpiece in his ear and could listen to everything McBride was saying.

Lovelace followed Kellerman as he panned his camera around the kitchen. Directly in front of them was a large oak kitchen table. Mackay sat at the table, facing them, with his arms outstretched and lying face down. A large kitchen knife protruded from his back.

'First question.' McBride said. 'What the fuck was Mackay doing in the kitchen in the middle of the night?'

'Perhaps he came for a drink?' Lovelace said.

There was a glass to Mackay's right containing an orange liquid.

'Perhaps,' McBride pondered. 'But why not just make a drink and go to bed? Lift Mackay a bit, would you? See what's under him.'

Lovelace walked over to the body of the late Ethan Mackay and felt his skin. He was cold.

'He's been dead for a while.'

'Care to hazard a guess at how long?'

'No.' Lovelace said. 'There are too many variables, and it's cold in here.'

With a gloved hand, Lovelace opened one of the many kitchen drawers. She found what she was looking for and returned to the body.

'What are you doing?' McBride asked.

'Taking his temperature.' Lovelace replied. She took the kitchen thermometer she had found and placed it on

Mackay's skin. She waited a few minutes and recorded the result. 'It may help forensics at a later date.' She added by way of explanation.

Secretly McBride was impressed.

Carefully Lovelace lifted Mackay's upper body from the table. Underneath him was a plate of food scraps.

'Looks like he came for a midnight snack.' Lovelace said.

'That would explain why he was sat at the table.' McBride noted. 'Describe the knife wound for me.'

Lovelace examined the knife. She turned and scanned the worktops just behind her. A knife block was standing next to a kettle. One of the knives was missing. She pulled all the knives out one by one and examined them. The carving knife was notable for its absence. She returned to Mackay's body and examined the knife handle. It matched those from the knife block.

'I'd say Mackay was stabbed with the carving knife. The entry point is approximately one inch to the left of the spinal column and just below the shoulder blade. The knife has been buried right up to the handle. There is some blood around the wound area but not much.'

'Good.' McBride said. 'Very succinct. If it is the carving knife, then it's probably at least six inches long. At that position in the body, it's likely to have ripped through the heart, killing Mackay instantly. That would explain the lack of blood. If the heart stops instantly, so does the blood flow. Any blood loss was probably contained within the body cavity.'

Lovelace stood back from Mackay's lifeless body and observed the scene. 'Whoever stabbed him did so while his back was turned.'

'Evidently.' McBride sniped.

Lovelace let it pass. 'There are two interior doors to the kitchen and one exterior door.' She walked over to the exterior door and tried the handle. 'It's locked, and we know no one entered the house from outside while Mackay was alive because of the security cameras.'

'So?' McBride asked.

'So the two internal doors are to Mackay's left and his immediate front. Both of which are clearly within his line of sight. Whoever killed Mackay did so while he knew they were in the room.'

'Good work, Lovelace.' McBride said. 'Anything else?'

'The killer used a knife that they found in the kitchen. They didn't bring it with them. The murder wasn't planned. It was a spur-of-the-moment thing. They may have been arguing with Mackay when he turned his back on them. They probably turned and looked for something to hit him with, and their hand fell on the carving knife. A few seconds later, and it was all over.'

'I concur.' McBride agreed. 'The evidence points that way. Who do you think might have the power to force a knife that deep into a human body?'

Lovelace had been wondering the same. 'Mackay is sat down. They're quite low tables and chairs. Whoever killed Mackay would have been standing up. If the knife is as sharp as I think, a fourteen-year-old girl could have launched the fatal blow.'

Or an old man. Or an old woman. Or any one of the guests in the Mansion House.

'Let's take a look at the knife then, shall we? Can you find any food bags or freezer bags anywhere?' McBride asked.

Lovelace returned to the kitchen cupboards and began rooting through them. She found a dozen or so bags of varying sizes.

'Good.' McBride said, carefully preparing the following sentence. 'I need you to carefully grip the knife handle whilst trying not to disturb any prints or evidence on it, and then I need you to pull the knife out.'

Lovelace looked at Kellerman, who moved the camera closer to the body. 'Are you ready for this?'

Kellerman looked green, and his nod lacked enthusiasm.

Lovelace reached over with her gloved hand and carefully withdrew the knife from Mackay's back. It took more effort than she was expecting. Carefully she laid it inside a large freezer bag.

'Good. Well done.' McBride said. 'That looks pretty sharp to me. We'll get forensics on it as soon as we can. Now please try to preserve any evidence on Mackay's body. You need to take the food bags and tie them over Mackay's hands and feet and one over his head. Can you do that?'

Lovelace didn't answer. Slowly and with much deference, she covered Mackay's extremities with the food bags and tied them up. When she had finished, Mackay looked like a macabre shop mannequin.

'Good. Now I need you to do the same with Mackay's food and drink. Please put them in bags and tie them up. Don't throw the drink away. Then I need you to scour the floor and retrieve anything on there. Anything at all. Bag it all up.'

It took Lovelace thirty minutes to clear everything up and store them in bags. When she had finished, the kitchen worktops were covered in twenty or more food bags with various fillings.

'That's good work.' McBride said. 'We're almost done here. We need to sort the body.'

'What do you mean?' Lovelace asked, but in her heart, she knew what he meant.

'It could be another day or more before we can get the body off the island. If the body starts to decay, so does any evidence. We need to stop the decay.'

Lovelace sighed. She looked at Kellerman and asked, 'what kind of freezers do you have on the island?'

Kellerman went even greener. 'We have some large freezers up at the prison. Ones you can walk into.'

'That will do.' McBride said.

'Anything in the house?' Lovelace asked.

'There's a chest-style freezer in the basement.' He said reluctantly.

'Big enough for a Mackay-sized body?' Lovelace asked.

'I'll show you.'

Kellerman walked by Lovelace and opened a door she had taken to be a pantry. In many respects, she had been right, and it was full of tins of food and spices and all manner of pantry-type foodstuffs. At the back of the pantry was another door that Kellerman opened. He reached for a light switch which threw a hard yellow light onto proceedings. A wooden staircase beckoned them down into a well-appointed basement. There were an extensive array of electrical appliances and, in one corner, a large chest freezer.

Lovelace looked inside. She began removing some of the items that were stored within. 'This will do.'

It took a few minutes to empty the chest and a little longer to carry Mackay's body down the stairs and into it. When they had finished, they took a moment to catch their breaths.

'I didn't realise a grown man could be so heavy,' Kellerman remarked as they returned to the kitchen.

'They're surprisingly heavy.' Lovelace admitted.

'That's good work.' McBride said. 'Not quite a forensic sweep but the best we could do in the circumstances. Mr Kellerman, I'll need you to arrange for a guard to be left at the kitchen door until we can get there. No one's to go in or out of the room for any reason. Make sure the doors are locked, and the guests are made aware.'

'Of course. I'll talk to Johnathon. We'll get Sampson to organise it.'

'Good. Miss Lovelace, you've proved quite useful, 1 but I'm afraid our work is not yet done. How are you with interrogation?'

'I'm sure you can guide me.' She said.

'Don't worry. I will. We'll set it up in Johnathon Preece's study. We'll get them all in one by one and see what they have to say for themselves.'

On the mainland, DCI McBride took a large gulp of his coffee and felt the liquid burn his throat. He switched his microphone off and turned to DS Sandhu. 'Found anything interesting?'

DS Sandhu looked up from her laptop and smiled. She was pretty when she smiled, McBride thought.

'A few things.' Sandhu remarked. 'A few things....'

Nine

McBride took a long sip of his coffee. His head no longer hurt, but he felt the drag of alcohol pull on his tiredness. He looked at his DS and marvelled at how she could look so fresh after their morning. He rubbed his temples and asked, 'how are they getting on?'

After Lovelace and Kellerman had concluded the initial sweep of the crime scene, McBride had given instructions on how he wanted the interviews to be conducted. They were in Johnathon's study, setting it up as DS Sandhu watched.

'Nearly there, I think.'

McBride followed Sandhu's gaze and watched as Lovelace positioned a camera to point at an empty chair. Behind that chair was another camera which pointed back at Lovelace. With the cameras, DCI McBride could watch both the interviewer and interviewee. Lovelace and Kellerman had moved Johnathon's large computer monitor so that it sat between the chairs. McBride's weary face looked back at them from the monitor.

'I think we're ready,' Lovelace said, addressing the monitor. McBride's face filled the screen. He had the chiselled, worn face of a man that had seen it all and had the scars to show for it.

'Okay. Good.' McBride said. He no longer spoke into Lovelace's ear. His voice came clearly through the computer's speakers. 'Let's start with Johnathon Preece.'

***

Johnathon sat in the empty chair and looked at Lovelace, who sat opposite him. Kellerman sat next to Lovelace with a notepad on his knees. McBride's face glowed at them from the monitor.

'Good morning again, Mr Preece.' McBride started. 'I trust the other guests have settled down a bit now?'

'They're a little agitated, understandably.' Johnathon replied, addressing McBride directly. 'It's all come as a bit of a shock.'

'Yes. I suppose it must have.' McBride said. 'And I apologise for the inconvenience of not being able to get to the island to conduct the preliminary investigation myself, but I'm sure you can appreciate the difficulties we face?'

'Of course. I'll do whatever I can to help.'

McBride smiled. 'Excellent. Perhaps you can start by telling us how you discovered Mr Mackay?'

Johnathon fidgeted in his seat. Lovelace thought he looked distinctly uncomfortable.

'Well,' he began slowly. 'After everyone had gone to bed, I returned to my office to do some work.'

'Is that normal?' McBride asked. 'It was very late.'

'For me, yes, it's quite normal. I often work into the wee small hours.'

Lovelace detected a hint of Scottish in his accent. It was subtle and understated, but it was there.

'Go on,' McBride prompted.

'Well, I heard Mackay come downstairs around one in the morning. I never heard him go back up. I must have fallen asleep in my chair. I woke up at about four and went into the kitchen for a drink. That's when I found Mackay.'

'He was dead?'

'Yes.'

'How do you know?' Lovelace asked.

'I checked his neck for a pulse. I couldn't find one. His skin felt odd too. I've felt it before, on a dead person. It doesn't feel right.'

'What did you do then?' McBride asked.

'I called for Mr Kellerman.'

'That's right,' Kellerman said. 'Johnathon telephoned me about ten past four. I have a room in the accommodation block. I came right over.'

'Whose idea was it to involve Miss Lovelace?' McBride asked.

Kellerman looked at Johnathon. He said, 'I think it was me. I remembered that Miss Lovelace had been a police officer, and it occurred to me that she would know the right thing to do.'

'Very sensible.' McBride stated. 'Tell me, Mr Preece, did you hear anyone else during the night?'

'No. As I said, I fell asleep shortly after I heard Mackay go into the kitchen.'

'You didn't go in and speak to Mackay yourself?' McBride asked.

'No.'

'Had Mackay ever stayed on the island before?' Lovelace asked.

'A few times.'

'Was he in the habit of going for midnight snacks?'

'I can't say that I know. I certainly wasn't aware of it.'

'Even though you sleep in your study?' Lovelace said, observing Johnathon's expression. 'Which itself is right next to the kitchen?'

Johnathon turned a shade pale. 'I see. You don't miss much, do you?'

Lovelace shrugged. 'It's a thing. I noticed your sleeping bag and blankets in your study.'

Johnathon paused for a long time, struggling to arrange his response in his head. How much did they know?

'My wife and I are estranged.' He said slowly. 'We have been for some years. We lead separate lives but continue to support one another, personally and professionally. It works for our daughter and us.'

'How long have you worked for Mackay?' Lovelace asked.

'Twenty years.' Jonathon said.

Lovelace saw the stress of all those years rush past Jonathon's eyes. 'Why did you work for him for so long?'

'He paid well. Very well. And I get to live in a beautiful house like this.'

'Alone and isolated from your family and friends?' Lovelace prodded.

She watched as Johnathon fidgeted in his chair.

'I…I…' Jonathon's shoulders sagged. He couldn't find the words.

'Mackay was blackmailing you, wasn't he?' McBride asked.

'No. No, of course not.' Johnathon said, but his denial lacked any real punch.

Lovelace leant closer. 'Tell me about it,' she asked.

'I can't.' He said, shaking his head.

'Very well,' McBride said, and his voice had taken on an edge that Lovelace found intimidating. 'Then we'll tell you. Please stop me if I get anything wrong.'

Lovelace watched the monitor as DS Sandhu passed McBride a sheet of paper.

'You were a prison governor at HMP Northend, one of Mackay's private facilities in the northeast. By all accounts, you ran the prison well and scored highly in Government tests. Until an inmate by the name of

Michael Hobson took his own life. Do you remember that, Mr Preece?'

Johnathon nodded.

'If you could answer the question, Mr Preece.' McBride continued. 'For the record.'

Johnathon looked up at Lovelace; his eyes had swollen with the memory.

'I remember.'

'Ethan Mackay did a good job covering up the mess, didn't he? He tidied it all up, made it go away.'

'It wasn't like that..' Johnathon began, but McBride interrupted.

'DS Sandhu spoke to his sister.' McBride said and left the words hanging in the air. Johnathon's face looked crestfallen. His shoulders sagged even more, and Lovelace watched as the life he had left, left him.

'I see.' He said calmly. 'Yes, I see.'

'According to Hobson's sister, he was in a relationship with a man at the time of his arrest. She'd met him a couple of times, but she didn't know him very well. We showed her your picture, Johnathon….'

'It's true.' Johnathon said, looking up at Lovelace and then at the monitor. 'I was in a relationship with Michael Hobson, if that's what you want to call it. We'd been out one evening for a drink, and Mike decided to drive home. To my eternal shame, I didn't try and stop him. There was an accident. A young woman was killed.'

'He got ten years, didn't he? Death by dangerous driving.' McBride continued.

'Yes.'

'And you manoeuvred behind the scenes to get him transferred to your prison?'

'Yes.'

'Where you were able to continue your relationship.'

'No.' Johnathon said firmly. 'No. Not once, not while he was under my care. Not once.'

'And then he killed himself.'

Johnathon's head dropped. 'Yes. He wasn't able to cope with prison life. It ate him up.'

'Then a local copper involved in the investigation into Hobson's suicide made the connection between you both.'

'Yes. I went to Mackay for help. He made it go away.'

'And continued to have you under his control ever since.'

'Yes. But you have to understand. It wasn't like that. Mackay never blackmailed me, not like that. I owed him my life and my career. He kept me out of prison. He saved my family.'

'He didn't,' Lovelace said. 'It was blackmail in all but name. He controlled you. He was coercive. Manipulative. He got what he wanted from you. He used you.'

'No!' Johnathon shouted. 'No, it wasn't like that. It wasn't like that at all!'

'Mackay knew you and your wife were separated. He knew your history.' McBride went on. 'He named your study "Ireland" after the gay serial killer to wind you up. It was his way of saying that he was in control. It kept you subservient to him.'

'NO!' Johnathon shouted. 'You've got it all wrong.'

'Let's leave it there for now, shall we?' McBride said calmly. 'If you could send in your wife next?'

Johnathon stood up. His face was red with rage and, Lovelace noted, fear.

'It's not what you think.' Johnathon said. 'You can believe what you want. People always believe the worst. People are cruel like that. But I didn't murder Mackay. He kept me safe and protected. And he paid me very well.' He threw up his hands. 'What do I have now?

Nothing. My life's ruined. No one will ever employ me again. Not now I've lost Mackay's support.'

He shook his head and left the room.

'Has he gone?' McBride asked.

'Yes,' Lovelace said. 'I think he believed Mackay supported him. I could see it in his eyes.'

'He probably did believe it. People like Mackay are very good at making people feel that way. They're abusers. That's what abusers do.'

'I'm not so sure..' Lovelace began.

'There's something else you need to know.' McBride began.

Lovelace's interest spiked.

'Hobson's sister never believed that her brother was driving the car that killed that young woman. She always believed that someone else was driving and that her brother took the fall for them.'

'Why would he do that?' Lovelace asked.

'Money.' McBride said. 'It always comes down to money in the end. Hobson told his sister that he believed he would only get a suspended sentence and that people behind him wouldn't let him go to jail. When he went to jail, he remained confident that his appeal would be successful. It wasn't. She said he rang her the night before he killed himself, fearing that he would be murdered in his cell. He said he knew things about some powerful people who couldn't let him live and wanted to tell her everything. He killed himself the next day.'

'Before he could tell anyone.'

'Quite. So I'd be careful to reserve judgment on poor Mr Preece for a little while yet.'

Lovelace sat back in her chair. She had met killers before. They very often looked harmless, like Johnathon Preece. She looked up as Elouise Preece entered the study.

'My turn, is it?' She asked.

***

'Before you start,' Elouise said, taking the seat that her husband had just vacated, 'I know all about my husband. We have no secrets.'

Lovelace watched Elouise's face for signs of duplicity. She saw none. There was, however, a small bruise just behind her right eye that makeup hadn't quite been up to the task of covering. It was a bruise she certainly didn't have before she invited Mackay into her bedroom the previous evening.

'Thank you, Mrs Preece.' McBride started, 'duly noted. My name is DCI McBride, and my colleague beside me is DS Sandhu. Do you have any objection to us asking a few questions?'

'Of course not,' she said confidently. 'Fire away.'

'Can you tell us about the altercation you had in the hallway last night with Grace Mahone and Ethan Mackay?'

Elouise didn't flinch, but Lovelace noticed how her eyes darted over to her. She looked at her for a few moments before looking back at the monitor.

'What would you like to know?' Elouise asked.

Lovelace wasn't fooled. Elouise was an intelligent woman. One of the three people in the hallway last night was dead; the other hadn't yet been interviewed. The only person who had been in a position to know what had happened, and to report it to the detectives, was sat right opposite, Elouise. Lovelace needed to adapt quickly.

'Just tell us what happened.' McBride said.

Elouise described the scene that she found when she opened her bedroom door. 'Ethan was holding Grace back forcefully. He had ripped open her robe. I had heard the altercation, and I stepped in to help.'

'That was kind of you,' McBride said, and Elouise couldn't detect the sarcasm though she suspected it was there.

'You invited Mackay back into your room?'

'Yes.'

'And you had sex with him?'

'Yes.'

'Does your husband know of your affairs?'

Lovelace caught the plural. It wasn't lost on Elouise either.

'I told you, Inspector. My husband and I have no secrets. We both enjoy the company of men.'

Lovelace smiled. She liked Elouise.

'Did he know you had sex with Mackay?' McBride asked.

'Yes, he did.'

'Did you know if Mackay had sex with Grace Mahone?'

For the first time, Elouise looked pained. 'I believe so. I don't think she was a willing participant.'

'He raped Grace?' McBride asked.

'She always consented, so I don't suppose you could call it rape.'

'But maybe she couldn't say no?' Lovelace asked.

'No one said "no" to Ethan Mackay.' Elouise stated.

'How did you get that bruise?' Lovelace asked.

Elouise's hand instinctively reached for the bruise. 'Ethan could get a bit carried away. He wasn't a violent man, not really. But he liked it rough, if you know what I mean.'

Lovelace nodded. She knew, and the more she learned, the more she disliked Ethan Mackay.

'What happened after you and Mackay had sex?' McBride asked.

'He stayed in my room for about an hour.' Elouise explained. 'Then he got dressed and left.'

'What time was that?'

'Between midnight and one o'clock. I can't tell you for certain, but it was around then.'

'And what did you do then?' Mcbride asked.

'I went to sleep, Inspector. I stayed there, alone, until I learned about Ethan's murder this morning.'

'Did you leave your room at any time?'

'No.'

'Did you hear anyone else leave their room at any time?'

'No.'

'And what did Mackay have on you, Mrs Preece?'

Elouise paused for a moment and stared at the monitor. 'What do you mean?'

'Ethan Mackay collected people.' McBride explained. 'Or, rather, he collected knowledge about people. Knowledge he could use to control and manipulate them. He knew about your husband's sexual preferences, and I'm sure he must have known about your living arrangements. But what did he have to control you?'

'I couldn't possibly say.'

'Couldn't or won't?' McBride asked.

'I'm not aware that Ethan had anything over me or that he tried to control me.'

'He tried,' Lovelace said, holding a stare that Elouise threw at her. 'You always seemed to be able to dodge his attempts.'

Elouise smiled. 'Oh, you mean the Thompson thing. That's something and nothing. If Ethan thought he knew something, then he was wrong. He was barking up the wrong tree.'

'Do you know about the Thompson and Bywaters case, Mrs Preece?' McBride asked. Before she could answer, he continued, 'It was a very famous case in the twenties. The Thompsons took in a lodger by the name of Frederick Bywaters, and it wasn't long before he and Mrs Thompson began an affair. It was all documented in a hundred or so love letters that Mrs Thompson wrote to Bywaters. It detailed all manner of things, including Mrs Thompson's desire to murder her husband and run away with Bywaters. She often wrote about how she had tried to poison Mr Thompson and how she had once put ground glass into his food. Of course, it all came to nothing until Bywaters grew impatient and stabbed Mr Thompson to death in the street. They were both hanged for it.'

'I'm aware of the case.' Elouise said softly. 'I believe they were wrong to hang Edith Thompson. She was a dreamer. A fantasist.'

'Why did Mackay name your room "Thompson"?' McBride asked.

'I don't know.'

'Mackay made some mention of women poisoners, I understand.' McBride went on. 'Did he mean you, Mrs Preece?'

Elouise stole another look in Lovelace's direction.

'I've never tried to poison Johnathon.' She replied.

'I never meant Johnathon, Mrs Preece.' McBride said firmly. 'I meant your first husband.'

Elouise's jaw went firm. Her brow furrowed, and Lovelace watched as emotional turmoil erupted behind her kind eyes.

'I see you've done your homework.' Elouise said at last. 'Very commendable, Inspector.'

'Not me, I can assure you, Mrs Preece. Behind every good detective is an even better DS. DS Sandhu does all the hard work for me.'

Elouise composed herself. Then she said, 'I was married at eighteen to a man ten years older. At first, we were quite happy. As happy as anyone, I suppose. Then he started to change. He became sullen and moody. As he got older, he got moodier and sometimes violent. I don't know what changed in him. But something did, and he turned to drink in a big way. I didn't cope very well, and to my eternal shame, I turned my back on him. I started to take lovers. It was my way of coping, I think. They gave me comfort and support and a little hope. And then I met Johnathon.'

'Why didn't you divorce your husband?' Lovelace asked.

'Dependency, I suppose,' Elouise said after giving it some thought. 'I didn't believe I could survive without my husband. He was fairly well off. He didn't need to work. I enjoyed the lifestyle he gave me, and I was quite content in my own little way.'

'And then you met Johnathon?' Lovelace said.

Elouise smiled, and it was a genuine smile. The memory was still good. 'Yes. Then I met Johnathon, and things changed. I fell desperately in love. We approached my husband together, and Johnathon demanded that he grant me a divorce. At first, he just shrugged us off and said he'd make sure we never got a penny of his money, but when we told him we didn't care about the money, he completely refused to divorce me.'

'And then your husband died?' McBride asked.

'You make that sound so much worse than it was.' Elouise said. 'Yes, he died. And no, I didn't kill him.'

'He had a heart attack, is that right?' McBride asked.

'Yes. That's right. He had a heart attack right in front of me. I tried CPR, but it was no use. He died in my arms.'

'Then you inherited his money and were free to marry Johnathon?'

'Really, Inspector. That's beneath you. But as you wish. Yes, I inherited what was left of my husband's money after he had tried to drink his way through it, and a year later, I married Johnathon. Shortly after that, my daughter was born, and I've lived the life I wanted ever since.'

'Thank you, Mrs Preece.' McBride said abruptly. 'That will be all for now. If you would care to send Grace Mahone to us.'

Elouise got up and left without saying another word. She closed the study door behind her.

'What do you make of that?' McBride asked.

'She doesn't seem worried by the link to the Thompson and Bywaters case. It hasn't fazed her at all.' Lovelace said. 'I think Mackay was barking up the wrong tree. Unless....'

'Go on.'

'Mackay didn't strike me as a stupid man. He would have done his homework. He would have found something. What if Elouise was telling the truth, albeit in a slightly altered way?'

'How do you mean?'

'She said her husband had a heart attack in front of her and died in her arms. Let's say that's true. Let's say she tried CPR for a bit. So far, all true. But what if she stopped? What if she waited a few minutes before calling an ambulance? What if she waited long enough for her husband's heart to deteriorate beyond help *before* she rang for help?'

'It's a motive for wanting Mackay dead.' McBride agreed. 'I'll get DS Sandhu to dig a little deeper.'

***

Grace Mahone walked into the study looking nervous. She sat on the chair Elouise had recently vacated and looked at Lovelace for guidance. There was trepidation and anxiety there, Lovelace thought. Grace Mahone was not a woman adept at dealing with sudden death. Lovelace smiled at her, and she relaxed noticeably.

'There's no need to look so worried, Grace,' Lovelace reassured her. 'The police want to ask a few questions about last night. Where you were, what you saw. That sort of thing.'

Grace fiddled with the hem of her skirt. 'Okay.'

DCI McBride loomed large on the monitor. 'Good morning, Miss Mahone. May I call you Grace?'

'Of course,' Grace said.

'Excellent. My name's DCI McBride, and my colleague is DS Sandhu. Are you okay with answering a few questions?'

'Yes. But I'm not sure how much help I can be. I didn't see anything.'

Lovelace watched Grace's eyes and her body language. Despite the nerves, she held herself well.

'Can you tell us about your movements last night? After the dinner.' McBride asked.

'Elouise told me you know about the little incident in the hallway,' Grace began, choosing her words carefully. She looked across at Lovelace. Was she a friend or foe? Lovelace watched the question play out behind her eyes.

124

'Tell us about that, Grace.' Lovelace asked. 'It had happened before, hadn't it?'

Grace nodded. 'Yes.' She said, with no explanation.

'Why did you stay with him? Why didn't you move on? Get another job?' Lovelace asked.

'He wasn't all bad, you know. He had his moments, he could be quite harsh, but he could be lovely, too. Occasionally. And I believed in the work we were doing. It was important to me.'

'You had a brother die in prison?' McBride asked.

Lovelace watched as the pain shot across Grace's face.

'Yes. He was a few years older than me. He was my hero. My big brother. He got in with the wrong crowd and ended up serving some time. After he died, I vowed to dedicate my life to his memory, to ensure that what happened to him couldn't happen to anyone else. Ethan Mackay may not be to everyone's taste, but I believed in him and what he was trying to do. We shared a common goal.'

'You shared his lifestyle too?' Lovelace asked gently. 'You shared the billionaire lifestyle, the international travel, the good food, good drink. The very best of everything.'

'Yes. I had all that too.'

'It would be a lot to give up.' Lovelace probed. 'Some people might put up with a lot to maintain that lifestyle?'

'If you mean did I tolerate Mackay's cruelty and advances to maintain my lifestyle, then yes. It was a conscious decision and one I have never regretted.'

'But last night, you resisted Mackay's advances? Why?'

Grace fidgeted uncomfortably in her chair. 'You had to be very careful to sense Ethan's mood. I may not have resisted on a different night, but he scared me last night. Elouise came to my rescue.'

'What did you do then?' McBride asked.

Grace looked at the monitor. She had forgotten he was there.

'I went into my room. I was there all night until I heard about Ethan.'

'Did you leave your room at any time?' McBride asked.

'No.'

'Did you hear anyone leave their rooms?'

'No.'

'Tell me about the names on the guest doors, Grace.' McBride asked. 'Did you have anything to do with them? Were you aware of Mackay's plan?'

'No. It was as much a surprise to me as to everyone else. I had no idea what Ethan was planning or what they meant.'

Lovelace leant closer. 'We think we know what most of the rooms meant, at least to Mackay. But what we don't understand is what he meant by "Lemon?"'

Grace shrugged her shoulders. 'I have no idea.'

Lovelace didn't believe her.

'Had you been to the island before?' Lovelace asked.

'No. This was my first visit. Ethan had been a few times as it was being built. But I had never seen the place before.'

'And what about the other guests? Had you ever met any of them before yesterday?'

Grace shook her head. 'No. Never. I'd seen the Preece's names on a lot of paperwork, but I'd never met them before. I'd also heard of Sir Malcolm. He was the topic of many a heated discussion that Ethan had had with a dozen different people. It was the same with Esther Friedman. She had become quite a thorn in Ethan's side.'

'Did you know any of the secrets Mackay may have had on any of the guests?' McBride asked.

'No. But it wouldn't surprise me if he knew every little detail of their lives. Ethan went to great lengths to find out what he could about people.'

'But you were never privy to that information?' McBride asked.

Grace considered her words. 'No. I wasn't. Ethan didn't always play entirely on the right side of the law. He knew people. Dangerous people. People that could fix things for him. Or find things out. He was always quite careful to keep me out of the loop.'

Grace looked over at Lovelace. 'It annoyed him that you were here.' She said. 'He didn't know anything about you other than what he had picked up in the papers. I wouldn't be surprised if some very dubious characters were looking into you.'

Lovelace laughed. 'They may get more than they bargained for! But I have no secrets. I wish them happy digging.'

'Everyone has secrets,' Grace said thoughtfully.

'They do, indeed.' McBride said. 'Thank you, Grace. If we need any more information, we'll come back to you.'

Grace stood up and straightened her skirt. Lovelace watched as she turned to leave.

'Would you send in Esther Friedman?' McBride asked.

Grace chuckled. 'Of course. However, you may regret not talking to her first. She's already seven sheets to the wind.'

***

Esther stumbled into the study, looking decidedly unsteady on her feet. She carried a glass of champagne in one hand.

'Well, hello. Isn't this cosy?' She said, lowering herself onto the chair.

'Miss Friedman, my name is DCI McBride. My colleague is DS Sandhu. Do you have any objection to answering a few questions?'

Esther looked at the face on the monitor. 'I don't know, Inspector. I feel I should have an objection, but I can't think of one. Oh, no, wait. I may have thought of one. Is this even legal?' She waved her free hand around the room, finally resting on Lovelace. 'I mean, this one's not even a proper badge-wearing member of your lot on top of the fact she's a suspect in a murder.'

Lovelace observed Esther carefully. Her every movement seemed controlled and contained. The drunkenness seemed to be an act, but to what end? Was she hoping they would lower their guard around her? Was she mining for information?

'Thank you for your concern, Miss Friedman, but I can assure you that it is all above board. As for Miss Lovelace being a suspect in a murder, I have it on good authority that is no longer the case.'

'I see,' Esther slurred. 'Very well, then, I suppose I have no objection.'

'Can you tell me your movements after dinner last night?'

'Not really, Inspector.' Esther said. 'I was rather drunk. It's all a bit hazy. I remember going off to get more to drink and then that kind young Grace putting me to bed. I may have invited her to join me. I do hope she can forgive me. I'm afraid I lose all self-control once I've had a few. I don't remember anything after that until that gorilla barred my way as I was going for coffee this morning.'

'Do you have an alcohol problem, Miss Friedman?' McBride asked.

'Only when I've run out, Inspector, but thank you for asking.'

Mcbride moved on swiftly. 'Why are you on the island Miss Friedman? You're no fan of Ethan Mackay's. You're less of a fan of his prisons. In the last twelve months, you've written a handful of exposes covering Mackay's business affairs and his prisons, and you've become a very vocal critic of the man.'

'Indeed I am. At least, I was.'

'Then why are you here?'

'Because I'm a journalist, Inspector. It's what I do. I am nothing if not fair and balanced. Ethan Mackay held out an olive branch and invited me to the island to see things for myself and make a balanced judgement on what he was trying to achieve.'

'He wasn't blackmailing you, then?' McBride asked bluntly.

'Good Lord, no!' Esther snorted. 'What on earth makes you think that?'

'Maybrick.' Lovelace added quietly. 'You told Mackay last night that he didn't know what he thought he knew. What did you think Mackay thought he knew?'

Esther was quiet for a moment. She had underestimated Lovelace. She had been quite drunk last night, but she was certain Lovelace hadn't been there when she had said that.

'I couldn't possibly know what a man thought he knew, now could I?'

'Maybrick was a Victorian cotton merchant who became a suspect in the Jack the Ripper murders.' Lovelace explained, knowing full well that Esther already knew this. 'He died in 1890, poisoned by his younger wife, Florence Maybrick.'

'And what has that to do with me?' Esther demanded.

'Is that why Mackay named your room "Maybrick?" After a Victorian female poisoner? Is that what he had on you?' Lovelace asked.

'That's very tenuous,' Esther said, smiling. 'I've never been married. How could I have poisoned a husband? Really, Miss Lovelace. One must do better.'

Esther drained her glass. 'Is that all?' She demanded to know.

'Not quite, Miss Friedman.' McBride said. 'What you've told us isn't entirely true, now is it?'

Esther slowly turned her head to the monitor. She looked rattled. 'I'm not sure I know what you mean, Inspector.'

'I mean,' McBride went on, 'that you have been married. It was a long time ago, I grant you, but even you must remember a small detail like that?'

There was a long pause when Esther looked directly at the floor, not moving her eyes for a second. Lovelace moved closer.

McBride continued. 'You were sixteen years old. He was fourteen years older than you. You were married for just two years when he died of food poisoning. I have to give full credit to my DS. She's bloody good at digging up the past.'

'So was Mackay, wasn't he?' Lovelace asked gently. Esther looked up and stared directly into Lovelace's soul. 'He knew about your husband, didn't he? He mentioned female poisoners and made a deliberate point of asking if you had ever poisoned one. What did he know, Esther?'

Esther sat upright. All pretence of drunkenness was momentarily lost. 'I was married, and it was a long time ago. I was happy in a strange sort of way. He pulled me out of a difficult home life and set me up. He died during a trip to India. I didn't murder my husband, Inspector. Mr Mackay didn't know what he thought he knew.'

'But you were intrigued enough to come to the island?' McBride asked.

'Yes. He dangled his little knowledge in front of me and tried to play me. I came to the island to see how far he would go. I also came to the island to write about my experiences here from a first-hand perspective. It carries so much more weight and I have a wonderful story to tell once we get off this god-forsaken island. Is that everything?'

'Just one more thing,' Lovelace said. 'Last night, you threatened to stab Mackay in the back. Did you?'

Esther rolled her eyes and laughed. 'No, Miss Lovelace, I did not. I meant it metaphorically, not literally.'

'And yet Mackay is literally dead, having been stabbed in the back.'

Esther rose from her seat. 'Not by my hand.' She said firmly. 'If that's everything? Perhaps next time you wish to speak to me in an official capacity Inspector, I would prefer it if I had my lawyer present.'

'Very well, Miss Friedman. Duly noted. If you could ask Sir Malcolm to join us?'

Lovelace waited until Esther had left the room. 'There's certainly a motive for murder there. If she did murder her husband.'

McBride agreed. 'We were only just able to find that out about Miss Friedman. I'm not hopeful we'll be able to dig any deeper.'

'Mackay did.' Lovelace said. 'Mackay found something. You need to keep looking.'

'DS Sandhu is looking forward to it.'

***

'I'm not sure I can be of any use to you,' Sir Malcolm said, puffing out his chest and allowing his large waistline to find its level. 'Went to bed after dinner and stayed there until I heard the others milling about this morning. I never left my room, and I never heard anything. The wind is quite loud, you know, what with the storm.'

'As I understand it,' McBride began, 'you were once vehemently opposed to Mackay's plans to build HMP BlackRock?'

'I was, yes.'

'What changed?' McBride asked.

'My mind, Inspector. That's what changed. I'm intelligent and prepared to alter my position should the evidence dictate. Mackay's plans intrigued me, and he convinced me of the importance of building a place like this.'

'Without your support, it was unlikely that BlackRock would ever have passed through Parliament?' Lovelace asked.

'That's right. It will be my legacy.'

'What did you make of Mackay naming your room after Dr Harold Shipman?' McBride asked bluntly.

'One of Mackay's little jokes.' Sir Malcolm replied. 'He was famous for making his little digs.'

Lovelace watched Sir Malcolm carefully. He was not good at hiding his emotions, but it looked like he had mentally prepared himself for this line of questioning. His face remained stoic.

'You looked quite upset when Esther asked you if you had any skeletons in your closet or whether you had them all cremated.' Lovelace probed.

'She's a pest. A hack. Nothing more. I don't know why I let people like her get under my skin. She's always digging in the dirt looking for scraps.'

'During dinner last night, Mackay made a few comments regarding Doctors and their patients,' Lovelace continued. 'He asked if you had ever slipped a patient something to ease their pain in their final moments. He made several comparisons between you and Harold Shipman, implying that you may one day be a guest at HMP BlackRock?'

Sir Malcolm held his composure, 'all part of the man's games. As I said, I shouldn't let it get to me so much.'

'Have you ever been accused of anything like that?' Lovelace asked.

Sir Malcolm considered the question for some time. 'I was a GP for a long time.' He said at last. 'I've tended to hundreds of people, the young and the old, the chronically ill and the terminal. People question your decisions from time to time, and rightly so. But I've never been accused of anything quite so serious as deliberately ending a patient's life. It goes against everything I believe in.'

'Thank you, Sir Malcolm, you've been most helpful. I think that's all for now.' McBride said. By the tone in McBride's voice, Lovelace could tell he had been warned to treat Sir Malcolm with due deference.

'Good. Well, if there's anything else I can help you with, please, don't hesitate to ask.'

Lovelace watched as Sir Malcolm struggled out of his chair and left the room. To McBride, she asked, 'is there anything there?'

'DS Sandhu's got her shovel out as we speak. It's early days yet, but there could be something….'

Lovelace waited patiently as McBride gathered his thoughts.

'So far,' McBride began, 'Sir Malcolm has led a blameless life. At least, on the face of it. He's had a few official investigations into his conduct but nothing more or less than you would expect from someone who has practised medicine for so long. People complain and make official complaints, and they have to be investigated. But…'

'But?' Lovelace prompted.

'But,' McBride continued, 'there's a pattern emerging that you wouldn't see if you were taking each case on its merit. Individually, nothing. Taken together, Sir Malcolm may have benefitted from the early deaths of some of his elderly patients.'

'Do you have any proof?' Lovelace asked.

'Not yet. We're waiting on several people to call us back. We'll know more in a few hours.'

'There will be proof,' Lovelace went on. 'Mackay would have found proof.'

'I agree,' McBride said, 'we'll keep looking.' He paused for a few seconds. Then he said, 'take care of yourself, Lovelace. You're stuck in a house with several people, each with a motive to murder Mackay. Murder can become a habit. Desperate people will murder again. Don't count these people as your friends. One of them is a killer.'

Lovelace was about to reassure McBride that she could look after herself when the power to the house cut out. Everything was plunged into darkness, and it took a few moments for her eyes to adjust.

'What happened?' She asked.

Kellerman put down the camera he had been holding during the interviews and said, 'power cut. It's not uncommon during a storm.'

'How long will it take to get back on?'

Kellerman shrugged his shoulders. 'A couple of hours. Maybe a day or two.'

'Is there no generator in the house?'

'No. Just to the prison.'

They were interrupted by Johnathon, who came into the room with a torch. 'Sorry. It looks like we've lost power. It's still dark outside, which doesn't help. I need to call the prison and make sure everything's okay.'

Lovelace looked at her mobile phone. 'I've got no signal. The transmitters must be down.'

'It would make sense if we have no power.' Johnathon said. 'Which is why I had an old-fashioned copper line installed from my office to the prison. Sometimes the old technology is the best.'

Johnathon picked up the handset to his landline telephone and began dialling a number.

'Does that connect to the mainland?' Lovelace asked.

'No.' Johnathon replied. 'Mackay wouldn't install one. I'm afraid we're perfectly cut off!'

Lovelace considered that for a second and then remembered McBride's warning.

Don't consider these people as your friends. One of them is a killer.

Ten

Georgia Hope took the stairs two at a time and landed on the floor of A-Wing in a flourish. Her hair was tied up in a tight bun at the top of her head, and wisps of golden locks framed her temples. She wore very little makeup, with just a touch of concealer. Her eyes glowed with the exuberance of youth, and she wasn't even a bit concerned about walking into a wing full of the country's most deadly and violent men.

She strode purposefully across the floor of A-Wing and stopped at the first cell. She lifted the flap of her Officer's uniform and reached for a set of keys that hung on a clasp around her waist. She selected a key and inserted it into the cell door. The door opened outwards, and she stepped to one side to allow it to open fully.

'Morning.' She greeted the inmate cheerily.

'You're late.' Came the gruff reply.

'Power cut,' Georgia remarked. 'Systems are down so I'm afraid we're doing it the old-fashioned way today.' She held up her keys and rattled them.

Patrick Hewell was a beast of a man, and his frame almost filled the doorway as he stepped forward. He looked up and down A-Wing and watched as other prison officers opened other cell doors. Georgia took a step back. His physicality dwarfed her. Despite this, she remained relaxed. Hewell had been in prison for more years than she had been alive, and despite his renowned grumpiness, he had never once assaulted a prison officer. Most considered him a model prisoner, respectful and polite, but it wasn't lost on any of them that he was serving a whole life tariff for murdering six young women in the early nineties. Yet prison life and the relentless march of age showed across his chiselled features. He walked slower and moved like an old man, proof his best years were a long way behind him.

Georgia stepped to the next cell and repeated her movements.

'Morning!'

Claus Fischer, German national and serial rapist. She shuddered. He always made her shudder. He had dark eyes that invaded her every time she went near him.

'Morning.'

Robert Askwith. Tall, handsome and well-spoken. The other female officers found much to like about Robert Askwith. In fairness, so too did some of the male officers. He was mild-mannered and respectful, and it was difficult to reconcile the man they saw to the fearsome and equally feared gangland enforcer that had been given a whole life tariff for torture and murder. Even the other inmates trod carefully around the man.

She stepped to the next door and unlocked it.

'Morning, Jack.' Georgia glowed.

'Good morning George,' Jack replied. He sat at his table reading a book. His reading glasses were perched at the end of his nose. 'Having issues today?'

Georgia liked Jack Lovelace. Everyone liked Jack Lovelace. He was kind, polite, thoughtful and friendly. She felt safe and warm in his company. He had a hypnotic personality. She liked that he called her "George." He was the only one that did.

'Storm's knocked out the power. We're doing everything the old-fashioned way today. At least until the computers are back up and running.'

'And how long might that be?' Jack asked.

Georgia smiled, 'well, the computers are back on, but I think they're having issues re-booting the programmes. Shouldn't be too long.'

Jack closed his book and placed his glasses into a leather pouch. 'If they need my help, they only need to ask!' He joked.

Georgia laughed. 'I'll be sure and let them know.'

Before he was arrested, Jack Lovelace had been a computer analyst and programmer. Georgia didn't doubt for one minute that he would be able to help. Sometimes the old boys just knew how to fix things.

Georgia opened the next cell door. Adam Sinclair. He was a new inmate to BlackRock and had not endeared himself to the staff or the other inmates. He stood at the door as it swung open. Instinctively, Georgia reached for her baton that hung by her side. Sinclair saw the movement and paused. *She was afraid.* He smiled, and his eyes burned. He liked it when they were afraid.

Jack Lovelace appeared by Georgia's side. He had seen her body language change as the cell door opened and watched as she reached for her baton.

'Everything okay, Adam?' Jack asked.

Sinclair was a small man with a thin, spindly frame. Most of the other inmates in A-Wing were twice his size. He looked at Jack.

'I just want my breakfast.' He said. Georgia took a step back, still gripping her baton, as Sinclair stepped out of his cell. He stopped inches from Jack.

'Is your girl coming to visit you again?' He asked.

'That's none of your business.' Jack responded firmly.

Sinclair's smile spread across his face and morphed into something else. Something sinister and cruel. 'It is my business.' He said and walked off.

'I don't like that man,' Georgia said softly once Sinclair was out of earshot.

'No one likes him, George.' Jack said matter-of-factly. 'No one likes him.'

Johnathon and Kellerman took a Defender from the pool of cars parked behind the accommodation block and headed towards the prison along the tarmacked road. Daylight had managed to push through the dark clouds that raced above their heads, but it was a grey light, and the car's lights came on automatically and lit their way. Kellerman drove across the mountain and battled against the wind that battered them. Once at the prison, they took the shortest route to the Citadel and were in the heart of the control room within minutes.

Gerry was sat at the centre of the control room, busy tapping away at his keyboard. He didn't look up as they entered. Four other staff members were heads down at their desks, busy trying to restart the prison's high-tech security systems.

Gerry reached out to a plate, picked up a sandwich, and took a large bite. He washed it down with a swig of full-fat coke. He looked up mid-swig as Johnathon approached.

Johnathon stood looking down at Gerry Holt and suddenly remembered why he preferred it when Gerry worked at the mainland office. The sight of him annoyed him. He was unkempt. His hair hadn't been brushed and stuck out at odd angles from his head. He wore a tatty, grey t-shirt that read "Fat people are hard to kidnap," and he was munching on his food with an open mouth.

'The power's been on for more than half an hour. Why aren't our systems back on?' Johnathon asked.

Gerry swallowed his food, and Johnathon noted that some still hung from the corner of his mouth.

'It's a work in progress.' Gerry said.

'Should it take this long?' Kellerman asked.

'It's a complicated system,' Gerry explained. 'It tried to re-boot everything all at once but given it hadn't shut down properly in the first place, there were a few corrupted files which caused the system to freeze. We're taking each element individually, fixing the code, and launching them one by one. It's going to take some time.'

'How much time?' Johnathon asked.

Gerry sighed. He hated non-techy people. Fucking Luddites. It took as long as it took. It wasn't a PC. You couldn't just turn it back on and expect it to work instantly. He threw his hands out in a "who knows" manner and said, 'how long's a piece of string?'

'That depends on where you cut it,' Johnathon replied curtly. He hated the tech guys. They never gave a straight answer to a straightforward question. 'And I'd like it if you cut this particular piece of string short.'

'We're working on it as fast as we can.' Gerry said, not trying to hide his exasperation.

'Good.' Johnathon said. 'Mr Kellerman, if you'd kindly stay here and oversee everything. Let me know the second we've got back full control.'

Kellerman nodded. When Johnathon had gone, he asked, 'is there a problem I need to know about?'

Gerry ran through a mental list of all the issues that he thought Kellerman ought to know about. The problem was that he didn't quite grasp what was wrong. There was something wrong. He could sense it. It was like a Formula One driver sensing an issue with the car long before the technicians realised something was wrong. He was as in tune with his software as Lewis Hamilton was with his car. *Something was wrong.*

'No.' Gerry lied. 'It's all under control.'

'Good. I'm going for coffee. I'll be back.'

Gerry watched as Kellerman turned and left the room. There was a break-out room downstairs with coffee and tea-making facilities. Kellerman wouldn't be long. He turned back and looked at his screens. What the fuck was wrong? There was code he didn't recognise and didn't seem to do anything. Was it corrupted code? Had the power cut caused it? It was possible, but he didn't like it. He had run through power surge and power cut scenarios during testing and hadn't seen anything like this before.

His fingers danced effortlessly over the keys. Bit by bit, the systems were being restored. It wouldn't be long before they had complete control once again. But the alien code bothered him. It made him feel anxious, and he didn't like feeling anxious.

***

Mrs Brent cleared the remains of breakfast from the table that had been set up in the lounge. As each guest had gone to be interviewed, they had returned to the lounge and eaten a hearty breakfast of sausages, bacon, eggs and haggis. Mrs Brent prided herself on making the finest full Scottish anywhere in the country, and none of the guests seemed ill-inclined to disagree with this. They each finished their breakfast with coffee or tea and, in Esther's case, a large glass of champagne. When they had finished, they all sat in silence among the chairs and sofas. Elouise placed a couple of logs on the burner, filling the room with a warm glow. She looked up as Lovelace entered.

'I'm afraid we're unable to make any more breakfast,' Elouise said, 'what with the power being down. I can get Mrs Brent to rustle up a sandwich if you like?'

Lovelace said no, that wasn't necessary. She had never been a big eater, and breakfast was her least favourite meal. She watched as Elouise carefully eyed her up and down. By being part of the investigating team, Lovelace noticed that the guest dynamic had changed. She was no longer one of them. She was very much the outsider. They were all watching her carefully.

Elouise walked over to a large jug and poured a cup of black coffee. She handed it to Lovelace. 'Do you take milk or sugar?'

'No. Black's fine.'

'So, any idea who killed Ethan?'

Lovelace blew into her mug. She felt every eye in the room turn to her. 'No. It's all in the hands of the police now. I've done my bit.'

'You must have an idea?' Elouise pressed. 'I mean, you've been at the heart of the questioning. You know all our dirty secrets.'

'I wouldn't be so indelicate as to share anyone's statements.'

'Well,' Sir Malcolm puffed. 'I have no secrets. There's nothing on me. No reason to kill Mackay. None at all.'

'Really?' Esther quipped, and the depth of sarcasm in that one word ripped a hole in the calm atmosphere.

'Now listen here, you old hack, mind your words, or I'll sue you for slander.' Sir Malcolm raged.

'Nonsense,' Esther retorted. 'You can't slander someone if you say it to their face, and I've no problem with speaking my mind. Mackay had something on you, and that's why you changed your position on BlackRock. He blackmailed you, and we all know it. What was it, eh? Some rich little old woman? Dead before her time? Were you bequeathed a valuable painting or jewellery? Eh? Come on, you can tell us!'

Everyone watched as Sir Malcolm's face turned a shade of red and his cheeks puffed up as if he were about to explode. And then, almost as suddenly as the rouge had risen up his face, it receded again. Sir Malcolm, Lovelace thought, was beginning to learn the art of self-control.

'What about you?' Sir Malcolm demanded to know, pointing an aged finger in Esther's direction. 'Why the bloody hell are you here? What did Mackay have on you? He must have had something. There's no other reason you'd be here!'

'He thought he had something, but he was entirely wrong.' Esther declared. 'He wasn't so much barking up the wrong tree as in the wrong forest. Stupid man. Certainly, nothing to kill him for.'

'But what was it?' Sir Malcolm asked again. 'There was something, wasn't there?'

'Well, if you must know,' Esther began, 'Mackay found out that I had been married before. A long time ago. It almost seems like a different life now.'

'Miss Friedman, you don't have to tell us anything,' Elouise said, 'it's not our business to know.'

'Yes, it is.' Sir Malcolm insisted. He pointed his finger at Esther. 'She's keen at digging the dirt on everyone else. I want to know what Mackay had on her!'

'My husband was a few years older than me,' Esther explained. 'He fell ill when we were touring India and died there. It was all unfortunate, but as I say, completely the wrong tree!'

'Didn't kill him, did you?' Sir Malcolm asked.

Elouise turned on the old man. 'Really, Sir Malcolm. That's very unkind.'

Esther stood up from her seat. 'If you must know, Sir Malcolm, I will tell you. Ethan Mackay wrote to me a little while ago detailing what he thought had happened between my husband and me. I have said it before, and I will say it again, he was barking up the wrong tree, but I was keen to come to BlackRock at his invitation to see what he would do with the information he thought he had. The truth is that my husband and I were part of a large party of travellers who all fell ill after eating the same food while in India. My husband was not a healthy man as it was, and he died. That's the simple truth of it.'

'Get him cremated before anyone could autopsy the body, did you?' Sir Malcolm asked.

'Really, Sir Malcolm. I think I've had enough of you for one day,' Esther said, and Lovelace saw the anguish in her eyes. 'I think I shall go and lie down for an hour or so.'

Esther nodded kindly in Elouise's direction and left the lounge.

'More than enough motive to kill a man, I'd say,' Sir Malcolm said, puffing his chest like a proud peacock.

'Why do you hate Esther Friedman so much?' Elouise asked.

'I don't hate the woman. Can't stand her, but hate's a strong word.'

'You really ought to be more circumspect,' Grace said. She had been sitting near the log burner, listening quietly to the exchange between Esther and Sir Malcolm. 'I don't know what Ethan had on you, Sir Malcolm, or anyone else for that matter. He never confided in me. But I know he knew something about you that he used to force you to change your stance on BlackRock. And I'd say Esther's just the sort of woman to find out what that is.'

Grace stood up. 'I think I shall go for a swim before the water gets too cold.' She looked across at Lovelace. 'Do you want to come?'

Lovelace nodded. 'If I can find a costume.'

'My daughter has a few. Feel free to take whatever you need.' Elouise said.

Grace swept out of the room. Elouise watched her fondly. Then her gaze fell on Lovelace. 'Come. I'll help you pick a costume.'

She slipped her arm through Lovelace's, and they left Sir Malcolm alone with his thoughts.

'You're a bit of a dark horse, aren't you?' Elouise said as they made their way from the lounge to the guest suites. 'Listening behind doors while no one knows you're there.'

Lovelace didn't know how to take the question. It didn't sound menacing, but it didn't sound friendly, either.

'I wasn't hiding behind doors.' Lovelace said. 'I was coming to bed. I heard the commotion and waited until it had finished. I wasn't snooping.'

'But you don't miss a thing, do you? I bet you already know who killed Ethan.'

Lovelace held back the smile that threatened to spread across her face. She had a bloody good idea.

'I have no idea,' she lied.

'And now you know all our secrets.' Elouise said as she opened the door to Lovelace's room and walked inside.

'I suppose I do.' Lovelace admitted.

'And yet, no one knows yours.' Elouise said. 'I wonder what secrets you have?'

'None that make me a suspect in Ethan's murder.' Lovelace stated.

Elouise walked over to a set of drawers and opened them. She rummaged around before holding up a two-piece swimming costume. 'I think this one would suit you best. It certainly suited my daughter perfectly.' She handed it to Lovelace.

'I always knew my husband was gay,' Elouise said suddenly. 'It didn't bother me. I suppose you'd call him bi-sexual. We enjoyed each other's company and had a beautiful family life. Our lifestyle suited us both. It continues to suit us both.'

'You don't have to explain to me,' Lovelace said. 'I don't judge. I take people for who they are.'

Elouise watched Lovelace's expression and saw no lie. 'Johnathon doesn't have it in him to kill anyone. He doesn't. He's not that sort of man.'

'What about you?' Lovelace asked. 'Could you kill anyone?'

'Oh, yes.' Elouise said promptly. 'Quite easily. I didn't kill Ethan, but I could have done it. Sometimes I wanted to, but I didn't.'

Elouise smiled fondly at Lovelace and turned and left the room.

How much of that, Lovelace wondered, was true.

***

Gerry Holt felt the pressure behind his temples. He rubbed them gently with his fingertips and tried to relax.

What was it that bothered him? Why did it bother him? He looked at the screens in front of him and squinted his eyes to narrow his field. He'd find it sooner or later, whatever it was. Perhaps it was nothing? He nodded enthusiastically. Yes, it was most probably nothing. A glitch that was caused by the power failure. Nothing more. He reassured himself that nothing was amiss, that the alien code was nothing more than a wound caused by the power failure.

One by one, the various controls on HMP BlackRock came back online. Two hours after the power failure and they were fully operational again. They still had no link to the mainland, but complete control of the island had been restored.

Gerry looked over at Kellerman, who had paced almost constantly since he had arrived.

'We're back on.' Gerry said, and Kellerman stopped pacing.

'Good. I'll let Mr Preece know.'

Gerry watched as Kellerman closed the door behind him. Then he turned back to the screens in front of him.

Everything was working perfectly.

But the doubt remained.

***

'It's still warm.'

Grace moved through the water like a nymph. She came up for air at the edge of the pool and looked up at Lovelace. Lovelace was wearing the two-piece swimming costume that had belonged to Elouise's daughter. She was boyishly pretty, Grace thought, with her unkempt hair and friendly face. She had a good figure, too, and was envious of the curves that framed her.

The pool room was dark save for the light that came in from outside. The atmospheric blue and purple lights surrounding the pool had been lost to the power cut, and the water was an inky black.

'Come on in.' Grace beckoned.

Lovelace sat at the edge of the pool and lowered herself in. They swam and chatted and giggled like schoolgirls for nearly an hour as the water slowly grew colder and colder. Lovelace had liked Grace from the moment she met her. She was warm and friendly, with beautiful green eyes and a sensual smile. She had a feeling they were going to be good friends.

They sat at the edge of the pool and dried themselves down.

'Ethan wasn't a bad man. Not really.' Grace said.

'He tried to rape you.' Lovelace countered.

Grace's head fell, and her damp hair fell over her face. Lovelace reached over and pushed it back to see her face. 'You're not to blame.' Lovelace said, cradling the back of her neck.

Grace looked up. 'He never raped me. Not like that. Not rape.'

'It's rape in all but the detail.' Lovelace said. 'See it for what it was. Mackay wasn't kind to you.'

A tear welled in Grace's eyes. Lovelace wiped it away with her other hand. She was wondering what to say next when Grace leant forward and kissed her. She held her head in her hand for a long moment before gripping her tighter and pulling her closer.

Eleven

Detective Chief Inspector McBride stepped outside the doors of the mainland headquarters and felt the wind howl in his ears. The rain was coming in sideways, soaking everything in its path. Satisfied the storm wasn't going anywhere anytime soon, he stepped back inside the building and shook his head until the water stopped dripping.

'Met office has the storm over us for at least another twenty-four hours.' Liam Swift said as he walked over to where McBride stood.

McBride looked at his watch. It was nearing midday. They had lost contact with the island almost three hours ago.

'What about the power?' McBride asked.

'Most of the East coast is offline. Power companies are struggling with the weather and the fact we're so remote. It could be another day until power is restored to the island. We'll be okay here. Our diesel generators will keep us going for a long time.'

'What about the prison?' McBride asked.

'Same. Ethan Mackay made sure there was full provision in case of power failure. We get quite a few this time of year.'

'At least they'll be comfortable in the Governor's house,' McBride said, more to himself than to Swift.

'No.' Swift countered. 'There was no provision for a diesel generator at the mansion house or the accommodation block. It was an oversight. We're having them retrofitted next month.'

'So they don't have power?'

'No. Nothing.'

McBride pondered this for a moment. Having no power wasn't the primary issue. People coped, and most people staying at the Mansion house were old enough to remember an age when power wasn't guaranteed. No, that wasn't the issue. The issue was the darkness. The darkness hid things. It hid people. There was a reason most crimes were committed under cover of darkness. What bothered McBride was the opportunity it gave the murderer to move about the house freely and unobserved. He had a horrible feeling that whoever the killer was, they hadn't finished yet.

He shook off the feeling. 'I should see how my DS is getting on.'

McBride walked back into the office where he and DS Sandhu had set up the incident room. Sandhu was deep in conversation as he sat down. After a few minutes, she placed her phone on the table and looked at McBride. A smile had formed on her lips.

'Now, that was an interesting conversation.' She said slowly.

'Tell me more.' McBride asked.

'Well, I didn't think we'd get much on Esther Friedman. Certainly nothing substantial. She was married a long time ago, and her husband died an equally long time ago. But I was taken by what Lovelace said. If Mackay had found something, there was something worth looking for. So I traced her marriage certificate and her husband's birth certificate, and I finally found his death certificate, which named his place of death as a small village in the west of India. So I rang the local police station and spoke to the Sergeant there. Strangely enough, we weren't the only people to have asked about this case recently.'

'We weren't?' McBride asked, intrigued.

'No.' Sandhu said, smiling. 'He remembers an Englishman coming to the village about six months ago asking about the case. He said he was working on a book about it. He showed some convincing credentials, certainly enough to convince the local authorities to assist in his research. They pulled all the files on the case and handed them over. The sergeant tells me they weren't particularly interesting—just official documents recording official details. In a nutshell, a group of British tourists fell ill in the village they were visiting as part of some pan-Indian tour. It was thought that they had all fallen ill through food poisoning.'

'All of them?' McBride asked.

'All of them. Including Esther Friedman, who was then Esther Latrobe. They all recovered except for Esther's husband, who took a turn for the worse and died a few days later. They're sending the files over for us to look at.'

'I sense there was nothing in the files to cast a shadow over Esther Friedman?'

'Not in the files, no.' Sandhu said cryptically.

McBride watched as his DS enjoyed her moment of knowing something he didn't. She was a good DS, and she relished the detail. The detail pleased her. He allowed her a few more moments to savour the feeling.

'But you found something?' He asked.

Sandhu nodded. 'My contact in India discussed the case with his father over dinner one night when his father told him he recalled the incident. His old man had been a policeman, too. Career paths run in families over there, much like they do here. The story he told was quite interesting.'

DS Sandhu paused. Then she said, 'although no crime was thought to have been committed, the police interviewed all the travellers who had fallen ill. No statements were taken, but my contact's father remembered that several of them had considered the possibility that Esther had poisoned them all but had fed her husband a larger dose to kill him. Because they all had become ill, it was considered less suspicious.'

'Did he say why they thought that?' McBride asked.

'Apparently, they argued the entire trip. Esther's husband was many years older than her, and she garnered some sympathy from some of the other ladies on the trip. He was violent and possessive. She was young and pretty and full of life. He was also wealthy, and the ladies on the trip were prone to gossip. They often discussed how they thought Esther would get rid of her husband. They enjoyed reading crime fiction a little too much. When they all fell ill, and Esther's husband died, their imaginations went into overdrive.'

'What did the police do?'

'Nothing. They had minimal resources where they were, so Mr Latrobe's body was flown to Delhi for an autopsy. It never got there.'

'What? What happened?'

'Esther Friedman happened. Before the authorities could react, she had her husband's body flown back to the UK on a private charter. He was cremated within hours of landing. The Indian authorities considered the case closed and didn't follow up with authorities here.'

'So Esther Latrobe becomes a wealthy young woman, morphs into Esther Friedman, and builds herself a powerful career.'

Sandhu nodded. 'Indeed she did.'

'And then Ethan Mackay goes a digging.' McBride commented.

'It's certainly a motive for murder,' Sandhu agreed.

'It is,' McBride said. 'But without proof, it would be hard to harm Esther's reputation. He'd be in danger of slandering or libelling her.'

'Perhaps he found proof?' Sandhu suggested.

'After all these years? It's doubtful.' McBride pondered the question for a moment. 'Or perhaps he was speculating? Esther admitted to being intrigued by Mackay's invitation to the island. It was the reason she went there, after all.'

'He didn't know what he thought he knew,' Sandhu said, repeating the words that Esther had used.

'But perhaps he knew enough to get himself killed.' McBride noted. 'Esther Friedman had had a lot to drink that night, and we know the crime wasn't premeditated. Perhaps she went down for a drink during the night and found Mackay enjoying his midnight snack. She was outspoken and not afraid of anyone. She would have had it out with him there and then. If he laughed at her, mocked her, and turned his back on her..'

Sandhu picked up the thread, 'then she turned and reached for the nearest thing to hit him with, and plunged a knife into his back.'

For the first time that day, McBride smiled. It was a theory, and so far, it was their best one.

***

Esther Friedman didn't find her way to her room for a lie-down, preferring to take a circuitous route to the bar instead. It was dimly lit. A single oil lamp that looked like it had seen better days stood on the bar emitting a dull orange glow. She walked over to it and turned it up. The light strengthened and cast everything nearby in a similar orange. The lamp felt odd, she thought. An anachronism. Why on earth did it even exist on such a high-tech island?

She went behind the bar and hunted down another bottle of champagne. She opened one and poured herself another glass. It was going to be a long day, and she was damned if she would suffer it sober.

She sat by the window, looked down over the pool, and watched as the very beautiful Grace Mahone stepped out of her robe and plunged into the dark waters. She was joined moments later by Lovelace, who was similarly attired in a pretty two-piece swimming costume. She was younger than Grace and slimmer in a boyish way, and Esther felt the pang of lost youth as she caught sight of her reflection in the window. She sat by the window as the two young women swam, giggled, and played in the water. She was still watching when they sat at the pool's edge and kissed. At first, it looked as though Grace had overstepped the mark, and Lovelace was about to pull away. Esther felt her heart twitch in sympathy for the young Grace Mahone. She had been there many times in her long life, and it pained her to see the same mistakes in the young. But Lovelace didn't pull away, and the two young women stayed in the embrace for a long time.

Esther watched it all, and she grew envious. Life had been hard. It was still hard. Age didn't make things easier. Men like Ethan Mackay and the odious Sir Malcolm Lambert had made it more complicated. She didn't like them. She didn't like them one bit. She had spent her life fighting men like that and was tired. She was so very tired of it all.

She watched as Grace and Lovelace came up for air. They stood holding hands by the side of the pool and slowly donned their robes. They held each other's hands like schoolgirls and left the pool area.

Ester turned to her drink and poured herself another glass. She didn't like the Lovelace girl, although she could not pinpoint why. Jealousy? Maybe. But no, she was too old for jealousy and too old for Grace. It wasn't that. What was it? She reached for her glass and looked down into the liquid. Someone had once told her that she would never find the answers at the bottom of a glass, but in her experience, that was exactly where she found them. She had had some of her best lightbulb moments at the wrong end of a bottle of champagne.

And then she had another one, and she was entirely surprised that she hadn't seen it before. Yes, that would certainly make sense. But why? Well, now that would be interesting. But she would need proof. But where to look?

***

Wayne Sampson, the island's head of security, stepped out of the accommodation block and braced himself for the onslaught of wind and rain. He pulled up the hood of his waterproof coat and twisted the bottom of it so that it held fast to his head. He ducked down and made a beeline for the Mansion House that stood, eerily dark in the afternoon gloom, barely two hundred yards away. He made the crossing quickly and stood in the entranceway dripping with rainwater.

He slipped his overcoat off and hung it on a free peg to one side of the doorway. In front of him, his two best guards sat on either side of the door to the kitchen, preserving the crime scene should the police ever make it to the island. He doubted if the storm would relent anytime soon. The last he heard, it was intensifying and was due to continue for a few days.

Maeve looked up as he crossed the floor.

'Afternoon, boss.' She said.

Maeve was one of his best, if not *the* best, guard he had. He hated putting her on such a dull assignment, but he knew he could trust her. They had worked together for years since she joined one of Mackay's early prisons. She had then been an average prison officer, content to deal with the usual run-of-the-mill stuff in a regular prison. He had watched as this small young prison officer had been cornered by three of the most fearsome-looking killers he had ever seen before knocking seven shades of shit out of them.

He had taken her to one side afterwards and asked her how she had done it.

'Brothers,' she said in a broad Belfast accent. 'Six of them. And their friends. At one time or another, I've had to fight my way through them all.'

She had a small scar just under her left eye, no doubt a relic of a vicious punch, but aside from that, she bore no other marks. When Mackay had offered Sampson a chance to build his own security detail, Maeve had been his first choice. They had since gone on to make a fearsome security team at BlackRock.

Maeve's colleague looked up. He was a beast of a man that stood six feet tall when stooping. He had arms the size of small trees and had to twist sideways to walk through doorways. He had been in the Paras for a short time but had received a dishonourable discharge for breaking an officer's jaw. When Sampson asked why, he shrugged and said, 'I fucking hate Ruperts.'

Despite being called Phil, he was now known as Rupert. Sampson had taken him on the understanding that if he ever punched a member of his team, he'd kill him. Rupert had seen tough men before and knew what they looked like. Sampson scared him, and he didn't doubt for a second that he would follow up on his threat. His eyes said it all. The eyes never lied.

'Everything okay here?'   Sampson asked.

'Yeah. We're all good.' Maeve replied.

'Sorry, it's a shit job.' Sampson looked at his watch. The afternoon was approaching the evening. 'I'll get some food sent down for you in a bit. I'll be back at ten to relieve you.'

'Sure, boss.' Maeve said.

Sampson's face twisted into what most observers would call a snarl, but it was his best attempt at smiling. The moment passed quickly. They were interrupted by a shrill, 'you there!' followed by footsteps as Esther walked quickly across the floor.

'Can I help you?' Sampson snarled.

Esther paused on her approach. She didn't like the gorilla. He had evil eyes. She stiffened her shoulders and approached with a little more caution than before.

'I wish to see the passenger list.' She said firmly.

'What passenger list?' Sampson asked.

'For the helicopter. The one that brought us here?'

Sampson looked at Esther enquiringly. 'Why?'

'Because I do. Can I see it?'

'If there was one, it's most likely stored on the computers. What is it you want to know?'

Esther paused. She was beginning to question everything she knew and everyone she thought she knew. The champagne dulled her senses a bit. What was it she wanted to know? Yes, of course, *that*. But would it be so simple? Surely not. No, perhaps there was another way. She would need to find a way to phrase it correctly to elicit the required response.

She looked at Sampson as Johnathon stepped out of his study.

'Never mind.' She said to Sampson bluntly. 'Mr Preece, may I have a moment of your time.'

The three guards watched as Esther was guided into Johnathon's study. Maeve gave the universally recognised hand signal for a drunk, and the three of them laughed.

Johnathon pulled a chair over for Esther to sit on, and he watched as she carefully sat down. He could smell the alcohol from where he sat.

'Is everything okay?' He asked gently.

Esther seemed distinctly uncomfortable. 'I'm not sure,' she said slowly, gathering her thoughts. 'I wondered if, perhaps, the passenger manifest would tell me, but now I think of it some more, I don't see how that could be possible. They would be too careful.'

Johnathon was intrigued. 'Who would be too careful?' He asked.

Esther watched Johnathon's face carefully.

'We've never met before, have we?' Esther asked, suddenly changing the course of the conversation.

'No. I don't think so.'

'So I have no idea who you are, and equally, you have no idea who I am?'

'I know you by reputation.' Johnathon said.

'Yes. Exactly that. *By reputation.*'

'I'm not sure I follow..' Johnathon began.

Esther tried to corral her thoughts. 'How many people in this house did you know before yesterday?' She asked. 'How many had you met?'

'My wife, obviously.' Johnathon said. 'Ethan Mackay and er….' He paused. 'That's it, I think.'

'You didn't know Grace?'

Johnathon shook his head. 'No, I don't think so. Yesterday was her first time on the island, and I don't think we've met before.'

'And Sir Malcolm?'

'Only by reputation and what I've read in the papers.'

'And Lovelace?'

'Again, only by what I've read in the papers. I know her father and her history.'

'I see.' Esther said, rubbing her temples and trying to clear the fog in her head.

'I'm not sure I do.' Johnathon said.

Esther stood up. 'I think, perhaps, I need another drink. I think more clearly then.'

Johnathon watched as Esther stumbled out of the door. She had had enough to drink, but it wasn't his place to say. He sat in his study for some time, wondering about what she had said and what she had meant by it all. None of it made a single bit of sense. He smiled. When did anything ever make any sense?

***

McBride and Sandhu had spent the afternoon fielding two dozen calls and a flurry of emails from all over the world. All the lines they had cast out for information had begun to get nibbles. One by one, they reeled them back in; by nightfall, they had collated a vast amount of data.

McBride finished his latest cup of sweet coffee and sat back in his chair. It had been an enlightening afternoon.

DS Sandhu had spent almost an hour on the phone with Mike Hobson's sister. Mike had always been a very private man and kept his personal life intensely private.

He only shared his relationships with his family when he felt they were more than just casual encounters.

'I sometimes met his boyfriends if we were out in town at the same time,' the sister said. 'I had never heard of his latest one, certainly not by name, and I'd only met him a couple of times.'

Sandhu had emailed her Johnathon Preece's photograph.

'Is this the man you met?'

'Yes. That's him.'

'Tell me about the night of the accident.'

'Mike never drank and drove. Never.' She began. 'It was out of character. Witnesses at the trial say they saw the car being driven dangerously moments before the crash. It seems he lost control and clipped a high curb. The car was flung to the other side, climbing the pavement and striking a young woman. She died at the scene.'

'Your brother was breath-tested at the scene, wasn't he?'

'Yes. He was nearly four times over the limit. But he wasn't driving.'

'But he admitted it was him in the driver's seat?' Sandhu pressed.

'He did. But he wasn't alone that night. Some witnesses claim that they saw a second man exit the car after the crash and leave the scene shortly afterwards.'

Sandhu knew this much to be true. She had read the witness statements that had sent Mike Hobson to jail for ten years. Some did mention seeing a second man who left the scene before the police arrived. No one saw him in or exiting the car, despite what Mike's sister claimed. Mike Hobson's statement alleged that he was alone and that he was driving the vehicle. It was all the police needed to secure a conviction.

'Tell me about Mike's time in prison.'

'It destroyed him.' She said. 'He couldn't cope. Eventually, he confided the truth to me. He said he had taken the blame for the crash to preserve his boyfriend's career. He was assured that powerful forces were at play and that he would never serve time. He believed them. When he eventually went down, he threatened to tell the world the truth, but of course, by then, it was too late. Who would believe him? And then he killed himself.'

Sandhu and McBride discussed the suicide afterwards.

'There was no reason to suspect foul play?' McBride asked.

The autopsy suggested not. But the sister did. And then the policeman made the connection between Johnathon Preece and Mike Hobson, which enhanced her conviction.

'So Ethan Mackay uses his power and influence to make the scandal disappear and owns Johnathon's allegiance.' McBride summarised.

'People have killed to free themselves from less harmful situations.' Sandhu agreed.

'It's a motive for murder.' McBride said. 'I wonder how capable Johnathon Preece is? Is he capable of murder?'

The question hung in the air.

***

Johnathon sat in the low light and poured himself a large glass of whiskey. The Chivas label twinkled in the flickering light of an oil lamp that sat in the corner of his study.

He was a free man at last. Mackay no longer had him. He savoured the whiskey and felt the strong liquid burn his throat.

His future spread out before him, and he could almost taste it. Elouise would be okay. They had lived separate lives, and now she, too, would be free from Mackay's pull. They were both free.

But Esther bothered him. What had she meant? *I really have no idea who you are.*

What did she mean?

And was it going to be a problem?

Twelve

'Tell me about Grace Mahone.'

DS Sandhu had won the argument. McBride had insisted that Chinese food would make for a better meal, but Sandhu had argued that an Indian takeaway would be better. Swift had sided with Sandhu; in due course, a menu was found, and food was ordered. The restaurant had complained that the weather was too bad to deliver, so Swift had sent a car.

'They're running off a genny,' the driver explained as he dropped off the food. 'They are the only ones open.'

McBride had scooped a large portion of food onto a piece of naan bread and shovelled it unceremoniously into his mouth. He followed it down with a mouthful of lager and said, 'tell me about Grace Mahone.'

Sandhu ignored the food trail around McBride's lips and said, 'pretty much everything she's told us is true. I can't find a lie anywhere.'

McBride pondered on this for a moment. 'Sometimes it's the truth they tell that gives them away.'

Sandhu had to admit that there was some truth in that. 'She is the youngest of four children. She's the only girl. Her eldest brother was convicted of murder at nineteen and given a mandatory life sentence. He died in prison six months later. He was killed in a fight.'

'Nasty.'

Sandhu agreed. Very nasty. 'What makes it worse is that he played no part in the murder. He and a party of other young men had gone out that evening, and one of them had taken a hunting knife as protection. It seems he was into all kinds of bad stuff, drugs, prostitution, and petty thievery. Nothing suggests that Grace's brother was into any of that. In fact, from what I can tell, he was a fairly naive and trusting young man. Grace idolised him. His friend stabbed a rival drug dealer to death, and they were all convicted of joint enterprise. It turns out they knew their friend carried a weapon, and it was on that basis that they were convicted.'

McBride nodded. He had no sympathy. Tragic though it was, violent crime was reaching endemic levels in the country, and sometimes a hard hammer was required to crack the nut.

'Grace took her brother's death hard.' Sandhu continued, pausing now and then to eat more food. 'She studied hard at school and achieved a first at Manchester University in Criminal Psychology. She joined Mackay as a Personal Assistant shortly after graduating. She's worked for him ever since.'

McBride finished off his glass of lager and poured himself another. The alcohol was dulling the edge of a stressful day.

'What does she gain by Mackay's death?' He asked.

'Nothing. If anything, she loses. She loses her job, her lifestyle, her whole life.'

'It would seem silly to kill the goose that lays the golden egg.'

'It would.'

'What about the name on her bedroom door? "Lemon." What does that mean?' McBride asked.

Sandhu shrugged. 'I have no idea. I've looked everywhere for some hint as to what that means, but I can't see it.'

'It must mean something,' McBride went on. 'From what I know about Ethan Mackay, everything he did had a reason and a purpose.'

'I'll keep digging.' Sandhu said. 'I'll find it.'

McBride smiled. He didn't doubt that for a second.

***

Grace rolled over and stroked Lovelace's face. 'You're cute when you sleep.'

Lovelace smiled. She couldn't remember feeling so relaxed and in tune with another human being. She struggled with people. She always had. It was easier to keep them at arm's length. She never let them get too close. It made life difficult. Grace had gotten under her skin, and she hadn't even noticed until she had reached over and kissed her. She had thought about pulling away but got lost in the moment and relished Grace's tenderness.

Once they had left the pool, they returned to Lovelace's room and spent the afternoon in each other's company, talking, giggling, and making love. Lovelace had fallen asleep like that, totally disarmed and happy. Something she hadn't been for such a long time. She lost herself in the moment, all her troubles forgotten.

'I should go back to my room,' Grace said reluctantly. 'I came here with nothing more than a swimming costume and a robe. I don't think I should go to dinner like that.'

'Perhaps not!' Lovelace laughed. 'Old Sir Malcolm would have a heart attack.'

'I was thinking more of Esther.' Grace argued. 'I think she likes me!'

'She has good taste.' Lovelace joked.

Grace smiled, and her face lit up. Lovelace reached up, cradled her head in her hands, and drew her slowly towards her until their lips touched.

'Will you come back tonight?' Lovelace asked.

'Try stopping me.' Grace replied, drawing back the covers of the bed and stepping out.

She picked up her robe from the floor and dropped it over her shoulders. She tied a bow at the front, reached down, and picked up her swimming costume. She turned and looked back at Lovelace as she reached the door. Lovelace had propped herself up with one arm and was watching Grace.

Grace smiled, opened the door, and disappeared into the corridor. She stood there for a moment, fighting the urge to open the door and go back in. Slowly, she thought to herself. Go slowly. Don't frighten her away. She let go of the door handle, turned to go to her room, and found Esther standing behind her in the darkness.

'You made me jump.' Grace said.

'Sorry. I suppose we're all a bit on edge.' Esther said, slurring her words.

'I suppose so..' Grace began, conscious that Esther must have seen her leaving Lovelace's room.

Esther held Grace's eyes for a long moment. It was difficult for her to comprehend what was happening behind those dark eyes. Esther held up the oil lamp that she was carrying so that it cast a strange orange light on the two of them. Their shadows danced on the walls behind them.

'People aren't what you think,' Esther said loudly. 'They're not at all who you think they are.'

'I'm not sure I know what you mean?' Grace asked nervously.

'People hide things. People hide. Their true selves. People are deceitful.'

Grace took a step back from Esther. She had a strange look on her face, corrupted by the odd light that drew confusing patterns on her face.

'I need to go to my room,' Grace said, fearful of what Esther would say next. She pushed past Esther and found the handle to her room. She turned and looked at Esther, who stood holding the lamp.

'You can't trust anyone, you see.' Esther said. 'Everyone lies.'

Grace opened the door to her room and stepped inside. Esther was an odd woman at the best of times, but drunk Esther was a new level of oddness. *Everyone lies.* What had she meant by that? Did she mean her? She was a nosey and curious old woman, Grace thought. There was a danger that she knew too much. Way too much.

Lovelace stepped back from the peephole. She hadn't been able to see much as the light from Esther's lamp had obscured her view. But she had heard what had transpired between the two women, and her heart burned for Grace.

Esther could be a very unkind woman, and she had seen the look on Grace's face. Grace had looked pained. Something Esther had said had struck a chord.

What had Esther said that made Grace look so stressed? *People hide.* Was that it? Had Esther seen Grace leave Lovelace's room a short time earlier? *People hide their true selves.* Was that it? Was Esther jealous? Angry, even?

Lovelace stood at the door and started to think. One or two things were beginning to make sense. But Esther was dangerous. Dangerous to herself. She'd need to keep a close eye on her.

***

So, Ethan Mackay was dead.

Elouise Preece felt the bruise that had developed under her eye. The memory came back, and she winced. She had seen his mood and knew very well what he could be like when the darkness gripped him, and she was older and stronger than poor Grace, so she had stepped in and taken the pain from her. And it had come quickly, too, and he had swung out and caught her under the eye.

And then she had consoled him. Mothered him. Tended to his bruised ego. Then his darkness lifted, and his other desires grew. The mothering changed, and she cared for his needs as she had always done for men like Mackay. And they always took what they wanted until they were sated and their passions ebbed away.

Mackay always took what he wanted. No one ever said no. And now he was dead, and she didn't feel a bit sorry for him.

Elouise passed through the dining room, lighting candles and setting oil lamps on tables. Mrs Brent had been sent to the prison to prepare dinner for the guests at the Mansion House. The Defenders were returning across the mountain and carrying the evening's meal through the storm.

She felt something she hadn't felt in a long time. She felt free. Mackay had lost his hold over her and Jonathon, and she felt the weight of anxiety leave her shoulders.

She had known Johnathon was gay almost from the first moment they met, but it hadn't changed how she felt about him. She had worked out from an early age that no one was ever really a hundred per cent anything, certainly not where sex was concerned. Most people were 99.9% something, and some were not. That was life, and she knew that Johnathon was somewhere in the middle.

She had been stuck in a loveless marriage to an older man and stayed in it because she couldn't see an alternative. He wasn't a horrible man, not really. She didn't love him, and then Johnathon came into her life, and things changed. The sex was incredible. Johnathon was a caring and thoughtful lover, and she fell deeply in love. But her husband was awkward, and he had refused a divorce.

It had seemed hopeless. He threatened to cut her off from his money, but it didn't matter to her, and she told him so, and that only served to increase his stubbornness. And then, one evening, he complained of feeling unwell, stood up from the couch and promptly fell, clutching his chest.

Maybe she had seen a way out. She could have been in the bath, kitchen, or anywhere. Who could tell?

So she went into the kitchen, made herself a cup of tea, and waited for a while. Caught quickly, they say, heart attacks can be survivable. Time. That's all she needed. Time.

She could hear the death rattle when she returned. His final moments were upon him. She dialled 999 and screamed for help. Her husband! He was dying! Come quickly! The operator talked her through CPR, and Elouise pretended to follow the instructions. When the paramedics arrived, she pumped so hard on his chest that she broke a rib.

She had tried everything, they said. She had tried so hard that he had bruises on his chest and cracked bones. There was nothing more she could have done—such a young age to be a widow.

A year later and she and Johnathon married.

Johnathon confessed that he enjoyed the company of men and women, and they had entered into an agreement whereby she never asked, and he never told. It worked both ways, too. Elouise found her pleasures when she needed them, and their lives worked perfectly well, and they had brought a little girl into the world, and her life was complete.

And then the crash and Ethan Mackay. It all seemed to happen at once. Her life was about to be turned upside down and ruined, and she couldn't stop it.

Mackay fixed it. Mackay always fixed it. But at what cost? He owned Johnathon, and by extension, he owned her. Mackay always seemed to know everything. He guessed how her first husband had died. Did you take your time? He had asked.

He knew about Johnathon and his lovers, and he knew about her. He knew everything, and he slowly forced his way into her life. Mackay was a parasite, but she humoured him. He had a powerful hold over her and Johnathon, and it was a hold she couldn't break.

But now he was dead. She was free at last.

Ethan Mackay's death was the second-best thing that had ever happened to her, and she couldn't have been happier.

'I say, this all looks bloody marvellous.'

She hadn't heard Sir Malcolm enter the room. He was a quiet old man, despite his size.

'Good evening Sir Malcolm. Can I get you a drink?'

Sir Malcolm was dressed smartly in crisp dark trousers, a well-pressed shirt and tie and an old tweed jacket.

He glanced at his watch, 'why not? Do you have sherry?'

'We have everything, Sir Malcolm. There is little else to do here but drink alcohol.'

Elouise poured a glass of sherry from a crystal decanter and passed it to him.

'I suppose there are some good walks around here?'

'There are,' Elouise said. 'But not in the winter. The island is a tough place to be caught outside this time of year. It's a small place, but very easy to get disorientated. If you walk the wrong way out of the Mansion House, you could end up walking right off the cliff and into the sea.'

'Indeed. Drowning must be very unpleasant, although I've heard it said that it's a calm way to go.'

'I shouldn't think you'd get a chance to drown,' Elouise said. 'If you didn't crack your head open on the way down, the sea's as likely to lift you back up and try again.'

Sir Malcolm shuddered. The way she said it was so... so cold.

Elouise saw the look that crossed Sir Malcolm's face. The thing about killing a person is that it's never the last time you think about it. Elouise had thought about it a lot. Sir Malcolm had recognised the look. He had seen it cross her face.

Awkwardly, she said, 'I must go and see if Mrs Brent has returned with dinner. Please help yourself to more sherry.'

Sir Malcolm watched as she hurried out of the room carrying an oil lamp. There was more to Mrs Preece than he had first thought. What depths were there to plunder, he wondered?

He was still considering the question when Esther came through the door in a flurry. She held an oil lamp in one hand and an empty champagne glass in the other.

'Ah. Good. Sherry. Pour me one would you?' She asked as she stumbled her way to a chair.

'I think you've had enough,' Sir Malcolm said coldly.

'I couldn't disagree more.' Esther retorted. 'It helps me think.'

171

Sir Malcolm reached for the decanter and poured Esther a glass of sherry before topping himself up. He handed her the glass and said, 'I don't like you. I don't like you at all.'

Esther took the glass with a cheery smile and replied, 'and I don't care.'

Sir Malcolm laughed for the first time since Esther had met him. 'Well, I don't like you, but I have some respect for you, even if you are an old soak.'

'Less of the "old", if you don't mind, I'm in the prime of life.'

'You know as well as I do that we are both far from the prime of our lives,' Sir Malcolm said with no animosity.

Esther looked at the old man and grudgingly admitted that her best days were behind her. That didn't mean good times weren't ahead, though, especially now that Mackay was dead.

'It hasn't done anyone any harm, has it?' Esther mused. 'Mackay getting stabbed, that is. Hasn't done any harm at all.'

Sir Malcolm nodded. 'I suppose not. He was a difficult man.'

Esther leant forward, 'what did he know about you?' She asked.

Sir Malcolm shuffled uncomfortably. 'Some things are best left unsaid.'

'I agree. But I might take a longer look at your life once we're out of here.' Esther said, holding Sir Malcolm's eye and closely watching his expression. 'I think it might make a rather good exposé, wouldn't you agree?'

Sir Malcolm held firm. 'You should be careful.' He said.

'I have nothing to hide. I told Ethan as much, and I'm telling you the same. There's nothing on me!' Esther said triumphantly.

'That's not what I mean,' Sir Malcolm said mysteriously, and he watched as Esther's expression changed to one of doubt and confusion.

Sir Malcolm raised the glass to his lips and let the amber liquid coat his tongue. In his mind's eye, he saw a broken Esther Friedman fall from the cliff's edge, and her head break as it caught the jagged edges of the granite rock before she plummeted into the foaming sea below.

Yes, the old hack should be very careful indeed.

***

'I need to ask you a question.'

Elouise had changed for dinner and sought out her husband in his study. She closed the door behind her and spoke the words as she did so.

Johnathon looked up from his book, and his reading glasses slipped down his nose. He took them off and slowly closed his book. 'Go on.' He said reluctantly.

Elouise took a deep breath and asked, 'did you kill Ethan?'

Johnathon's expression held fast. There wasn't a flicker of emotion that she could see.

'No.' He said, at last, carefully watching his wife's expression. 'Did you?'

Elouise pulled up a chair and collapsed into it. She was tired, and Ethan's murder had cast a shadow over everyone. She believed him, but still, the anxiety lingered.

'No, I didn't.' She said slowly, dropping each word carefully. 'But I wanted to.'

Johnathon took her hand. 'Everyone who ever crossed the man's path wanted him dead. There is no shortage of people with a motive. Even I wanted to kill him sometimes.'

'They'll start digging, you know. Into our pasts. They'll look for things we may not be too proud of.'

Many years ago, Elouise confessed to Johnathon that she had delayed calling an ambulance when her first husband had had a heart attack. In turn, he had admitted that it had been him driving the car that killed the young woman when his lover had taken the blame. Their secrets had bound them even tighter together.

'There's no proof of anything.'

'But we let Mackay control us because of what we thought he knew.' Elouise argued.

'Because we felt he knew more.' Jonathon said. 'The more I think on it, the more I'm convinced he had nothing. We can't stop the police investigation. They're bound to look. But I'm convinced they'll find nothing.'

Elouise stiffened. 'I'm scared, Johnathon. I'm really scared.'

Johnathon squeezed his wife's hand. 'Everything will be okay. I'll take care of everything, I promise.'

Elouise forced a smile. She wiped a tear from her eyes and stood up. 'Mrs Brent's due with the dinner shortly. Will you be joining us?'

Johnathon nodded. 'I just need a quick change of clothes.'

'Okay.' Elouise turned to leave, then suddenly turned back to face her husband. 'It will be okay, won't it?' She asked.

'Yes. It will all be okay.'

Secretly he feared that the story hadn't yet been entirely played out. There was still more to come, he thought. He just didn't know what form it would take.

Thirteen

The Citadel was bathed in the harsh light of a dozen security lights that swept over BlackRock. The storm continued to rage overhead, and the rain that had fallen constantly for over twenty-four hours now fell as snow. It was whipped up into a frenzy around the glass windows of the Citadel and the crenellated top of the enormous walls surrounding the prison.

Gerry sat at his bank of computer monitors and idly watched the storm blow its white passenger over the prison grounds. He was humming quietly to himself and chewing on a chocolate bar. Two other technicians sat at their desks, monitoring their screens.

Since they had fully restarted the computers that controlled BlackRock, Gerry had found himself notably relaxing. There was a niggle at the back of his head, but he had seen more reasons to ignore it than to be concerned about it. But still, *there was a niggle,* and he didn't like niggles. Whatever people thought of Gerry Holt, he told himself, he was nothing if not thorough.

He glanced over at Emily, who was tapping away at her computer. His eyes casually wandered the length of her body. He found everything he saw to his taste, and he found himself lingering on her body for longer than was appropriate. She sensed him watching her and looked up. He thought she had a cute way in which she pushed her glasses back up her nose with the fingers of her left hand, and she did that now, all the while keeping eye contact with Gerry.

'Everything okay?' She asked. She had been warned about Gerry and kept him at arm's length for most of the time they worked together. She had been rostered on to the night shift with Gerry and Carl, and while she enjoyed Carl's company, Gerry made her skin crawl.

'Have you taken a look at the code I sent you?' Gerry asked.

Emily looked across at Carl, who rolled his eyes.

'It makes no sense to me.' Emily admitted. 'I should think it's just a corrupted file from the power surge.'

Gerry nodded and turned back to his screens. Yes, it probably was. Just a corrupted file. Nothing more.

His eyes wandered back to the scene outside the window, and his thoughts turned back to Emily, and he let his imagination run free.

***

Sampson trundled through the snow and looked up as he approached the Mansion House. No lights guided his way, and he made most of the journey by memory. He was painfully conscious that if he missed the house in the blizzard, he could easily walk off the cliff and into the freezing North Atlantic. He wasn't entirely unhappy when the front of the building appeared a few feet in front of him.

He shook off the snow in the entrance hall and hung his coat on one of the free hooks. Maeve and Rupert were still where he had left them several hours ago. They had pulled up chairs on either side of the kitchen door and were playing cards in the light of an old oil lamp. Coke cans sat on the floor around their feet, along with the remnants of snack food they had gathered from one of the free vends in the accommodation block.

Maeve looked up as she heard him approach.

'Evening, boss,' she said as she folded her cards on the makeshift table they had created from an unused bin.

'Don't stop your game on my account,' Sampson said.

Rupert threw his cards onto the table on top of Maeve's and said, 'I think I'm done. There's only so much money I can lose in one night!'

Sampson smiled. Maeve was unbeatable at poker. He knew. He'd tried. What surprised him the most was that Rupert never learnt his lesson.

'I'm here to relieve you both,' Sampson said, looking at his watch. 'There's some curry over at the accommodation block. You should probably hurry before the other greedy bastards eat it all.'

Rupert didn't need telling twice. A man his size required feeding, and he was starving. He got up, grabbed his coat from the back of his chair, said good night and left.

'Never get in his way when there's food on the table,' Maeve joked. She looked at her boss as he sat on the chair that Rupert had vacated. 'You want me to do a double shift?' She asked.

Good old Maeve, Sampson thought. Dependable.

'No. Get off. Get something to eat and get some sleep. Let's hope tomorrow's not so fucking dull.'

Maeve stood and collected her coat. 'Night, boss,' she said, turning and leaving.

Sampson's eyes followed her figure as she walked away and into the darkness. He pulled her chair closer and lifted his feet onto it. He sat back in his chair and let his mind wander.

It was going to be a long and very dull night.

***

'It's snowing.' Liam Swift said as he walked back into the office.

McBride and Sandhu were still where he had left them a few minutes earlier. While they had finished the remains of their takeaway food and their conversation had once more reverted to Ethan Mackay's murder, Liam had gone off searching for alcohol. He raided the visitor's waiting suite and acquired a bottle of wine, champagne, gin and a selection of mixers. He also clutched a bottle of single malt under his arm.

'I'll take that,' McBride said, lifting the whisky from Liam's grip and pouring himself a large glass.

Sandhu poured herself a glass of wine, and Liam dropped into a chair next to her and opened the champagne.

'I don't think it would be wise for you to venture home tonight,' Liam said. 'We have several rooms on site for staff to use. They're clean and comfortable.'

'That's very kind,' Sandhu said, but she doubted if she would get a chance to use them. Once he got the wind under his sails, there was no stopping McBride. It wouldn't be the first time they had pulled an all-nighter. She sensed that Mackay's murder had re-ignited the fire she knew burned in his soul. He loved a good mystery, and they hadn't faced one like this for some time. She was looking forward to working it out.

'Right,' McBride began, draining the liquid from his glass and pouring himself another. 'What do we know about Sir Malcolm Lambert?'

'There's not much about Sir Malcolm that isn't known,' Sandhu admitted. 'Every part of his life is well documented. He's one of the most respected Members of Parliament, having been elected to his East Mercia constituency in 1990, and has served in two Conservative governments. His star's on the wane, but he commands a serious amount of respect in the House.'

'He was opposed to BlackRock?' McBride asked.

'He was, and while he opposed the building of the prison, it was unlikely to get support in Parliament. He was a thorn in Mackay's side.'

'Has he always been opposed to Mackay?'

Sandhu shook her head. 'No. Quite the opposite. Sir Malcolm was quite firm on law and order and prison reform. He backed a firmer response to crime and campaigned for harsher sentences and more prisons. If anything, his early support for Mackay put Mackay in the frame. It helped him build his prison empire.'

'But he opposed BlackRock.' McBride stated matter-of-factly.

'He did.' Sandhu agreed. 'Until he didn't.'

McBride left that fact to hang in the air. It was an important fact. Why did he suddenly stop opposing BlackRock? When Sir Malcolm changed his mind, Mackay's plans passed Government approval, resulting in HMP BlackRock being commissioned.

'He said he was an intelligent man,' McBride said, thinking out loud. 'He said he took all the evidence and changed his mind. Is it far-fetched to believe that that may be so?'

'Not at all,' Sandhu admitted. 'But we're talking about Ethan Mackay, a man with a reputation for digging up people's secrets.'

'Only if they were buried.' McBride stated cryptically.

'I don't follow?' Sandhu said.

'Lovelace said that Esther had commented about Sir Malcolm's patients being cremated or buried. The implication is that Sir Malcolm may have been able to cover his tracks by having his victims cremated or only targeting those he knew would be cremated.'

'Well, I spoke to the British Medical Association, who confirmed that Sir Malcolm has had a few complaints made in the past, but none of which were held up, and none about the death of a patient. His record's almost spotless.'

McBride stared into the space in front of him. 'He's not a stupid man,' he said quietly. 'I don't sense a god complex in Sir Malcolm, but I sense a greedy man. A man motivated purely by money and power. If he targeted victims, they would be old, probably with little or no family and quite rich, but not necessarily so. A few grand here and there to the respected doctor would go largely unnoticed.'

Sandhu sighed. 'I've been digging, but Sir Malcolm hasn't practised for thirty years. It will take some time to find the records and poke around. Even if we find one or two deaths that fit the profile, finding evidence will be something else.'

'Mackay did.' McBride said. 'Every time we come back to that. Mackay *knew*. He knew people, and he knew their secrets. More than that. He would have had proof. Mackay knew everyone's dirty little secrets on that island, and I'm certain that's what got him killed. Knowledge is a powerful and dangerous thing. In the wrong hands, it's lethal; in this case, it's the *knowing* that gets you murdered.'

***

Lovelace sat on a comfortable chair in the bar and watched as the ice began to gather on the window ledge.

'I was hoping I'd find you here.'

She looked up as Elouise stepped into the bar carrying an oil lamp. She placed it on the bar and walked around the other side. 'Can I get you another drink? What are you having?'

Lovelace held up her gin glass and showed the printed side to Elouise. 'I don't know how to pronounce it,' she admitted, 'but it's bloody nice.'

'Fynoderee.' Elouise said, successfully mastering the tongue twister. 'Jonathon picked up a case when he was on the Isle of Man. It is very nice. I think I'll join you.'

Elouise measured two large glasses of the Manx gin, dropped ice into them and poured in a tonic. She carried the glasses over to where Lovelace sat and took a chair opposite. 'I do fear that if I have to stay on the island for too long, I may become an alcoholic!'

'I think Esther is there waiting for you,' Lovelace joked.

'Yes. She's certainly a strange one.' Elouise paused and looked at Lovelace for some time.

Lovelace held her gaze and then asked, 'you said you were looking for me?'

'Yes,' Elouise said slowly, 'yes, I did, didn't I? You see, I was wondering whether I can trust you. I'm still not sure.'

'Why do you need to trust me?' Lovelace asked. 'Once we're off this island, we'll probably never see each other again.'

'That's true.' Elouise agreed. 'I get the feeling I can trust you. There's something about you. I want to talk, you see. I get the feeling you may be the only one to understand.'

Lovelace leant forward and smiled. 'You're worried because of my relationship with the police?'

'Yes. Yes, I am.'

'Because of your secrets?' Lovelace went on. 'Because of the secrets you and your husband share and whether or not the police will discover them, reveal them, and destroy your lives?'

'I knew you'd understand.' Elouise declared.

'I do. I also know that your husband was driving the car that killed the woman that Mike Hobbs was convicted of killing. I also strongly believe that your husband has never fully come to terms with that or that Mike Hobbs later took his own life. I suspect your husband feels regret and shame, and guilt. I think you have been the one to hold him together.'

A tear welled in Elouise's eye. She wiped it away with the back of her hand. 'He confessed to me after Mike killed himself in prison. The guilt was eating him away. It was killing him. And Mackay had him under his control. Johnathon felt trapped. So I went to see Mackay to try and sort the mess out, but I seemed to make it worse. I became another of Mackay's lovers. He used Johnathon to control me and make me do what he wanted. I was mad to think I could appeal to his better nature. He didn't have one. Johnathon discovered the affair, and I think the last breath of life left him. He became a shell of a man that was merely going through the stages of life in the hope that death would come soon.'

'But Mackay's came first?' Lovelace said.

'Yes.' Elouise said, 'but not at Johnathon's hands, I'm sure.'

'But he is responsible for two people's deaths?' Lovelace countered.

'By the consequences of his actions, not by any malicious intent.'

'What was your intent when you let your first husband die?' Lovelace asked, feeling guilty for the way that she asked it.

Elouise smiled, and Lovelace watched as the stress and anxiety left her body. She physically relaxed in front of her as the tension ebbed away.

'Yes,' Elouise said at last. 'I left my husband to die. It was almost too easy, and I've never had a moment's regret. Not one.'

Lovelace looked deep into Elouise's eyes. 'I think you are a competent woman,' Lovelace said. 'I admire your conviction.'

Elouise chuckled, but it was a nervous chuckle. 'I suppose it will become an actual conviction soon? Now the police are looking into it.'

Lovelace shook her head. 'Not necessarily. I don't know what Mackay had on you, but all he had on Johnathon was his testimony about how Johnathon had gone to him for help after the crash and how they convinced Mike Hobbs to take the fall with the promise of no prison time. But that's testimony that a dead man can't give.'

'That's quite a motive for murder.' Elouise said.

'It is,' Lovelace agreed. 'For both of you. But if you're going to survive what follows after this, you and your husband need to get your act together. You have a daughter that needs you both. Make sure you're there for her.'

Elouise looked deep into Lovelace's eyes. 'You know who killed Mackay, don't you?' She asked.

Lovelace swallowed her gin. 'I think so.'

'Be careful.' Elouise advised. 'Someone on this island has already killed Mackay to keep a secret.'

'I'm quite a capable person in my own right,' Lovelace said.

'Yes. I believe you are.' Elouise reached over and took Lovelace's hand. 'I think I can trust you. I'm sure of it, but I can't for the life of me think why. Look after Grace, will you? She's a beautiful young woman.'

Lovelace smiled. 'She is, and I will.'

Lovelace observed Elouise's expression carefully. It seemed that the gossip about her and Grace had already begun. BlackRock was fast becoming a difficult place to keep a secret, and it concerned her. Who knew what, exactly?

Johnathon walked into the bar carrying a lamp. He had changed for dinner and was dressed in a dark suit with a salmon shirt. His cufflinks sparkled in the light of a dozen candles.

'Mrs Brent has just pulled up. Shall I get her to unload everything in the lounge? Seems silly to all gather in the dining room.'

Elouise drained her glass and stood up. 'I'll sort it.' She threw a glance at Lovelace and smiled warmly. 'Thank you.' She said softly, and Lovelace felt the warmth in those two words.

Elouise took a lamp and disappeared from the bar. Johnathon placed his light on the table in front of Lovelace and asked, 'can I get you another drink?'

'I really shouldn't,' Lovelace said unconvincingly.

'Why not?' Johnathon asked. 'Have you any plans for this evening?'

Lovelace's mind quickly pondered her plans with the beautiful Grace Mahone but felt it was probably best not to share them with Johnathon. 'Well, when you put it like that, I suppose it would be rude not to?'

Johnathon smiled, took Lovelace's glass and wandered over to the other side of the bar, searching for gin. He poured Lovelace's drink first and then poured himself a small beer.

'I'll take one of those,' Grace said as she wandered through the door, using the torch on her phone to light her way. She sat next to Lovelace and waited while Johnathon poured another drink.

'I saw that fella from security a little while ago,' Johnathon said to no one in particular. 'He was sitting outside the kitchen getting himself comfortable for the night shift, by the look of it. All on his own, he was. I don't like the man. He bothers me, but I can't for the life of me think why. I'm not sure if I'm comforted by the fact he's in the house or bloody terrified by it.'

'He certainly has a look about him,' Lovelace agreed.

'Esther calls him the "gorilla",' Grace said.

'I think the old dear's lost the plot,' Johnathon absently said as he dropped a double measure into a gin glass.

'Who?' Lovelace asked.

'Mrs Friedman. Esther. She's wandering around the house talking all sorts of nonsense.'

Lovelace watched Grace's expression, but she concealed her emotions well.

'How do you mean?' Grace asked.

Johnathon placed Grace's drink on the table before her and sat opposite the women.

'She was blabbering on about the passenger list earlier. God knows why. I think her bloodstream must be almost a hundred per cent proof by now!'

'She was talking to me about people hiding their true selves earlier.' Grace admitted. 'She said something about people being deceitful.'

Lovelace watched Grace with interest. It was fascinating that she should share that when she didn't need to.

'I wonder who she meant?' Grace asked.

'Everybody has secrets,' Lovelace mused.

Johnathon nodded sagely. 'They do. And I suppose the person we put up in front of others is not necessarily our "true self." I suppose we are all guilty of being deceitful in that way.'

And yet, Lovelace mused, neither Johnathon nor Elouise had hidden their true identities from each other. They had trusted each other, and it had formed an unbreakable bond that even Mackay couldn't break. Lovelace looked across at Grace and watched as the shadows thrown by the candles danced lightly across her face. She felt she knew Grace, that she understood her. If they were going to create an unbreakable bond between themselves, they would have to be honest with each other sooner or later. She didn't think Grace was ready to do that yet, but the time was fast approaching.

They were interrupted by Elouise's return.

'Dinner will be served in the lounge tonight. It's a help-yourself sort of thing. Mrs Brent has made a huge pot of curry and managed to rustle up some pieces of bread and rice. Shall we?'

She led the three of them one by one through the darkened corridors to the lounge. The wood burner was fully ablaze, and Sir Malcolm stood next to it with a poker in one hand and a glass of wine in the other. His face looked tinged with red in the half-light, and Lovelace wondered if the old man had gotten too close to the fire.

Esther was sat in one of the easy chairs and was tucking into a bowl of steaming curry with a passion and furiousness that only someone that had drunk too much could show. She didn't look up as the others entered and helped themselves to food from a large pot that had been carefully arranged on a side table.

Lovelace sat on the vast sofa beside Grace and delved into her food. The atmosphere in the room was tense. Elouise and Johnathon sat apart but close to one another. Sir Malcolm perched himself on an armchair and carefully ate his curry with a knife and fork. Esther continued to eat furiously and spoke to no one. Grace dived into her food by scooping it up with a slice of naan bread and shovelling it into her face with none of the sophistication that her name would suggest. Lovelace followed suit. Sometimes it was the best way. Now and then, Lovelace paused to watch the others. She could feel the anticipation in the air. Everyone could feel it, but no one could quite place it—none except Lovelace.

Trouble was coming, she thought to herself. But where would it come from first?

Fourteen

Lovelace rolled over, and her arm reached out to the space next to her, but it fell on empty air. Her head was still a bit foggy, but she was sure someone should be there. She waited a moment while the fog lifted and her mind sorted for clarity in the darkness.

Grace. Grace was gone.

Lovelace pushed herself up on one arm and waited for her eyes to become accustomed to its new reality. Slowly the shadows in the room took on solid form, and she could make out a figure silhouetted at the window.

She stepped out of bed and drew a robe about her shoulders. She joined Grace at the window, and the two stood for some time, marvelling at the changing landscape.

'It's beautiful, isn't it?' Grace said softly.

Lovelace followed Grace's eyes and breathed in the beauty that mother nature had landed at their feet.

The sky was bright, the brightest she had seen in many days. A full moon shone from a star-lit horizon and cast everything before it in a harsh winter's light. Across the landscape in front of them, a white blanket had been laid, and Lovelace followed it as far as the mountain.

'What time is it?' Lovelace asked.

'About four, I think. I couldn't sleep. The light woke me.'

As they spoke, a cloud passed in front of the moon, and it was as if someone had turned off a light. Everything plunged back into darkness before the cloud passed over, returning everything once more into the light.

Lovelace looked at the sky beyond the landscape and watched as more storm clouds raced towards them. The wind was still there, pushing everything towards the island and pushing up the snow into large drifts.

'Looks like another storm's on the way.' Lovelace said, slipping an arm around Grace's waist and moving in closer.

She felt Grace shiver.

'I don't like this island,' Grace said at last. 'It smells of death.'

Lovelace turned Grace's face so that they were looking at one another. 'I'll protect you,' Lovelace said, and she had never been more determined about anything in her life.

Grace smiled, and Lovelace caught the doubt before they were plunged into darkness.

Grace pulled Lovelace closer to her, and they stood like that for some time.

'I should go back to my room,' Grace said slowly.

'Stay,' Lovelace insisted. 'Wake up with me.'

'Not here. Not in this place.' Grace said, choosing her words carefully. 'His presence is still here. I can feel him. I don't want that to.. to poison us.'

Lovelace felt the sincerity. Mackay was a big personality in life as well in death. She would take Grace far away from Mackay's influence when it was all over.

Grace broke free from their embrace and kissed Lovelace.

'I don't want to fuck this up,' she said honestly. 'I do that sometimes.'

'I understand,' Lovelace said. 'We'll have plenty of time together when it's over.'

'I'm glad you understand,' Grace said. She stepped back from the window and headed to the bedroom door.

She opened it and turned back towards Lovelace, who was now little more than a shadow in the distance. 'I'll see you later.'

Lovelace watched as Grace closed the door behind her.

***

The knocking on the door at stupid o'clock was beginning to piss Lovelace off. Her watch said it was just after seven in the morning. She slipped her feet from the duvet and reached for her robe. It was cold, and she shivered as the robe's fabric dropped down over her body.

She reached the door as the knocking restarted. She had wondered if it was Grace, but it sounded more like a man's knock. Firm but lacking in any great conviction. It was as if whoever was at the door wanted to wake Lovelace up without disturbing her.

She opened her door and was faced with a nervous-looking Johnathon in mid-knock. Kellerman stood behind him, and Lovelace felt a pang of dé-Jà-Vu. The last time they had done this, someone had been murdered.

By the looks on their faces, it had happened again.

'Oh, right. Sorry, we didn't mean to wake you..' Johnathon stuttered.

'Clearly, you did,' Lovelace remarked with no attempt at hiding her displeasure, 'otherwise you wouldn't be stood at my door knocking on it.'

'I think he means we would rather not have been waking you up. Again.' Kellerman said, and a look of fear was written across his face.

'What is it?' Lovelace asked.

The two men looked at one another and then at Lovelace.

'Someone's died.' Kellerman said, picking his words carefully.

'Someone?' Lovelace asked. 'Who?'

Johnathon found some inner strength and told Lovelace everything he knew in a single sentence.

'Shit.' Lovelace exclaimed. 'Wait here. I'll get dressed.'

Fifteen minutes later, Lovelace sat in the back of a Land Rover Defender. Kellerman was sat in the front passenger seat, and Johnathon had climbed in the back with Lovelace.

Lovelace had donned a pair of thick jeans and a solid pair of walking boots that she had found in Emma's room. She had also laid her hands on a thick woollen jumper and a storm coat. She had dropped a woolly hat on her head and wasn't entirely displeased by the look she had randomly created—modern chic with an air of practicality. One look outside her bedroom window had told her what sort of day they were in for.

Now she was sitting in the back of a heated Defender, driving through three feet of snow while a blizzard raged in the air around them.

Kellerman turned in his seat to talk to Lovelace. 'We'll have to take the long route around the mountain. The mountain pass is entirely blocked.'

Lovelace was not surprised. The storm she had foreseen last night was well and truly upon them. She sat in her seat and gazed out of the window.

The driver handled the four-by-four with consummate ease. He pointed the huge car in the general direction of travel and was never disappointed in the result. Lovelace relaxed as she grew confident that he wouldn't carelessly drive them off the edge of the island to their deaths. As they passed close to the cliff edge, Lovelace watched as the storm delivered terrifying waves the size of small houses into granite rocks. Seaspray fell as ice onto the windscreen and was quickly wiped away. She felt relief as the driver passed close to the cliff's edge and then out, back inland, towards the mountain's base. The road twisted and turned before joining the mountain pass as it snaked off the hilltop. The driver pointed the car forwards as he felt it try and step sideways, and after a few minutes, the bright lights of BlackRock greeted them.

The three of them opened the doors to the Defender simultaneously and crossed the small distance to the front gate quickly. Lovelace was grateful for her choice of footwear as the tread on her boots dug into the snow and held her upright. They were greeted by prison staff and quickly shown through security. Lovelace was subjected to a cursory pat-down, as were Jonathon and Kellerman, although Lovelace sensed that it was merely a tick-box exercise rather than a full search. Once the search was completed, a series of doors were electronically unlocked until they found themselves outside once more, and Kellerman led the way, head down, to A-Wing. Once through the outer security fence, they entered the building unimpeded by locked doors.

'This way,' Kellerman instructed, and Lovelace and Johnathon followed until they stood outside Jack Lovelace's cell door. The door indicator glowed a solid red.

'Have any prisoners been allowed out of their cells yet?' Lovelace asked.

Johnathon shook his head. 'No. We've been in lockdown since the body was discovered.'

'Who discovered the body?'

'Georgia Hope. She's one of our best prison officers. She was doing a routine walk-through at about four this morning when she noticed blood coming from under the cell door.'

'Were the doors locked?'

'Yes.'

'All of them?' Lovelace queried.

'All of them.' Johnathon insisted. 'This cell door was opened remotely from the Citadel.'

'Had the doors to the cells been opened through the night?' Lovelace asked.

'No. Gerry's pulled up a spreadsheet with timestamps from last night. None of the cell doors were opened after lights out at ten. They were all closed until the cell door was opened this morning.'

Lovelace stepped past her father's cell door to the next one in line. The door to this was open, and two male guards stood on either side looking fearsome. Blood had seeped out from under the door into the corridor. From where she stood, Lovelace could see footprints in the blood.

'First responders attempted CPR, but it was clear immediately that he was dead. I'm afraid they may have contaminated the scene a bit.' Kellerman stepped to Lovelace's side and looked into the cell.

Lovelace stepped in next to him and took in the scene around her.

Clichéd though it was, there was no other word for it than "bloodbath." Lying on the floor in front of them, face down, was Adam Sinclair. A chair and a computer were directly in front of Lovelace and just in front of the body. Blood spatters covered every inch, reaching as far up as the ceiling.

Lovelace carefully stepped into the cell and examined Sinclair. He had a wound to his neck that spread from one ear to the other. It was a deep wound, too, and the torn carotid artery was visible beneath the blood. Despite herself, Lovelace winced. It was a painful way to go, and death would have come quickly. She looked at the scene and then stepped out of the cell.

'Suicide.' She said without any emotion. 'He was stood in front of his desk with his back to the door. The blood spatter on the wall suggests this. He was determined. The wound is deep. What sort of weapon did he use?'

She watched as Johnathon shot Kellerman a look.

'What is it?' Lovelace asked.

Kellerman moved in closer. 'We haven't been able to find the weapon.'

The words hung in the air and cloyed at them.

'What? How the fuck is that even possible?' Lovelace asked.

Johnathon shrugged. Kellerman looked worried.

'We've had two independent teams search the cell. We've spoken to Miss Hope and the first responders. No one has seen a weapon.'

Lovelace turned her expression upside down, looking for the sense in it. Her confusion betrayed her usual unflappability. 'So Adam Sinclair cuts his own throat in a locked cell that hasn't been opened through the night, without a weapon?'

'That's about the size of it.' Johnathon agreed.

'That's just not possible.' Lovelace mused.

'And yet, here we are.' Kellerman added.

Indeed. *Here they were.*

'It's why we asked you here,' Johnathon said. 'We thought you might be able to shed some light on it.'

Lovelace shook her head. 'The simplest solution would be that Sinclair cut his own throat, and one of the attendant prison officers later removed the weapon. But to what end?'

'We've been strict with our protocols.' Kellerman insisted. 'All the prison officers and first responders were removed to a clean room after Sinclair's body was found. They insist that they never removed a weapon from the cell, and subsequent searches have held to their statements. We've carried out a detailed finger-tip search of the route between Sinclair's cell and the clean room. Nothing. No Weapon.'

Lovelace pondered this for a moment.

'Okay. Then Sinclair was murdered, and the murderer took the weapon away.

'That can't be possible,' Johnathon said with a note of exasperation in his voice. 'No one entered Sinclair's cell from the moment he was locked in it until Miss Hope noticed the blood coming from under his door at four this morning.'

'When you have eliminated all which is impossible, then whatever remains, however improbable, must be the truth.' Lovelace said, hoping she had remembered the quote correctly.

'Sherlock Holmes,' Kellerman nodded.

'But it is impossible,' Johnathon argued. 'No one has been inside this cell.'

'Not impossible,' Lovelace countered. 'It's improbable, but that adds weight to the quote. It's not impossible to hack a computer and change data. Improbable, for sure. But not impossible.'

'Gerry assures me that his system is impenetrable.' Johnathon insisted.

'Fine.' Lovelace said bluntly. 'Then let's have a chat with Gerry, shall we?'

***

Gerry sat at his desk munching on a bacon sandwich brought up from the kitchens. Brown sauce hung from the corners of his mouth, and he ate with his mouth open, a trait that Lovelace felt demanded a serious slap about the back of the head with a brick. She sensed that people would feel that about Gerry regardless of his eating habits.

'Not possible.' Gerry said arrogantly, whilst continuing to bite into his food. 'My system's impenetrable. There's no way it's been hacked.'

'But it's possible?' Lovelace pressed.

'Nope. No-way. Not a chance.'

Lovelace perched on the edge of Gerry's desk and looked him straight in the eye. 'So you're telling me that while the computer systems of other companies, like the NHS, telecoms companies and government agencies, can be hacked, your system can't?'

'Yup.'

'Why?' Lovelace asked.

'Because they don't employ me.' Gerry said.

'What about the corrupted code?'

Lovelace looked up at a pretty twenty-something that sat behind Gerry. Gerry turned at the same time and threw the young woman a menacing look.

'What corrupted code?' Johnathon asked. 'Gerry?'

Gerry turned back to his computer. 'It's nothing. Some of the systems struggled to reboot properly after the power cut. The switch to generator power complicated things. It corrupted some of the files. I haven't figured out where they've come from or what will happen if I delete them. I'm looking into it.'

'Could it be a hacker?' Johnathon asked.

Gerry considered this for a brief moment. Too brief, Lovelace thought.

'No. As soon as the power was cut, we lost connection to the outside world. The corrupted code came during the reboot. Even if it was some hack, there's no way anyone could get into the system to make it work.'

'Unless they were on the island,' the young woman said, smiling. Her colleague that was sitting next to her gave a wry smile. They were enjoying Gerry's discomfort. Gerry wriggled uncomfortably in his chair.

'Is that the case, Gerry?' Johnathon asked. 'Is it possible for someone on the island to hack the system?'

'No.' Gerry insisted. 'My system is beyond most people. No one on this island can get into this system without me knowing. They'd leave a trace. There's always a trace.'

'What do you think?' Lovelace asked, directing the question at the young woman. 'Miss?'

'Emily,' she said, 'Emily Saunders. Gerry's right. They would leave a trace, and we should be able to find it.'

'Are you looking?' Lovelace asked.

Emily shook her head. 'No.'

Johnathon looked at Gerry. 'Why aren't you looking?'

'Because no one hacked my fucking system,' Gerry replied angrily. 'There's nothing to look for.'

Lovelace watched as Johnathon adopted his "I'm the boss" look.

'Right,' he said, 'last night between ten o'clock and four this morning, someone let themselves into Sinclair's cell and cut his throat. He didn't do it to himself. That means someone got in and out and changed the log to cover their tracks. The only place on this island with working computers is the prison. That means someone in this prison has done that. I need you to find out who.'

Gerry waved his arms in exasperation and was about to say something when Johnathon spoke first. 'That's not open for debate. That's an order. No one leaves this office until you have something for me to work with, am I clear?'

Gerry looked defeated. 'Fine. But no one hacked my system.'

'Good,' Johnathon said, 'that's settled then. There's a direct line to my office at the Mansion House. Call me when you have something.' He looked across at Lovelace. 'What next?'

'Can we talk to the prisoners nearest to Sinclair's cell? They may have heard something.'

Johnathon led the way out of the Citadel, followed by Lovelace and Kellerman. Gerry turned to look at his colleagues, and the look on his face warned them that he was not best pleased.

Carefully, Emily asked, 'where do we start?'

Gerry laughed. 'We? We don't start anywhere. If you think you're clever enough, knock yourselves out, but I'm not wasting my time looking for something that's not fucking there.'

He stood up and grabbed a can of cola from his desk. 'If you need me, I'll be in the break-out room, sleeping.'

***

They set up an informal interview room next to the cellblock. Lovelace had refused the offer of a formal interview room, preferring to keep everyone at ease. Tea and coffee were brought up from the kitchens, along with a selection of treats. Taking a centre chair between

Johnathon and Kellerman, Lovelace poured herself a large black coffee.

They started the interviews with the prison officers on the floor during the night. One by one, they came in, drank coffee, nibbled biscuits and re-lived the previous evening's events from their perspective until Georgia Hope raised the alarm. There were no significant differences between the statements. It had been a quiet night. Floor sweeps were conducted on the hour, every hour and had been duly recorded in the activity log. No one saw anything that could shed light on the incident. They all inadvertently gave each other alibis. No one, including Georgia Hope, was outside the other guards' observation.

'You found Adam Sinclair?'

'Yes.' Georgia said to Lovelace's question. 'It was on my four o'clock floor sweep. I noticed blood coming from under Sinclair's door and radioed for assistance. The door was opened remotely, and I went in and began CPR. It was clear he was long dead, but you must try, right?'

'And you saw no weapon? Or anything that could be used as a weapon?'

Georgia shook her head. 'I'm sorry, but no, I didn't.'

The first inmate that walked into the room dwarfed the guard that walked by his side. Lovelace looked up at a man in his mid-fifties with receding grey hair tucked neatly to the side of his head. He had arms the size of small trees, and he walked in the manner of a man with far too much muscle on his legs. His voice, when he spoke, was soft and tinged with a northern brogue.

'What's this about?' He asked, refusing the offer of tea. 'I've missed breakfast.'

Lovelace leant forward, carefully watching his eyes. 'Adam Sinclair's been murdered.'

'Good.' He said. 'I hope he suffered.'

'Why do you say that?' Lovelace asked.

Patrick Hewell shrugged. 'He deserved it. Couldn't have happened to a nicer man.'

Lovelace was familiar with Patrick Hewell. His crimes were well documented. 'You killed women yourself, didn't you?' She asked.

'He killed children. Young girls. Nonces don't live long in prison.'

'Did you kill him?' Lovelace asked.

Hewell chuckled. 'I wish it had been me. I'd have wrung his neck until his eyes popped out. But no. I was stuck in my cell all night.'

'Did you hear or see anything?'

'If I did, I wouldn't tell your lot.'

When he had gone, Lovelace turned to Johnathon. 'He's a bloody big fella.'

Johnathon smiled. 'He is. And yet, he's the perfect prisoner. We've never had a moment's issue with him.'

Claus Fischer, the German serial rapist, was next. Lovelace found his presence unnerving. He had a way of looking at her that made her feel dirty. He answered the questions succinctly and without elaboration. Nothing he said drove the investigation forward.

She shuddered as he left. 'I don't like him,' she said to the air in front of her. 'I don't like him at all.'

Robert Askwith came in next, and Lovelace felt herself relax in his presence. He spoke gently, and his accent was touched with Estuary English, although Lovelace suspected a different lineage. His words were well-clipped and perfectly enunciated, and he replied to Lovelace's questions honestly and briefly. He was shocked to hear of Sinclair's death but not surprised. He had dealt with a few people like Sinclair in the past and expressed regret that it hadn't been him that had killed him. 'Sometimes, they just need a bloody good beating.'

Lovelace saw scars on his knuckles and how some of his fingers were twisted with arthritis, and she wondered if he was now paying the price for his "enforcement" days.

Jack Lovelace stepped into the room and beamed at seeing his daughter. 'I hear that Sinclair chap's been done in? Is that true?' He asked.

'It is. It happened last night between ten o'clock and four this morning.'

'Bloody hell. Well, I can't say I'll shed a tear for him. Couldn't have happened to a nicer man.'

'You're not the first to have said that,' Lovelace said. She watched as her father took a chair and sat down. He did so slowly, keeping his back straight as he went. He's getting old, Lovelace thought as she poured him a milky coffee.

'Well, people speak their minds in places like this.' Jack went on, stirring four spoonfuls of sugar into his mug. 'We've nothing to lose. We are considered the lowest people in society, and, in many cases, this is truly deserved, but even we have standards. Child killers and molesters are a world apart from the rest of us. They don't deserve the air they breathe.'

'But still…' Lovelace began.

'But a man is dead,' Jack continued, 'and you must at least be seen doing something to catch his killer, eh?'

'Something like that,' Lovelace admitted. 'Did you see or hear anything last night?'

Jack took a long sip of his drink and laid the mug on the table in front of him. 'Even if I did, I wouldn't say. You'll not find many people in this place who will. Screws included. No one likes Sinclair's kind. We all prefer them dead.'

Lovelace was about to say more when a security guard entered the room. He walked over to Johnathon and whispered in his ear.

'I think this is a good place to conclude the interviews.' Johnathon said, and Lovelace could see the alarm in his eyes.

Jack stood up and smiled at his daughter. 'Good luck at finding his killer. You'll need it. You have no shortage of people who wanted him dead.'

Lovelace turned to Johnathon once he had left and asked, 'what is it? What's happened?'

Johnathon struggled with the words. 'My chief of security has gone missing. They can't find him anywhere.'

Fifteen

Despite having a small scar under her right eye, Lovelace found Maeve to be disarmingly pretty. She was stood by the door to the kitchen when they had returned to the Mansion House. There were two chairs and the remnants of snacks lying on the floor where Wayne Sampson, head of security, had left them.

'He relieved Rupert and me about eight o'clock last night. It was the last time we saw him. Rupert and I went back to the accommodation block and grabbed something to eat, and I went straight to bed. There's nothing else to do here, even when the power's switched on. We grabbed breakfast this morning and came over to relieve Sampson at about eight.'

She was pretty, Lovelace decided, but her eyes were the most profound black she had ever seen. She spoke with a strong Belfast accent, but her words were clipped and well-enunciated. Still, the eyes troubled Lovelace. There was a darkness behind the darkness, which put her on edge.

'Where's Rupert now?' Lovelace asked.

'When we couldn't find the boss, I took up position outside the kitchen, and he went looking for him.'

Lovelace noticed a radio that clung to Maeve's waist. 'I assume you've tried to call him?'

'I have,' Maeve explained. 'The radio has a twenty-kilometre range, but the mountain gets in the way. There are repeaters littered over the mountainside, but they only work if there's power. There's full radio coverage on this side of the mountain and the other side, but the two can't communicate. I've been calling on the radio since we found Sampson missing. Rupert called the prison using the landline in Mr Preece's office, and they've been trying up there, but still nothing.'

The front door of the Mansion House swung open, and Rupert calmly strolled in. He paused in the entranceway, stamped the snow from his boots, and shook the ice from his coat.

'Anything?' Maeve asked.

Rupert shook his head. 'He'd be a damned fool to go out in this weather. There are no tracks to speak of, but the snow was covering mine almost the minute I made them. If he went outside, we could never tell.'

Lovelace turned and addressed her questions to Maeve. 'Is this typical of Sampson? Would he abandon his post?'

'Never.' Maeve said firmly. 'He's an old soldier. He'd never leave his post without good reason.'

'Is that his coat?' Lovelace asked.

Maeve picked up a jacket draped over the back of one of the chairs. 'Yeah. It's his. He knows better than to go outside without a jacket in this weather.'

Lovelace watched as a hint of emotion swept across Maeve's emotionless expression. She was worried, Lovelace thought. This was definitely out of character for Wayne Sampson.

Lovelace turned and faced Johnathon and Kellerman, who had remained in the background since they had reached the Mansion House. 'Before we jump to conclusions, we need to organise a thorough search of the island. He can't just have vanished. He must be somewhere.'

In her mind, she added, *or at least his body.*

Johnathon looked as though he had read her mind. He had gone even paler than before. 'That'll be easy to do at the prison. There's plenty of staff there. Maeve, could you organise a room search of the accommodation block, just in case he's taken himself off for a kip? Rupert, if you wouldn't mind standing guard at the kitchen door. We still need to keep the crime scene clean for when the police get here.'

'I can organise a search crew to scour the island.' Maeve said. 'It won't be thorough, what with the weather, but it's best we do it now while it's light enough.'

'Yes. Do that.' Johnathon agreed. He doubted that Sampson would be outside, but it was better to be safe than sorry.

Lovelace waited while Maeve spoke into her radio. When she received no reply, she looked at Johnathon and said, 'may I use your telephone?'

'Of course. Whatever you need. Consider my office open for as long as you need it.'

As Maeve disappeared into Johnathon's office, Lovelace said, 'we ought to search the Mansion House. Perhaps if you and Mr Kellerman started down here, I'll recruit Grace to help me look upstairs.'

Grace appeared at the foot of the staircase as she mentioned her name.

'Hello. What's going on?' She asked.

Lovelace smiled at the sight of Grace, who was dressed in a pair of light-coloured jeans and a cream hoodie. She took her to one side and explained what had happened in the last couple of hours.

'Fuck! Sinclair's dead and your chief of security is missing? You don't think he killed him, do you?'

Lovelace took a step back. Interesting. She hadn't thought of that. But why would Sampson want Sinclair dead, and why didn't he take his jacket?

Lovelace turned and faced Johnathon and Kellerman, who were anxiously awaiting further instructions.

'Tell me what you know about Sampson.'

'Not a lot, if I'm honest with you,' Johnathon said. 'He was one of Mackay's men. I wouldn't have employed him, but it wasn't my decision. He'd been one of Mackay's fixers for years.'

'That's right,' Kellerman agreed. 'He could be a nasty piece of work, but Mackay took to him. He had a violent streak and a mean temper. He wasn't a man to cross.'

Lovelace remembered something that Esther had told her a few days ago. 'Didn't he kill someone once? A prisoner?'

'That's right,' Johnathon said. 'His temper got the better of him, and a young man lost his life. It was in one of Mackay's early institutions, and Mackay pulled a few strings and made the scandal disappear. Sampson has been at Mackay's side ever since.'

'Any reason you can think of why Sampson might want Sinclair dead?'

'That's your thinking, is it?' Johnathon said doubtfully. 'Apart from the fact that no one likes Sinclair's sort, I can't see it myself. Sampson has a first-class career at BlackRock. It would make no sense for him to risk it all for a piece of work like Sinclair.'

They were interrupted by Maeve, who returned from Johnathon's office.

'There's a search underway at BlackRock, and a team is being prepared to sweep over the island. If he's up there, we'll find him. I'll go and start over at the accommodation block. That shouldn't take too long.'

'Before you go, Maeve,' Lovelace asked, 'how well do you know Sampson?'

'Yeah, quite well. I've worked for him for a few years now.'

Lovelace leant in so that she was just out of Rupert's hearing.

'Would you say you know him intimately?'

Maeve glanced over her shoulder at her colleague and then back at Lovelace. Her emotions were beginning to betray her face, Lovelace thought.

'I'm not sure that's any of your business.' Maeve answered, trying not to let her emotions get the better of her.

'You were close, weren't you?' Lovelace continued. 'Were you lovers?'

Maeve nodded. 'Yes. But I still don't think that's any of your business.'

'You're close to him.' Lovelace pressed. 'Probably closer than anyone on BlackRock, and you know him intimately. So, if you're worried, then so am I.'

She watched as Maeve relaxed a tiny bit.

'Did Sampson ever mention Adam Sinclair?'

'A few times. We were in charge of Sinclair's security during the prison transfer. Why? Is this about Sinclair's murder?'

'It could be.' Lovelace admitted.

'You're mad if you think Sampson killed Sinclair. Why the fuck would he?'

'You tell us,' Lovelace challenged. 'Is there any reason why Sampson would want Sinclair dead? Did he have a pet hatred for child killers? Did he know any of Sinclair's victims? Could someone have paid him to execute Sinclair?'

Maeve was about to refute all the allegations out of hand when she paused and thought about them. She had seen something in Lovelace that told her to be truthful. Flat denials were of no use to either of them.

'Okay, firstly, I can't think of any reason Sampson would want Sinclair dead,' Maeve began carefully. 'But if I'm honest, none of us will lose any sleep now that he is dead. Good riddance. Secondly, he had no particular hatred of sick fucks like Sinclair. It's what we do here.

We look after people like that so they can wallow in their guilt and prevent them from ever hurting another child again. We have to look after many of these people, some much worse than Sinclair, and Sampson has never expressed any intention of inflicting harm on any of them. In answer to your last question, absolutely someone could have paid Sampson to kill him, and in answer to your next question, if the money were right, Sampson might have done it too. But he wouldn't have gone missing afterwards. He would have fronted it out, and you'd probably never have found the evidence to prove he did it. He certainly wouldn't have run away or topped himself with grief for what he had done because I know he's done worse.'

Lovelace smiled at the accurate portrayal of the man she had met. There was no doubt in her mind that Sampson could kill Sinclair, but it didn't fit the nature of the man she had seen. He could have done it, and he may have done it, but she didn't think he had. Unfortunately, that didn't explain where he was now or what had happened to him.

'Thank you, Maeve. If you could organise the search of the accommodation block, we'll set up a search of the house. We'll meet in Johnathon's office when we're all done.'

Maeve gave a respectful nod in Lovelace's direction, and a smile gathered in the corners of her mouth, but she repressed it, turned, and walked out of the Mansion House and into the storm.

Lovelace addressed Johnathon and Kellerman. 'Okay. Start down here. Search every room. Don't leave a single corner unexplored.' To Grace, she said, 'come on, you're with me.'

***

'Do you ever feel that the most dangerous people on this island aren't the ones behind bars?' Grace said as they made their way up the staircase.

It had indeed occurred to Lovelace. There was an active killer in their midst, and she was pretty sure she could lay the deaths of several people at the feet of the guests of the Mansion House. She was also sure she knew who'd murdered Mackay and the killer's motive. She could only guess how Sampson's involvement linked to her hypothesis. If she was right, and she was sure she was, Sampson was long dead. Now it was just a case of finding his body.

Lovelace reached out and took Grace's hand. 'We need to stick together,' she said as they reached the top of the staircase and turned towards the lounge. 'We're safer together.'

Grace smiled warmly and squeezed Lovelace's hand. There was something about Lovelace that warmed her and scared her in equal measure. Grace thought herself a good judge of character and felt instantly attracted to the young woman, but she couldn't help but sense that she didn't honestly know who Lovelace was. It wasn't lost on Grace that from four o'clock in the morning when she had left Lovelace's room, no one inside the Mansion House had an alibi during the time that Sinclair was killed and Sampson had gone missing.

As they made their way towards the lounge, they met Elouise coming the other way, carrying a lamp to light her way through the dark corridors.

'Hello. You two are up early.'

Briefly, Lovelace explained the events that had unfolded that morning.

'Shit. Johnathon must be going out of his mind.'

'He does seem a little stressed,' Lovelace admitted. 'I don't suppose you've seen Sampson at all during the night?'

'No.' Elouise said. 'I went to my room right after dinner, and I've been there ever since. I didn't even know Sampson was in the house.'

'Have you just come from your room?' Lovelace asked.

'Yes. Why?'

'And you're sure Sampson's not there?'

Lovelace saw a grin stretch across Elouise's face in the half-light thrown by the lamp.

'No. He's not my type, nor has he ever been.' Elouise said. 'If you don't mind, I should go and check on Johnathon and see if Mrs Brent has arrived with breakfast yet.'

They watched as Elouise's shadow followed her to the end of the corridor and disappeared.

Grace squeezed Lovelace's hand. 'You're obsessed with sex,' she remarked drily.

'Two things in life truly motivate people.' Lovelace said. 'Money and sex. I think Mrs Preece has plenty of the former and seeks more of the latter. I certainly wouldn't have put it past Sampson to give up his post on the promise of some skirt.'

They entered the lounge and found Sir Malcolm bent over the wood burner with matches in hand. The curtains had been opened, and the little light outside came in and brightened everything up.

'Bloody wood's damp.' Sir Malcolm grumbled. 'Can't get the damn thing to light.'

'Have you been trying long?' Lovelace asked.

'Half an hour or so. Why do you ask?'

'Did you come straight from your room, or have you been downstairs yet?'

Sir Malcolm stood bolt upright and puffed out his chest. 'Why? What's this all about?'

Lovelace explained what had happened that morning, and she watched as Sir Malcolm slowly deflated.

'I see.' He said slowly. 'Bad show. Yes, indeed. A bad show.'

Lovelace waited as Sir Malcolm toyed with a thought in his head. Then he said, 'I went to the dining room first to see if breakfast had been served. When I saw that it hadn't, I came straight here and started to light this bloody thing. It's cold in this house without the central heating.'

'And you never went anywhere else?'

'No.'

'And you were in your room the whole night. You never went out or saw Mr Sampson?'

'No, I did not,' Sir Malcolm said firmly. 'I saw those other two outside the kitchen, and as far as I was aware, they were there the whole night.'

'Just a couple more questions, Sir Malcolm, if you don't mind. Did you know Wayne Sampson before you arrived on the island? And did you know Adam Sinclair or any of his victims?'

Sir Malcolm shot Lovelace a stern look and was about to refuse to answer such questions when he changed his mind and said, 'for what it's worth, I never met either man before in my life. Of course, I knew of Adam Sinclair, and I can't say I shall mourn his passing, but I didn't know him or any of his victims. As for the other chap, I didn't know him from Adam.'

Sir Malcolm turned and drove a poker deep into the wood burner. He stood back proudly as a flame caught and dark smoke bellowed out of the opening. He closed the door, opened the vents wide, and watched with deep satisfaction as bright flames licked at the glass.

Lovelace and Grace slipped out of the lounge and into the dining room. It was empty, and Lovelace noticed that the table had been laid for breakfast. They performed a cursory search of the room and then made their way to the bar and cinema room. From there, they dropped into the pool area and back up to the bar. No one was around.

'Should we search the rooms?' Grace asked.

They looked in Lovelace's room first and then Grace's. Neither of them expected to find anything but were relieved when they didn't. They knocked on Elouise's door and went in when no reply came.

'Shouldn't we ask first?' Grace asked.

Lovelace shook her head. 'Probably better this way. Just be quick.'

They searched all the places someone could hide or where a body could be hidden and replicated the search in Sir Malcolm's room. They found nothing.

They stood outside "Moriarty" for some time before Lovelace opened the door and went in. Mackay's room had been untouched since his murder, and they both felt awkward searching it. They sighed with relief when they found nothing and crossed the corridor to Esther's room.

They went in when no reply came to their knocking, and they found Esther's room as they expected to find a room belonging to a middle-aged woman. It was neat, the bed was made correctly, and one of the windows was opened slightly, allowing the freezing winter's air to stream in. Grace went over to the window and closed it.

'It's too bloody cold for that,' she said as Lovelace searched the room.

'Nothing. It's like the man's a ghost.' Lovelace said as they stepped outside into the corridor. 'Come on, let's see what the others have found.'

Johnathon was sitting at his desk, nursing a mug of steaming coffee. Kellerman was perched on the edge of an armchair nearby and was staring ominously into space. Maeve was standing with her arms crossed by a bookcase.

'Anything?' Lovelace asked. She scanned the faces of the people in the room, and their expressions told her everything she needed to know.

'Every room in the accommodation block has been searched,' Maeve began, and Lovelace noted the strain in her voice. 'A few of us swept over the grounds, but the weather's pretty shit. He could be out there, and we could have passed within an inch of him and not seen him.'

Lovelace didn't doubt that for a second. It was not a day to be outside.

Johnathon said, 'Kellerman and I searched downstairs. We've looked in every corner and in every room. He's nowhere to be found.'

Lovelace felt a great deal of sympathy for Johnathon. The strain was wearing him out. His face had a grey patina, and his eyes looked devoid of life. Elouise would need all her strength to pull him back from the edge.

Lovelace turned to Maeve and said, 'you said you were in your room at the accommodation block all night? Can anyone alibi you?'

Maeve unfolded her arms and looked like she was placing herself in the offensive. That was interesting, Lovelace felt. She didn't know how to defend, only how to attack.

'What the fuck are you implying?' Maeve demanded.

'Did you know Adam Sinclair or any of his relatives?'

Maeve took a step forward. 'Are you fucking accusing me of something?'

'Just answer the fucking question,' Johnathon said, exasperated.

Maeve looked at the prison governor with renewed respect. She had never once heard him swear.

To Lovelace, she said, 'no, I didn't know Sinclair, and I had no reason to see him dead. I have no alibi for last night. I was alone. I saw Sampson for the last time when he relieved us of guard duty.'

'Mr Kellerman?' Lovelace asked.

'What?' Kellerman asked, stunned to have been dragged into the conversation.

'Same questions. Did you know Sinclair or any of his victims? Where were you last night? Can anyone alibi you?'

'Never met Sinclair before he came here. I was alone in my room in the accommodation block all night until Johnathon came for me around four thirty this morning. I didn't know any of his victims.'

'Johnathon?'

'Same.' Johnathon said. 'I was in my lounge downstairs all night. I think I saw Sampson at his post around midnight. I heard my office phone ringing at about twenty-five past four this morning, and Sampson wasn't at his post then. The phone call focussed my mind quite a bit. I never gave Sampson another thought. As for his victims, I'm afraid I couldn't even tell you their names.'

'I didn't see him outside the kitchen when we left this morning to go to the prison.' Lovelace admitted. 'I didn't give it much thought.'

'What about your alibi?' Maeve asked, directing the question at Lovelace.

Grace stepped up. 'I was with Lovelace in her room until about four this morning. I returned to my room about then.'

'Well,' Kellerman said, 'that excludes both of you from killing Sinclair. He was found at about four this morning which means you both have an alibi at the time of his murder.'

'But that doesn't shed any light on what has happened to Sampson?' Johnathon remarked. 'Where the bloody hell has he gone?'

Elouise opened the door to the study and peeped around. 'Mrs Brent has arrived with breakfast if anyone is interested?'

One by one, the trail of people left Johnathon's study and made their way across the reception area. They were almost at the staircase when Lovelace stopped abruptly.

Of course. How stupid. That made perfect sense.

All eyes were upon her when she looked at where Rupert was standing guarding the kitchen and said, 'has anyone looked in the kitchen?'

Rupert stepped aside, and Lovelace opened the door to the kitchen. She was followed into the room by Grace, who always remained within inches of her. Johnathon and Kellerman came in next, followed by Maeve. Elouise made her excuses and stayed outside.

The kitchen was exactly as Lovelace remembered leaving it. Nothing had been disturbed.

Well, not exactly nothing.

Lovelace walked over to the knife block and looked where a second knife had gone missing. The first knife had been used to kill Mackay and was wrapped up safely for forensics to examine, and now a second place in the knife block was empty.

'There's a knife missing.' She said quietly.

They spread out across the large kitchen and looked into every corner. Nothing.

Kellerman went to the back door and tried the handle. It was locked.

Calmly, Lovelace walked over to the pantry door and opened it. Blood was evident on the walls and over the tins on the shelves, and she followed its course as it led down the stairs to the cellar.

Kellerman walked up behind her with a lamp in his hands. There was so much blood on the walls, and a hand print could be seen running through it, as though someone had reached out to support themselves as they had fallen into the cellar.

Slowly they climbed down the stairs. Kellerman stood at the front, his lamp held aloft.

At the bottom of the stairs lay Wayne Sampson. He was lying on his back, and his soulless eyes stared out from a blood-spattered face. A single knife wound ran deep from ear to ear, reminding Lovelace of Adam Sinclair.

Sixteen

DCI McBride considered the evidence that DS Sandhu had diligently laid before him. Even though they were just a day or so into the investigation, the corner of the office that Liam Swift had made available to them was awash with folders, papers, emails and statements. Putting it all into some semblance of order from which he was supposed to derive a solution seemed daunting. It was a task that appeared even more daunting given that they were entirely cut off from the crime scene, the witnesses, the body and the potential suspects. Sometimes McBride wondered if he was ever going to get a smoking gun still in the hands of the killer, with the body growing cold at his feet. He doubted it, but he lived for the day when the complex jobs didn't flow his way.

DS Sandhu had spoken crisply and with a brevity that he admired. He hated talkers. Sometimes he wanted to grab people by the shoulders and shake them violently while crying, 'get to the fucking point!'

'Ethan Mackay, forty-four-year-old Scottish Billionaire and philanthropist.' Sandhu began. 'By all accounts, one of the most respected and admired businessmen in the UK, if not the world. Behind closed doors, however, he's not the kind-hearted man his brand managers would have you believe.

'From the evidence we have collected so far, from those on the island and some who aren't, Ethan Mackay collected people, or, rather, he collected information on people which he used to control and exert pressure on them.

'The first case in point would be Sir Malcolm Lambert, Member of Parliament for East Mercia, Father of the House, former doctor and recent backer of the controversial HMP BlackRock. Without Sir Malcolm's support, it would have been doubtful that BlackRock would ever have been given the green light from the government. Until about two years ago, Sir Malcolm was vocal in his opposition to BlackRock, until one day he suddenly changed his mind.'

'The question is,' McBride added, 'did Mackay exert pressure on Sir Malcolm, and if he did, what form did that pressure take?'

'Exactly.' Sandhu agreed. 'If the gossip on the island is anything to go by, then it seems that Mackay may have had something on Sir Malcolm from his time as a family doctor.'

'Anything there yet?' McBride asked.

'Nothing concrete. But we'll keep looking.'

'Good. What about Esther Friedman?'

Sandhu took a sheet of paper that was lying face down on the table next to her. 'Journalist, mid-fifties. Been a thorn in Mackay's side for years. She's almost as bad as Mackay for drilling into people's past looking for dirt, but in her case, it's to sell newspapers. She's bloody good at it too.'

McBride frowned. That last point troubled him. He knew of Esther Friedman and begrudgingly admired her skill set. She would have made a formidable detective. But she wasn't a detective and had no idea of the lengths people would go to keep their secrets safe. Someone had already murdered Mackay, and killing again was just as easy. Murder begets murder.

'Anything more on Esther Friedman's first husband?'

Sandhu shook her head. 'Nothing. It's a dead end. If there was any proof that Esther murdered her first husband, it's lost in the fog of the past.'

'What about Mackay's assistant?'

'Grace Mahone,' Sandhu said, reading from another sheet. 'Thirty-three years old. She's been Mackay's PA for almost twelve years. She's clean. She has no past to speak of, certainly no skeletons lurking around.'

'Everyone has a history.' McBride said, speaking from experience.

'She probably does, but nothing criminal or shady. Perhaps she's a closet pyromaniac or something?' Sandhu said, laughing at her joke.

'Maybe.' McBride agreed. 'But has she worked for Mackay for twelve years because she wanted to or was forced to? Any clues about her room name?'

'"Lemon?" Nothing. I can't seem to grasp what that means.'

'It means something.' McBride said. 'Mackay did nothing without reason. Perhaps if we can work that out, we may learn more about Miss Mahone. Okay, what about Mrs Preece?'

'Elouise Preece, forty-nine years old, married to Johnathon Preece, HMP BlackRock's Governor. She has one daughter, Emma, who is currently studying at Edinburgh University. She was married before Johnathon Preece to a man twenty years her senior. He died of a heart attack.'

'Any more on that?' McBride asked. 'Any legs to Lovelace's theory?'

Again, Sandhu shook her head. 'No. Nothing. Nobody who knew her previous husband ever doubted her story. The medical report stands up to scrutiny. If Elouise Preece did wait before calling the emergency services, there's no proof.'

'But Ethan Mackay knew enough to name Elouise's room after Edith Thompson, a woman hanged for murdering her husband so she could be with her younger lover. The parallels are striking.'

'They are,' Sandhu agreed. 'Maybe Mackay was playing cruel mind games with her? It's certainly his style.'

McBride scratched his head. 'What about Johnathon Preece?'

'All the evidence we've gathered would suggest that he was driving the car that killed that poor young woman. But like everything else, there's very little evidence. Certainly, no proof that I can find. It's all guesswork and hearsay.'

McBride rocked back and forth in his chair. Many threads were leading in different directions and with different results. Ethan Mackay knew something about one of the guests on BlackRock that resulted in his death. In their little ways, each of the guests potentially had a secret worth killing for to keep hidden. But which secret was the one that sealed Mackay's fate?

'What about Lovelace?' He asked.

'Anything you want to know about Lucy Lovelace is freely available on the internet. There must be a dozen or more books written about her father. Lucy is twenty-nine. Her father, Jack Lovelace, is in prison on BlackRock for the rape and murder of at least a dozen young girls and women. He was a computer scientist who worked alongside Thames Valley Police during the investigation set up to catch him. He managed to hoodwink the detectives for at least two more years, during which five more women were murdered. When the police net finally closed around him, he cut his wife's throat in front of his two daughters, Zoe and Lucy, and then set fire to the house in a murder-suicide attempt. The police were able to rescue the girls and arrest Jack Lovelace. He was given a whole life tariff for the murders, and the two girls were taken to Japan by their paternal aunt and uncle, where they remained until Lucy returned a few years ago to take up her studies at Oxford. After that, she joined Thames Valley Police.'

McBride raised an eyebrow.

'Recently, she was involved in investigating the Night Prowler murders in Oxfordshire when Adam Sinclair was arrested. Lovelace was arrested after the investigation for the murder of a young man in Oxford town centre, for which she has since been exonerated. She quit the force soon after.'

'And now she's on BlackRock with her father, Adam Sinclair and a murdered Ethan Mackay.'

'I can't see that as anything but a series of random and unconnected events.' Sandhu remarked. 'Lovelace has no motive for Mackay's death. She has no reason for wanting him dead whatsoever.'

McBride was inclined to agree. He didn't think Lovelace was involved with Mackay's murder. On a side note, he asked, 'what happened to her sister?'

Sandhu threw her arms up in a display of frustration. 'God only knows.' She said. 'She's completely off the grid. I can't find a trace of her anywhere. It's like she's a ghost.'

McBride shook his head. It probably wasn't important. He looked up as Liam Swift came into the room bearing coffee.

'Thought you might like one of these,' Swift said, laying the mugs on the desk. 'There's a call for you, too. Line three.' Swift nodded at the telephone on the desk. Button three was illuminated.

McBride picked up the receiver, pressed the button and barked, 'McBride.'

Sandhu watched as her boss sat up straight in his chair.

'Who is this?' He growled. 'No. Absolutely not. No fucking comment.'

He slammed the phone down on the receiver with such force that it leapt back out of its cradle.

'Boss?'

'Fucking press. They've got wind of Mackay's murder. It'll be all over the news before we can say boo.' McBride turned and looked at Swift. 'You'll need to increase security at the gate. The vultures are hovering.'

'You think they'll come in this weather?' Swift asked doubtfully.

'They'll come.' McBride assured him. 'For a story like this, they'll come.'

***

'We ought to process the crime scene.' Lovelace said to the small group who had returned to the kitchen.

She looked around at the pallid faces of those around her. Johnathon had pulled up a chair and slumped into it. Kellerman stood behind him, looking nervous.

Maeve had taken the discovery of Sampson's body hard. She was standing by the back door, shaking, desperately trying to control the emotions that bubbled beneath her demeanour. She looked like she was about to burst into tears.

Grace had remained close to Lovelace the entire time. It was as though she gained strength by being near her. Lovelace turned to her and squeezed her hand.

'Should we?' Kellerman asked. 'Should we go near him?'

'We can't just leave him there!' Maeve growled. 'We should cover him or something.'

Johnathon mumbled something incoherent and sank his head into his hands.

Lovelace turned to Maeve and said, 'I know this is difficult for you, but I need you to keep yourself together. I need your help.'

She watched as Maeve stood upright and nodded. 'Okay. I can do that.'

'I know you can,' Lovelace said sweetly. 'I need you to go outside and tell your colleague what has happened. He's to remain at his post and not let anyone through that door. No one, that is, except Elouise Preece. Find her for me and ask her to come here. Then I need you to go back to your room and compose yourself. I'll be across in a little while. We'll need to search Wayne's room. I'd like it if you were there.'

Maeve took a deep breath and dug deep into her reserves of strength. She nodded at Lovelace as she left the kitchen.

Lovelace turned to Kellerman. 'Mr Kellerman, I think we can easily assume that you are now the de facto boss of BlackRock.' They both looked at the shell of Johnathon as he sat slumped at the kitchen table. 'I need you to go back to the prison and oversee the security up there. Sinclair's killer is still at large, and I need someone on site that I can trust to keep me abreast of the situation.'

Kellerman didn't say anything. He nodded and left the room.

Lovelace looked at Grace. 'Are you okay to stay with me?' She asked.

Grace slipped her hand into Lovelace's and said, 'I wouldn't want to be anywhere else.'

A few minutes later Elouise came into the kitchen. She draped her arm around her husband's shoulders and squeezed him. 'Johnathon? Johnathon, what is it? What's wrong?' She looked up at Lovelace. 'What's happened?'

Briefly, Lovelace explained Sampson's murder. 'I think your husband has come to the end of his rope. I'm not sure he can cope anymore. I think it's time for you to step in.'

Elouise searched deep into Lovelace's eyes and saw the compassion there. She turned to her husband and said, 'Johnathon, look at me.'

Slowly Johnathon lifted his head.

'I think you should stay in my room tonight, what do you think? And when we can get off this island, we should go and get Emma and go somewhere warm and never think about this place again. What do you think?'

Johnathon's voice cracked as he said, 'I think I'd like that.'

Elouise put her arm entirely around Johnathon's shoulders and coaxed him out of his chair. 'Come on, let's get you away from here.'

As they reached the kitchen door, Elouise looked back at Lovelace and mouthed the words "thank you."

When the door closed behind them, Lovelace walked over to the entrance to the pantry and placed her hand on the door. She looked back at Grace, who hovered nervously nearby, holding a lamp aloft. 'Find some towels. The larger, the better. And some gloves. I think there's some in the drawer over there.'

Lovelace opened the pantry door, which swung into the kitchen. The cellar door swung outwards too. She opened it and stood there looking at the blood spatters when she felt Grace at her side. She took a pair of vinyl gloves and slipped them on her hands. Grace did the same.

Lovelace took the lamp from Grace and held it up to the wall.

'For whatever reason, Wayne Sampson was stood here, having just opened this door. Whoever killed him stood directly behind him. They must have already had the knife in their hands. But why were they going down into the cellar? What were they going there for?'

Lovelace pondered the question for a moment. Then she said, 'the moment the door was open, the killer struck. They came forward and cut his throat in one swift movement.'

'How do you know it was one movement?' Grace asked.

'I saw the knife wound when we found the body. There's only one cut. Whoever did it must have tilted Sampson's head back to expose the throat and brought the blade to bear hard and fast. He wouldn't have died instantly. I think he turned, and the killer pushed him as he did so, forcing him to topple down the stairs. He's reached out to grab the wall, see. His handprint slides that way. He fell down the length of the stairs and lay at the bottom, where he died. You can see the arterial blood flow down until he reaches the bottom. He would have lost consciousness soon after reaching the bottom and died soon after that.'

Grace shivered.

Together they walked down the stairs, trying as hard as they could not to step in the blood. It was a futile attempt. There was so much of it. They stood at the bottom for some time, looking at the body.

'What do we do now?' Grace asked.

'Nothing. I can barely see in this light as it is. I shouldn't think there's much evidence to collect. If there is, it can wait for the police.'

'What about... what about the body?' Grace asked.

Lovelace shrugged. 'There's no point putting him in the freezer with Mackay, there's no power, and it's cold enough in the cellar. Do you have the blankets?'

Grace held out the several blankets she had found in one of the kitchen cupboards. Carefully they laid them over Sampson's body until he was fully covered.

'That's the best we can do for now. Let's get out of here.'

Grace turned and climbed the stairs. Lovelace followed with the lamp in hand. She turned when she reached the top and looked back down into the cellar. The light from the lamp cast everything at the top of the stairs in a faded yellow light, but the stairs themselves receded into blackness. Lovelace shivered. Devil's island was beginning to live up to its nickname. Soon she would name it the Island of Death.

And Death was waiting.

***

Jack Lovelace donned thick gloves and pulled a large coat over his shoulders. He stepped out of A-Wing and into the cold air.

The wind tugged at his clothes, and the snow lashed at his face. He strolled confidently away from the prison door and through the thick snow until his way was barred by the twenty-foot prison wire that ran around the wing. He stood at the main entrance and stared at the electronic lock. It was glowing a firm red. The world had decreed that he would never get further than that red light until he died. He was angry with the world. BlackRock was no place for a man like him.

He turned as he heard footsteps crunching the snow behind him. George was approaching with a beaming smile. He liked George.

She came up and stood next to him. She wore a thick prison officer's uniform with a fur-lined collar, and a black beanie sat on her head.

'The light's not going to go green as much as you would like it to, Jack. Sorry.'

He was about to say something wry and witty, but the wind caught the words as they gathered on his lips and pushed them back into his mouth.

'What are you doing out here?' Georgia asked. 'It's bloody freezing.'

Jack closed his eyes and felt the cold worry the skin on his cheeks.

'It's invigorating!' He exclaimed. 'It's beautiful. It's Mother Nature at her imperial best. Can't you feel it? Close your eyes. Just live in the moment.'

Georgia closed her eyes and drank in the experience.

'There's something about being amidst a storm that makes you feel the most alive. But also insignificant. It's like the world is not about us. We are merely temporary visitors within its midst. We are all nothing. The storm is everything.'

Georgia felt her emotions stir. Jack could be an old charmer when he turned it on.

'Come inside, Jack. It's almost lunchtime.'

They turned and crunched their way back through the snow. Jack turned at the door to the men's wing and looked back through the falling snow at the gate. He could make out the red led glowing in the distance. George was right. There was no point wishing it green.

***

Lovelace braced herself at the door to the Mansion House and placed her hand on the door handle. She turned to look at Grace.

'Ready?'

Grace was pulling a large overcoat over her shoulders and tucking a scarf between it and her neck. A black beanie sat proudly on her head. She looked cute, Lovelace thought.

'Ready!' Grace declared, and Lovelace twisted the handle.

The wind grabbed at the door the second a gap appeared and threatened to rip it from Lovelace's hand. She held on to it firmly and stepped outside. The snow lashed at her face, and the wind howled about her ears. She waited until Grace had passed through the door and closed it carefully behind her. Together they dipped their heads against the onslaught and hurried across the ground until the accommodation block loomed in front of them. Maeve was waiting beyond the glass doors, and she opened them as the two young women arrived. They hurried inside, and Maeve shut the door behind them. Lovelace stamped her feet to remove the snow and pulled her hat from her head. Her hair, even in normal times a law unto itself, leapt into the free space and ran amok with the freedom. Lovelace ran a hand through it to calm it down, then turned and smiled at Maeve.

She'd been crying, Lovelace noticed. Her eyes, though clear of tears, were puffed at the edges and swollen slightly. She had made an effort to compose herself, and Lovelace admired that, but the grief was tangible.

'Are you okay?' Lovelace asked.

'I will be. Probably not today, though.'

'Probably not tomorrow, either,' Lovelace said. 'But one day.'

Maeve nodded. 'I want to know who did it. I'll fucking kill them.'

Lovelace didn't doubt for one second that Maeve could follow through on that threat. There was a darkness to the young Irish woman that gave Lovelace pause for thought. She was a woman to be wary of.

'Can we see Wayne's room?'

'This way,' Maeve beckoned, and the three of them walked away from the front door and down a long corridor that ran across the front of the building. The wall to the outside world was glass-fronted, and there was enough daylight outside to light their way. They stopped at the door at the far end of the corridor. Maeve turned to the last door and placed her hand on the handle. She paused, gathering her strength.

'You don't have to come in.' Lovelace said. 'We can do it.'

'No.' Maeve said firmly. 'I want to.'

She twisted the handle and walked inside. The room was bright and airy. Two windows were looking out into the storm, and one of the smaller windows had been opened to let fresh air in. It was brutally cold inside the small room.

'He always had a window open,' Maeve said softly. 'It didn't matter how cold it got outside. There was always a window open. He hated being hot indoors.'

Lovelace took a moment and surveyed the room. It was a maisonette-type flat rather than a room. The front door opened into the kitchen area, including a cooker, a freezer and a washing machine. A black marble breakfast bar separated the kitchen from the lounge, and a small area beyond that contained a small corner sofa, a coffee table and a television. French windows looked out into the landscape beyond, and a slight snow drift started climbing up the glass.

'Are all the rooms like this?' Grace asked.

Maeve chuckled. 'Fuck no. The ground floor is like this and is for managers only. Everyone else has a smaller version on a single floor. The block's a three-storey building.'

Lovelace moved into the lounge and looked about. An open staircase led to the bedroom upstairs. Everything was clean and tidy and organised in an almost regimented way. Most notable of all was the lack of any personal items.

'What sort of man was he?' Lovelace asked. She knew the answer to the question but was intrigued about how Maeve would reply. She knew men like Wayne Sampson and had met many of them in her lifetime. He was tough and hard as nails. He took no prisoners and expected no mercy in return. He was quiet, almost painfully shy, and would slip into a corner on social occasions. He fostered no relationships beyond the Brothers in Arms esprit de corps typical of old soldiers. He would have been violently loyal to Mackay. The unusual element was Maeve. She was cute in a dark way, and Sampson would have appreciated her strength and determination.

'He could be a difficult man to know,' Maeve began slowly. 'He didn't make friends easily. I don't think he had any friends on the island. Certainly none he'd have a drink with.

'He was fiercely loyal. He believed in what Mackay was doing here. We all believe in the potential for redemption in most people, but some don't deserve that consideration. Some people deserve to be here and never leave. It meant something to Wayne that he was part of this. It made him feel good about himself.'

'What was he like in private?' Lovelace asked.

'Shy. Reserved. He had his demons like all of us, but mostly he could be a lovely man.'

'And how would you describe your relationship?'

Maeve considered the point for some time. She did not attempt to rush her answer. Slowly, she said, 'we were lovers. Nothing more, really, as much as I wanted it. He didn't bond easily. If I'm honest, it was mostly just about the sex. Apart from getting drunk on this island, there's little else to do, particularly in the winter. Most of the staff are either drinking or fucking. Sometimes both.'

'But he meant something to you?' Lovelace asked.

'He did.'

'Was he having sex with other staff members?'

'Yes. As I said, everyone was at it.'

Lovelace dug no further. She knew all she needed to know about Wayne Sampson. There was nothing complicated or mysterious about the man, despite the legend he had built around himself. He was a hired thug, little more than a mercenary, who screwed around. It went no more profound than that.

They made a relatively light search of Sampson's room. Beyond some toiletries in the bathroom and one or two personal items in his bedside drawer, nothing in the flat could shine any light on the man or who may have wanted to kill him.

Maeve opened the door to let them out. 'I'm going to stay here for a bit. Before I go back to work..'

Lovelace and Grace returned to the front door and let themselves into the storm. They made the crossing quickly and stood in the entrance hall to the Mansion House, shaking off the snow and ice.

'What now?' Grace asked.

'Well, I need a drink.' Lovelace said, slipping off her large overcoat. 'Then I thought we might investigate the other past-time that keeps the staff on this island occupied through the dark and stormy days.'

Seventeen

She loved London. Something about the place was lacking in other cities, and she had been to most of them. Even today, in the midst of winter, with dark clouds rushing overhead in the fierce wind and the rain lashing at the windows, with the gloom and darkness pressing against her, she never felt happier.

It was only lunchtime, and you could be forgiven for thinking that the evening had already closed in. It was so dark outside. The orange street lamps bathed the street outside in a surreal, other-worldly glow that reflected off the rain-soaked road.

She bit down on her sandwich and bathed in the beauty of it all. She barely noticed as her phone buzzed quietly beside her.

She glanced at it casually. She had never been one to be dictated to by technology, preferring to live in the here and now, but there was something about the way it vibrated on the small table beside her that seemed to suggest it knew something that she ought to know too. It didn't. Twitter had informed her that someone, somewhere, was doing something that she might be interested in. She wasn't. Her phone didn't know her at all.

She swallowed her sandwich and drank coffee from an expensive-looking bone china cup.

Her phone buzzed again. This time it wanted to tell her about some "Breaking News" that it was sure she would be interested in this time. As she glanced away, she caught the word "BlackRock."

Now she was interested.

She opened her phone and clicked the link. The BBC news site flashed up before her. She read the report slowly, drinking in every word.

Ethan Mackay dead at 44. Unconfirmed reports say that the Scottish billionaire and philanthropist has been found murdered whilst visiting the site of HMP BlackRock, the island prison off the West coast of Scotland. Insiders say that Mr Mackay was part of a VIP tour of the island, including Sir Malcolm Lambert, MP, the Sunday Times Journalist Esther Mackay and Lucy Lovelace, daughter of the Cherwell Valley Strangler and the detective who brought the Night Prowler to justice so recently. It is understood that the island is currently cut off from the mainland due to Storm Irene. More follows…

Fuck.

She opened google and searched for the telephone number for the operations centre at BlackRock. She found it quickly and dialled it. It rang off after ten rings. She rang it again. And then again.

She found another number in her phone book and dialled that. It answered on the second ring.

'Hey. You okay?'

'Sorry. I haven't got time to talk. Can you get a telephone number for me?'

'Sure. Whose?'

'Whoever's running the police investigation into Ethan Mackay's death.'

'Fuck. Ethan Mackay's dead?'

'Focus Will. Can you get the number?'

'Already on it. Hang tight. Fuck, Ethan Mackay's dead. How?'

'They're saying he's been murdered.'

'Shit. Yeah, here it is. Detective Chief Inspector Latham McBride. I'll text you the number.'

'Thanks, Will. Talk later.'

She hung up. The number came through seconds later. She dialled it and waited.

In the operations centre for BlackRock, MacBride watched his phone light up for the thirtieth time in as many seconds. The vultures were coming.

He reached forward, turned his phone to silent, and turned it over so that he didn't have to see it light up every few seconds.

She waited for a second and rang again. Each time she tried, it went to an answering machine.

She looked up at the waiter as he came by to clear her plate.

'How far do you think Glasgow is from here?' She asked.

'Edinburgh's about seven hours,' he said, thinking about it. 'Glasgow's probably about the same. Probably more like eight or nine today.'

'Why's that?'

'Heavy snow just as you reach the Lakes. It wouldn't be a nice drive up there today.'

She drank the last of her coffee and dropped a ten-pound note on the table.

The rain was unrelenting, and it drove at her as she made her way through the quiet streets. It was cold, too, and she could feel the ice in the air. Ten minutes later, she turned a corner and a luxury car dealership, awash with bright neon lights, beckoned her in.

A salesman came over with a towel and welcomed her in.

'Not a nice day for it. Can I get you anything? A hot drink? Tea, coffee, hot chocolate?'

'Just a car.' She said.

Stunned, the salesman asked, 'do you have a particular one in mind.'

She did. She had seen it earlier as she had walked past.

'That one.'

She pointed to a matt black Range Rover Sport.

'Good choice, madam.' The salesman said, oozing charm. 'Would you like to sit in it for size? I can organise a test drive.'

'No need.' She said. 'I'll take it.'

The salesman licked his lips in anticipation.

'How would you like to pay? We have several finance options available for you. We can deliver to you early next week.'

'I'll take it now,' she said firmly. 'With a full tank of fuel, please.'

'Madam, that's an eighty thousand pound car.'

'I know.' She said. She reached into her pocket and pulled out a small wallet. She selected a card and handed it to the salesman. 'I don't need anything except that car and a full tank of fuel.'

The salesman walked away with her card and spoke to what she suspected was the manager. He picked up a telephone and made a call. Five minutes later, the salesman returned with her card.

'The car will be ready in ten minutes. We're sorting the fuel now.'

Twenty minutes later, the powerful car stormed out of the city towards the M25. She would be there in seven hours, delivering terrible news to the poor, unsuspecting DCI McBride.

***

Given the height of the Citadel and how it stood atop the crenellated ramparts of HMP BlackRock, it was no surprise to those that worked there that it was a constant whipping boy for the storms that raged about it. The windows that peered out into the fading light of day were lashed with sleet and snow and, now and then, freezing salt water that was swept into the jagged cliff edge by the mighty North Atlantic sea that constantly growled in the background.

Emily stood at the glass window, watching the waves crest the cliff edge and spray water over the snow-covered ground. She was nursing a steaming cup of coffee and the beginnings of a migraine. Carl sat at his desk behind her, tapping away at his keyboard. They had been at it constantly since Gerry had absolved himself of any responsibility for his software. It was a nightmare. Despite his self-attributed genius status, Gerry had created one of the most complicated systems she had ever worked on. There were thousands upon thousands of lines of code, and most of them were so intricate that she had to deconstruct them, line by line, to fathom any understanding.

'Take a look at this,' Carl said, twisting his monitor around so she could see better.

Emily turned in and leant in over Carl's shoulder. She was so close he could smell the coffee on her breath and the slightest whiff of perfume. It was sweet and intoxicating.

'What am I looking at?' Emily asked.

'This bit of code, here. It seems to have embedded itself into the system during the reboot. It wasn't there before. I've run a dozen sweeps of the software. It's alien code.'

'It doesn't make any sense,' Emily mused.

'No, it doesn't.' Carl agreed. 'Taken individually, it makes no sense. But there's a lot of it, and taken as a whole, it looks like another program has piggybacked into Gerry's software. It's like some parasite, feeding off the system.'

'Can you delete it?'

'I've tried. There's no getting rid of it.'

Emily shook her head in frustration. They needed Gerry. He was the only one that knew the intricacies of his software. 'Do you know what it does?' She asked.

Carl shrugged. 'Fuck knows. It doesn't seem to do anything.'

'It has to do something..' Emily said, leaving the statement to hang in the air.

She dropped her coffee on the desk next to Carl's and sat in her chair.

'I suppose we'd better keep digging.'

***

Elouise found Sir Malcolm in the lounge prodding at the wood burner with a poker. Daylight was fading fast, and Elouise swept around the room, lighting candles and putting oil lamps on tables.

'Bloody weather doesn't look like it's letting up,' Sir Malcolm grumbled. He closed the door to the burner and reached out for the glass of whiskey he had poured a few moments ago.

'Indeed.' Elouise replied. She wasn't in much of a mood for talking.

'Can't believe it's taking the Electricity Board so long to restore the power,' Sir Malcolm continued. 'Bloody poor show.'

'Quite.' Elouise said absently. 'I shall have to write to my MP.'

Sir Malcolm chuckled. 'Yes, yes. You should. Who is he?'

'No idea.' Elouise replied. 'But I daresay his lights are on at the moment.'

'Well, you leave it with me, my dear. I'll have a chat when we get out of here.'

Elouise lit the last candle and made for the exit. The last thing she needed was to be stuck with Sir Malcolm for the evening. She paused as she walked past him.

'Can I get you a top-up?' Elouise asked as Sir Malcolm slumped into a large armchair.

'Why not? Can't do any harm, eh?'

She reached for a crystal decanter that sat on a small silver platter and poured him a large glass.

'Thank you.'

As she reached the door, she turned and asked, 'have you seen Esther at all today?'

'No, thank god.' Sir Malcolm said. 'Or did I see her at breakfast?'

'No. She wasn't at breakfast. I thought perhaps she was sleeping off her hangover.'

Sir Malcolm chuckled. 'She did have rather a lot to drink. And it gets much harder to recover as you get older. It's a terrible thing, age, you know. I don't recommend it.'

Elouise closed the door behind her. She stood in the darkness for a moment, thinking about Sir Malcolm.

He sometimes came across as a bumbling old fool, but she didn't doubt the intelligence behind those old eyes for one minute. He was a wily old fox and certainly not one to be underestimated.

Had Ethan Mackay underestimated Sir Malcolm Lambert? If, what everyone thought was true, that Sir Malcolm had nobbled a few of his older patients, then he was a man to be wary of. Murder gets easy after the first time.

She sighed as she remembered the moment her first husband died. The death rattle still haunted her. But was that murder? Was she a killer? Was it a crime to let someone die and not step in to save them? She didn't know the answer despite searching for it every day since then. She wondered if she would ever come to terms with what she did or didn't do that night.

Her mind drifted to Johnathon. He was a weak man who couldn't entirely accept the person he was, even if others had. The crash was unfortunate, and it eroded his mental health quite considerably. He had been on a downward spiral ever since. Then his lover died, and he felt the responsibility all over again. And then Ethan Mackay happened, and that's when Johnathon had retreated into his head. She had seen it coming and felt guilty for doing nothing to prevent it.

She walked away from the lounge and along the corridor until she came to her bedroom door. It was dark, but her eyes had become accustomed to it, and she knew every corner of the house intimately. She paused nervously as she reached for the handle. As she opened the door, the light from an oil lamp reflected off the plaque. "Thompson."

Fuck Ethan Mackay, she thought. Long may he burn in Hell.

She sat at the edge of her bed and ran her fingers through Johnathon's hair. He looked like a lost boy, curled up and defenceless under her sheets. She had given him a sleeping tablet from her collection, and he had washed it down with a large glass of water. Sleep had come soon after, and she had watched him for some time before completing some chores.

He was still sleeping, and his chest rose and fell with each breath he took. She thought it would be much simpler if his breathing just stopped. So much easier for Johnathon and so much easier for her.

No. She couldn't do that. Not to Emma. Not to Johnathon. There would be tough times ahead, but she would cope. She had to. Her family needed her.

She blew out the oil lamp and left her husband to sleep.

She knocked gently on the door opposite. Lovelace appeared a few seconds later. She wore a long white robe, and her hair was a mess. Elouise could see Grace in the background as she quickly threw on some clothes.

'May I come in?'

Lovelace stepped back from the door, and Elouise walked in.

'I'm sorry to interrupt. I need some company.'

Grace walked over and took Elouise by the hand.

'Is everything okay?' She asked.

Grace led her over to the edge of the bed and sat her down. Lovelace poured a glass of wine from one of the bottles she had acquired earlier and gave it to Elouise.

'You must think me a silly old fool.' Elouise began. 'But I'm just so very tired of it all. I'm tired of this place and the death and the pain and the stupid old men and the angry men and, to be fair, all of the bloody men.'

Lovelace smiled. She poured Grace a glass of wine and then filled one up for herself.

'I can drink to that.' She declared.

'I didn't mean to intrude,' Elouise said, 'but you two are still young and full of life. I wanted to share that for a moment to remind me that life is worth the effort.'

'Of course, it's worth it.' Grace declared firmly. She smiled at Lovelace, who smiled back.

'I'm intruding!' Elouise said, standing up. 'I should leave you in peace.'

'Don't be silly,' Lovelace argued. 'Stay. Drink wine. Help us plot the downfall of stupid men. Here, let me top you up.'

Elouise Preece relaxed for the first time since she landed on BlackRock.

***

Kellerman was tired too. And fed up. Everything that could go wrong on BlackRock had gone wrong, and he felt the weight of the responsibility sit heavy on his shoulders. It was too much that Ethan Mackay had been murdered on his watch, but Sinclair too, and now that stupid security guard. He had liked none of them but had not wished them dead. It was all getting too much. What the bloody hell was going on?

He trundled through the snow and pulled his collar up against the wind. It blew over the prison's outer wall and swept everything into a frenzy. He made a beeline for the Citadel and was relieved when he entered its front door, and a wave of warmth greeted him.

He divested himself of his outer clothing and climbed the staircase to the operations room.

It was empty save for two technicians who were head down at their monitors.

'Where's Gerry?' He asked.

Emily looked up at Kellerman and then at Carl. Kellerman's arrival had caught them off guard.

'He..er..' She stuttered. 'He's taken a break. I think he's in the break-out room downstairs.'

'How long's he been there?'

'Not long.' She lied. She had to work with Gerry, and there was no point in worsening the situation.

'I see.' Kellerman said.

He turned, left the room, and took the stairs two at a time. He found Gerry reclined in one of the break-out rooms surrounded by empty cola cans, sandwich wrappers and half-eaten chocolate bars.

Kellerman walked over to Gerry's prostate figure and prodded him firmly in the ribs. Despite his weight, Kellerman felt his index finger slip between his ribs. Gerry shot up in agony and squealed.

'What the fuc..!'

He stopped as he saw the look on Kellerman's face.

'Oh, it's you.' Then, slowly, he said, 'I.. er… I must have drifted off.'

'How long have you been down here?' Kellerman demanded.

'Not long.'

'You're a liar. Don't lie to me.'

'I'm not lying.'

'Okay, tell me what you've done so far to sort this bug out?'

Gerry paused. He had no idea what the two of them had done upstairs.

'Right. Follow me.' Kellerman demanded.

Reluctantly, Gerry fell in behind Kellerman as he climbed the stairs back to the operations centre.

'You two.' Kellerman said, pointing at Emily and Carl. 'Get in one of the Defenders and return to the accommodation block. Take the rest of the night off. You,' he said, turning to Gerry, 'sit the fuck down and fix that bug. Now! I'm going to be sat by your side the whole night until it's done.'

***

Liam Swift had fielded a dozen or more requests for a statement since the news of Mackay's murder had broken. He politely and firmly declined them with a simple 'no comment.'

The news stations were not happy with that, and within the last hour, a local television crew had pitched up at the front gate and had started recording pieces to camera. The weather had been no deterrent.

He felt his heart miss a beat as his phone started to ring again. He took a deep breath and prepared his brief statement.

'Swift. Oh, it's you. What? Wait there.'

He strode purposefully to where the police had set up their office and walked up to DCI McBride.

'They've been trying to get hold of you. Your phone's turned off?'

McBride looked up. His face had grown weary. 'What is it?'

'The Electricity company are at the substation that feeds BlackRock. Here,' he handed his phone to McBride, 'you should talk to them.'

'DCI McBride.'

DS Sandhu watched her boss's face for clues as to the conversation he was having. She found none and waited patiently while he ended the call. He handed the phone back to Swift.

'Well?' Sandhu asked. 'What is it?'

'It seems the storm wasn't responsible for the power cut on BlackRock,' McBride began. 'They're at the substation now. There's considerable fire damage. Fire investigation officers are on their way to take a look.'

'A fire?' Sandhu asked. 'Could it have been an accident?'

McBride shook his head. 'No. It was deliberate. It was arson.'

'That doesn't make any sense.' Sandhu mused. 'Why would anyone want the power cut to the island?'

Not just "why," McBride thought. "Who?"

*****

Elouise felt the warmth of the wine as she stood up to leave. She took a moment to balance herself and grabbed an oil lamp from a table.

'I don't know what we're doing for dinner. Poor Mrs Brent is getting too old to run about in this weather. Perhaps I'll have something sent down from the prison kitchens. I'm sure it's good food,' she added doubtfully.

Lovelace and Grace watched as she reached the door. She was a little unsteady on her feet.

'I must go and check on Miss Friedman. I don't think I've seen her all day.'

Elouise closed the door behind her and walked across to "Maybrick."

Fuck Ethan Mackay, she thought again. She rapped on the door and waited for a reply. When none came, she tried the handle and opened the door. She leant in and cried out, 'Miss Friedman. Esther. Are you there?'

Still no reply. She opened the door further and walked in. There were no candles alight, and an oil lamp sat on a nearby table, also unlit. Elouise shone her light around the room. Esther's bed was unmade. The duvet covers were folded as if she had recently climbed out of bed. Her clothes were folded neatly on a nearby armchair.

Elouise was about to give up the search, thinking that she and Esther had yet to cross paths, when something unusual caught her eye.

She walked over to the window and drew back the curtains. Very little light swept in from outside. The evening had fully set in.

Elouise shone her torch over the windowsill and along a line back to Esther's bed.

It couldn't be, could it?

Seconds later, she convinced herself it could.

The more she looked, the more evident it became. Blood. Lots of it, covering the floor, the table, the windowsill and the glass. *So much blood.*

Esther's blood?

Where the fuck was Esther?

Eighteen

Elouise and Grace stood behind Lovelace as she ducked down and inspected the blood. Grace pulled out her phone and switched on the torch. She handed it to Lovelace, who scanned the blood trail from where it began at the bed to where it ended at the windowsill.

'It's definitely blood.' Lovelace agreed.

'Esther's?' Grace asked tentatively.

'No way of telling whose blood, but it would seem probable that it was Esther's.'

'There's so much of it!' Elouise exclaimed. 'What do you think happened?'

Lovelace looked up at the two women holding their lamps aloft. 'It could have been a nosebleed.' She suggested.

Elouise scoffed. 'But the blood. There's so much of it.'

'It always looks worse outside of the body,' Lovelace explained. 'A small wound can look like a massacre when the blood's spread everywhere.'

'That's true,' Grace agreed. 'But why did she go over to the windowsill and not the bathroom?'

Good question. She was pretty and intelligent, Lovelace mused.

'And given there are already two bodies in the house, it's not too much of a stretch to think that Esther may have gotten into trouble.' Grace continued.

Lovelace turned her attention back to the blood trail from the bed to the windowsill. Something on the bedside table caught her eye, and she focussed the torch on it.

'What is it? What have you found?' Elouise asked.

Lovelace had shielded the two of them from what she had found. She stood up and turned to face them. 'Blood. Matted blood and hair on the edge of the table.'

'She fell?' Elouise asked.

'Or was pushed.' Grace said.

'Either is possible.' Lovelace agreed. 'But as Grace said, there are already two bodies in this house. This would suggest that Esther has come to some harm.'

'But she could have fallen?' Elouise insisted. 'She was very drunk last night, and she is an older woman and less secure on her feet than the rest of us. Perhaps she got out of bed to use the toilet, fell and hit her head?'

'That could have happened, couldn't it?' Grace asked. Her face was lit up by the lamp she carried. The shadows danced playfully about her features. Lovelace saw the anxiety there.

'It's possible,' Lovelace admitted reluctantly. 'But it doesn't explain why she made her way over to the window?'

'People have been known to act erratically after a concussion.' Elouise explained. 'Perhaps she didn't know what she was doing? She could have got up and gone to open the window and fallen out?'

'True.' Lovelace said. 'Or she could have been attacked, dragged over to the window and thrown out. It's a fair distance to the ground.'

'Either way,' Grace mused. 'If she went out of the window, she should still be there, right?'

Lovelace walked over to the window and threw it open. 'Was the window open or closed when you came in?' Lovelace asked as the wind chased itself into the room.

Elouise paused. The truth hit her sideways. 'It was closed.'

Elouise looked back at the two women. The truth reached Grace as Lovelace's eyes met hers.

'Esther couldn't have closed the window behind her if she had fallen out.' Lovelace said, giving voice to the reality they were faced with. She leant out of the window and stared into the void. She could only just make out the floor, which was blanketed in thick snow. She pulled the window closed and looked back into the room.

'I can't see a thing. We should wait until the morning.'

'But what if she's out there?' Grace pleaded. 'What if she's waiting for someone to find her? We should at least check?'

'Grace is right,' Elouise said. 'If Esther has been attacked and thrown out of the window, the killer may not have had time to move her. She may still be alive. We owe it to her to at least make sure.'

Lovelace relented even though she knew it was futile. The fall in the bedroom was likely to have brought Esther to the edge of death. The fall from the window would have finished her off. The cold would have long since killed her, even supposing she had survived both of those events.

'Okay. Let's take a look.'

Elouise found an array of equipment in Johnathon's living room that was ideal for the search they were about to undertake. Even though it would take just a few short minutes to walk around the building, it was lost on none of them that the storm was continuing to rage fiercely. Elouise found walking boots, sticks, waterproof coats, gloves and trousers, and she handed them around and began to climb into her boots. She waited while Lovelace and Grace found suitable attire that fitted and slowly climbed into them. She smiled for the first time that day. They looked bright and silly in their mismatched clothing, like teenagers on their first-ever hiking trip.

'How do I look?' Lovelace asked, perfectly aware that she looked ridiculous.

'Stunning.' Grace said. 'How about me?' She turned full circle and posed for Lovelace.

'Cute.' Lovelace said. 'Chavvy, but cute. All you need now is a spliff, a bottle of White Lightning, and an abandoned bus shelter, and you'll be good to go!'

'Well, I think you both look wonderful.' Elouise said, envious of the deep rapport the two young women had developed. She missed that closeness. She feared she'd never find it again. 'Right. Let's go, shall we?'

The oil lamps proved useless in the wind and blew out almost the first second the three stepped out into the night. They returned to the reception area and waited while Elouise disappeared into Johnathon's study. She returned a few minutes later, holding two large torches. She handed one to Lovelace and held on to the other one. They stepped back out into the night and switched the torches on.

The bright lights swept out into the darkness. Everywhere was a blanket of white, and it reflected at them. Lovelace pitched her torch down, covering the first couple of feet in front of her, and Elouise followed suit. She watched as Lovelace led the way and Grace fell in beside her, linking her arm through hers.

They walked around the building in silence, mainly because all they could hear was the wind as it raged overhead and the sound of the North Atlantic as it battered the cliff face a few hundred yards ahead of them. Even if they could talk, the words would have been lost in the frenzy. Instead, they dropped their heads and carefully kept within a few feet of the building's edge. Now and then, Lovelace paused and looked up, carefully studying her whereabouts according to the building's peculiar structure. After a few minutes, she stopped, and the other two women huddled in close.

'I think this is it. She should be around here somewhere.'

The two torches were swept up and down the building and out into the land beyond. They only had a few yards of good visibility before the snow obscured their view. The snow was deep here. Drifts had built up the side of the Mansion House and stood eight feet tall.

Lovelace shone her torch up the building until the light fell on Esther's window.

'I'm sure that's her window,' Lovelace bellowed, and the words barely made it out of her mouth.

Elouise understood the context. She shone her light up to the window and worked out the lay of the building from memory. Lovelace was right. They stood underneath Esther's room. If Esther was here, she was covered in several feet of snow. She lay her torch down in the snow, walked over to the drift, and began slowly moving handfuls of the stuff away from the building. Grace joined her, and Lovelace followed Elouise's example, laid her torch beside her, and shone the light at the place where she thought Esther would have landed.

It took a few minutes to clear the snow away from the building. Lovelace felt herself sweat inside her thermal coat despite the cold. When the vast majority of the drift was removed and no body had been found, they started clearing snow further away from the building.

It took half an hour of digging before Elouise gave it up as a bad job. She looked at Lovelace and shook her head. Lovelace placed her hand on Grace's, and Grace looked up.

'It's no good,' she said, leaning in as close as she could. 'She's not here.'

Grace dropped to her knees and looked at what they had cleared. She didn't want to admit it, but it was an undeniable truth. If Esther had fallen out of the window or been pushed, they would have found her by now. They had cleared so much snow, and the troughs began filling back up. Reluctantly, she stood up, and the three of them returned to the building.

She had to be dead, Grace thought as they trundled through the snow, and she couldn't understand it one bit. None of it made sense.

***

The snow had started not long after she had passed Stafford. It came in dribs and drabs for the first hour and was nothing more than a visual inconvenience. As she had passed Manchester and pushed the Range Rover towards the Lakes, the snow had intensified until the visibility had become seriously reduced. She pulled off the motorway at Tebay services and bought a strong black coffee. She sat at a window, watching the landscape change and slowly sipped at her drink until the caffeine revived her.

She tried calling the elusive DCI McBride but to no avail. The number for the operations centre just went straight to an answering machine. There was nothing for it. She had to push on. Time was running out.

She filled up the car at the filling station and restarted her sat-nav. It was another two hours to Glasgow, then possibly another hour to BlackRock Mainland Operations Centre.

She dropped the car into drive and slipped back onto the motorway. She slowly edged her speed up as fast as she dared and activated cruise control. She took her foot off the accelerator and relaxed back into her seat.

Two, maybe three hours. After that, who knew?

***

It was bitterly cold inside the Mansion House when the three women returned. They divested themselves of their outer clothes and stood in the reception area shivering.

'I feel I ought to inform someone,' Elouise said, looking at the others for guidance.

'Who?' Grace asked. 'There's no one to tell.'

'Perhaps Mr Kellerman?' Elouise suggested. 'I could reach him on Johnathon's phone. And then, if the power is switched back on, he can inform the police on the mainland.'

'Who can't get here anyway.' Lovelace pointed out.

'I know,' Elouise said, 'but I think I'd feel better all the same. Why don't you two go to the lounge and get warm? I'm sure Sir Malcolm has lit the fire already and is undoubtedly standing over it with poker in hand!'

They watched as Elouise disappeared into the darkness, then turned and walked up the staircase to the upper level.

Sir Malcolm had kept a good fire going in the burner, and a delightful wave of warm air greeted the two as they entered the lounge. He had pulled up an armchair within poking distance of the stove, and his face had taken on a deep red glow, though Lovelace wasn't sure whether that was because of the heat or the whiskey he was drinking.

'Ah, there you are,' Sir Malcolm exclaimed, looking up from his drink. 'Bloody hell, you two look freezing. You haven't been outside, have you?'

'We have,' Grace admitted, slumping into the large corner sofa. She was followed by Lovelace, who sat next to her.

'What the bloody hell for?' Sir Malcolm asked.

There was a pause as the two women looked at one another.

'We were looking for Esther,' Lovelace said slowly.

Sir Malcolm threw them a quizzical look. 'Why would you think she'd be outside in this weather?'

Slowly, Lovelace explained the circumstances that led to the search outside.

'Good god,' Sir Malcolm said. 'You don't think someone's done her in, do you?'

'It would seem likely, Sir Malcolm. The blood seems to indicate it.' Lovelace explained.

'But who would want to kill an old woman like Esther?'

'Well, you for one,' Lovelace said abruptly, then instantly regretted it. She looked across at Grace, who was trying to suppress a smile.

'What the hell do you mean by that?' Sir Malcolm demanded to know.

'Just that there was no love lost between you two. You were hardly friends. She'd been making digs at you almost the entire time we've been here.'

'That was the nature of the woman. If I killed every woman I ever met that made snide little digs at me, there wouldn't be many of you left.'

Lovelace avoided looking directly at Grace. She could see her stifling a laugh in the corner of her eye, and she didn't want to be caught up in a fit of giggles. That wouldn't please Sir Malcolm one little bit.

'Well, there's a motive,' Lovelace countered. 'Esther was a digger, like Ethan Mackay. They liked to collect dirt on people and control them. Sometimes I wonder if they didn't find out something that got them killed. By all accounts, you have something to hide.'

'Now look here!' Sir Malcolm blustered, and his face grew redder.

'Is everything okay?' Elouise asked as she entered the lounge bearing glasses and a bottle of brandy.

'We're discussing what may have happened to Esther and whether it's related to Ethan's murder,' Grace said. 'Lovelace was just musing at the possibility that they both may have found something incriminating about Sir Malcolm which has led to their deaths.'

Elouise gave Lovelace a disapproving look. 'I see.' She walked up to the coffee table and placed the bottle of brandy down on it, followed by the fat-bottomed glasses she was carrying. 'Brandy, Sir Malcolm?'

She didn't wait for an answer. She poured him a large glass and handed it to him. 'The way I see it is that any of us here in this house has the motive and opportunity to kill Ethan Mackay or Esther. Or both.'

'What about Lovelace?' Grace demanded to know.

Elouise poured three more glasses of brandy and handed them out, taking the last one for herself. 'As far as motive goes, I couldn't say beyond that Ethan and Esther were both very good at seeing the bad in people and routing out their secrets. Perhaps they routed out a secret about Miss Lovelace that we don't know about?'

Lovelace raised her glass. 'A valid theory.' She admitted.

'After all,' Elouise continued, 'you know an awful lot about everyone else in this house, but we know very little about you.'

'Nonsense.' Grace said, rising to Lovelace's defence. 'I knew all about her before we ever met. Her life's no secret. And what about that Sampson man and the prisoner who died? What motive has she for killing them?'

Elouise pulled up an armchair nearer to the burner and dropped into it. She sipped at her glass of brandy and savoured the burn as the liquid slipped down her throat.

'She arrested the man at the prison. Adam Sinclair, wasn't it? Nasty little man. I think he tried to kill you, didn't he?'

Lovelace nodded and said nothing.

'Motive enough for wanting a man dead.' Elouise insisted.

'But she can't have killed him,' Grace cried. 'We were together at the time he was murdered. She and I are the only ones with an alibi for his murder.'

'Good point,' Elouise admitted. 'Provided your alibis can be trusted. But okay, I'll let the Sinclair murder pass. I don't think it's possible for someone to leave the Mansion House in the middle of the night, in this weather, drive to the prison and get inside without being seen. I think we can safely exclude all of us from the Sinclair murder.'

'Quite. Most unlikely.' Sir Malcolm said, enjoying the exchange between the women. 'But what about this Sampson fellow? He was murdered in this house, wasn't he?'

'He was,' Elouise said. 'And I don't believe anyone has an alibi for his time of death. That puts us all in the frame.'

'But why?' Grace asked. 'Why kill Sampson? And how was he lured into the kitchen from his guard post?'

Elouise rotated her glass slowly and watched as the light from a dozen candles reflected off the amber liquid. 'I have a theory about that,' she started slowly. 'I don't know why he was killed, but let's say for argument's sake that he found out something about Ethan's murder that made him a target.'

'Like what?' Sir Malcolm asked.

'I don't know.' Elouise admitted. 'Perhaps he didn't know what he knew either.'

'So how was he lured into the kitchen?' Lovelace asked, intrigued to hear what Elouise had to say. She had a theory too.

'I'd say he could have been lured into a quiet spot in the kitchen on the promise of one of two things that can sway even the strongest of men. Food or sex.'

'Well, that knocks me out of the running!' Sir Malcolm laughed.

'Why?' Grace asked. 'You're not married, are you, Sir Malcolm? Have you ever been married?'

'Why, er… I haven't, but I don't see how that is relevant here.'

'No, actually, I agree with you.' Grace said. 'Being married doesn't mean you can't have sex with men. And the ability to lure a man away from his post on the promise of sexual favours doesn't exclude men, either.'

'Really. I must protest!' Sir Malcolm stuttered.

'She's quite right, of course, Sir Malcolm.' Elouise agreed. 'Any one of us in this house could have lured Mr Sampson away from his post and killed him. Any one of us.'

'Including Johnathon,' Lovelace pointed out.

'Yes, Miss Lovelace, I certainly wouldn't have put it past my husband to do that sort of thing, although I don't think he would have had the stomach to cut a man's throat in cold blood.'

Lovelace agreed. She didn't think Johnathon had it in him either, but their theories aligned.

Elouise drained the remains of her glass and stood up. 'One of us in this room is a cold-blooded, vicious killer. It could be me, although I know it isn't, which in my head cuts the suspect list to just four. I can't see Johnathon killing anyone if I'm honest so I think it's one of you three.'

Grace sat up. 'Well, I know it's not me, and I'm certain it's not Lovelace. As far as I'm concerned, it's down to you, your husband, and Sir Malcolm.'

Elouise smiled. 'Miss Lovelace?'

'I wouldn't like to say,' Lovelace remarked carefully. 'I think everyone is capable of murder given the right set of opportunities.'

'Sir Malcolm?' Elouise asked.

'Feels like a woman's crime to me. Besides, I think your husband's a bit of a case, if I'm honest. Not sure he's got it in him, and I know it's not me, so it must be one of you three.'

Elouise smiled and turned to leave the room. 'The prison's sending food down with the change of shift. I think I need to eat. I'll have it brought up here, where it's warm.'

When she had gone, Lovelace refilled everyone's glasses and sat back down on the sofa. She felt Grace watching her. Sir Malcolm leant back in his armchair and closed his eyes.

Softly, Grace said, 'I wonder where Esther is?'

The words hung in the air, cloying at them. She was dead, of that Lovelace was certain. The question wasn't "where?" but "who next and when?"

Nineteen

She saw little of the landscape save what the powerful lights of the Range Rover highlighted as she pushed the motor into the mountainous Scottish countryside. She had slowed considerably since she had left the motorway and drove westward, ever closer to her destination. The snow fell heavily, and she manoeuvred the vehicle gently through the twisty snow-covered roads. The big four-by-four relished every moment and tackled every mile with a sure and steady foot. It still came as a relief as she crested a small brow of a hill and the bright neon lights of BlackRock's mainland operations centre came into view.

She was astonished to find film and news crews on either side of the approach to the main entrance, and she had to park almost a hundred yards away from the main gate. She grabbed her thick coat and stepped out into the freezing wind.

No one paid the young woman much notice as she trudged through the thick snow to where a tall metal security gate barred her way. She wandered its length, trying to get the attention of one of several guards who had squeezed into the Guard's Office for warmth. They seemed to be enjoying the moment as she could hear them laughing and chatting.

'Excuse me,' she said to a young man in a large black overcoat standing behind a camera a few yards away. 'Is there a bell or something?'

'They won't talk to the press.' He said, 'miserable sods won't even bring us coffee.'

She smiled and turned back to the guards' office. It had large glass windows facing out on all sides, slowly misting up from the inside. Within, hot drinks were being consumed, and here and there, she noticed a plume of smoke rise from what she assumed was a vape of some kind.

There was nothing else for it, and the distance to the guards' office wasn't that far. She leaned down and rolled a giant snowball between her hands. The problem was the metal fence that barred her way. She'd need to pitch the ball high enough so that it rose above the fence, but slow enough so that it arced downwards to the window. Her first attempt caught the top of the fence and obliterated itself, casting its remains into the wind. The wind caught the second attempt mid-flight, and it disappeared into the night. The third dropped too short, and the fourth fell far to the right-hand side.

As she rolled the fifth, she could see the cameraman take a keen interest in what she was doing. She took a step back, drew her arm back and launched the snowball into the air. At first, she thought she had pitched it too slowly, and she waited to see it hit the top of the fence. Once it had cleared the top, she knew it was good. It cut a perfect arc in the well-lit night sky and dropped at a perfect angle into the window. For a moment, no sound came, and she wondered if, perhaps, she'd made it too soft. Then came a crack that echoed into the night. Shit. There must have been a stone in it.

'Nice shot.' The cameraman applauded.

'Thanks.' She replied, clapping loose snow from her hands.

'I think you might be in trouble,' the cameraman laughed as a couple of pissed-off-looking guards came out of the office.

'Well, it certainly attracted their attention.' She admitted, approaching the fence.

'Did you do that?' One of the guards with a broad Glaswegian accent demanded to know.

'I did.'

'That's criminal damage, that is,' he said, deeply offended.

Another guard stood by his side and agreed. 'Could have you arrested for that.'

'Yes. Good. While you sort that out, I need to speak to the person in charge.'

'No visitors.' The Glaswegian said curtly. 'No Press.'

'I'm not the Press,' the young woman said. 'And I think he'll want to know what I have to say.'

'Go away.' the other guard said.

'He'll want to hear what I have to say.' She insisted. 'If you don't listen to me, I think you'll both be looking for new jobs by the end of the week.'

The guards looked at one another and then at the young woman on the other side of the fence.

'Wait here.'

The two disappeared into the guards' office and conversed with the other guards. One of the men, with a big bushy beard, turned and looked out of the window. She watched as he spoke on his radio.

Inside the operations centre, Liam Swift was pacing nervously. He heard his name come over the radio, and he stopped and spoke into his.

'What is it?'

'Some girl at the gate trying to get in. Says she has information for you.'

Swift looked at his watch. It was getting late. Too late for guests.

'Did she say what it was?'

'Nope. Said it was important, though.'

Probably just another journalist trying to get a quote for tomorrow's papers, he thought.

'Tell her to come back tomorrow. We may have more news then.'

'Roger that.'

Swift slipped the radio back onto his belt and waited for the static to end. He hated journalists.

The Glaswegian guard stepped out of the office and crunched his way through the snow to where she waited.

'Come back tomorrow.' He said.

'It's important.' She insisted.

'It can wait until tomorrow. Come back then.'

Frustrated, she turned and walked back to her car. She got in and turned the heating up.

Now what?

***

Georgia Hope glanced at her watch. She was five minutes into her fifteen-minute break, and she couldn't help but feel that the night was going to be a long one. She didn't care much for the night shift. It wasn't very interesting, and there were usually fewer people on shift to talk to. She'd begin her floor walk at ten o'clock and slowly send the prisoners back to their cells. One by one, the doors would be locked behind them until they were all safely put away, and the prison would take on a whole new life.

She drank coffee from a large mug and crunched on a chocolate bar. It was approaching a quarter to ten.

She leaned back in her chair and took a moment to enjoy the peace. It would be busy for half an hour or so, and then the rest of the night would drag on interminably until tomorrow began afresh.

***

Gerry was beginning to get frustrated. Kellerman sat at his side and watched him as he worked, and it was slowly grinding his nerves.

'There's nothing wrong with my software.' Gerry declared.

'Something's wrong with it.' Kellerman insisted.

Gerry sighed. There was no telling some people. 'I could look at this alien code all night and still make nothing of it. It's a corrupted file that somehow got stuck in the system. It doesn't do anything.'

Kellerman could sense Gerry's annoyance, and in some small way, it pleased him. Gerry was one of the most annoying people he'd ever met, and returning the favour felt oddly satisfying. On the flip side, it had been a long day, and he didn't much care for being in Gerry's company for any longer than he needed to be. But still, he had an uneasy feeling that he couldn't shake. He glanced at the digital clock on the wall in front of him. It was nearing ten o'clock, and he was starving.

'Okay. A couple more hours, and then we'll call it a day. What time does the night shift start?'

'I'm it,' Gerry replied. 'You sent the other two home.'

Shit. That was silly.

'It's okay,' Gerry added, soothing Kellerman as he went on. 'Not much occurs after ten, and the day shift will be here before the sun gets up. I've got all I need for a comfortable night.'

Kellerman wondered what made Gerry comfortable through the night and then shook his head. He probably didn't want to know.

'I'll go and see if the kitchen has anything for us to eat. I'll be back in a bit.'

Gerry watched as Kellerman left the citadel. He heard the door bang as he left the building, and watched as Kellerman made his way across the yard and through the falling snow.

He turned and faced his monitors, and the pulse in his head began to bulge. The alien code was seriously beginning to give him a headache. Despite having told Kellerman that it was most likely a corrupted code from the power cut, he couldn't help but sense some order. Man-made order.

But for the life of him, he didn't know what it was meant to do.

***

'I think I shall go to bed.' Elouise declared, rising to her feet. She was exhausted, and her head ached.

Dinner had been brought from BlackRock and delivered to the lounge, where the four of them had sat and eaten. It had been a quiet and subdued affair, and no one spoke. Afterwards, they sat in silence and listened as the storm continued to rage outside. Periodically, Sir Malcolm left his armchair and poked the burner before pouring himself more whiskey.

Elouise had kept her guests' glasses topped up, but Lovelace had noticed the strain in her movements. Her eyes looked sad, and she drank her drink slowly, not enjoying it.

At almost ten o'clock, Elouise stood up and declared her intention to go to bed.

'Johnathon needs me.'

Sir Malcolm's eyes had already closed, and the sudden movement in the room brought him around. 'What's that?' He asked.

'I'm going to bed, Sir Malcolm. Is there anything I can get for you before I go?'

'No, no. I'm quite all right. You get off, my dear.'

Grace turned to Lovelace and said, 'I'm rather beat myself. I might go up too.'

'I'll come with you,' Lovelace said, standing up, and she was relieved to see that Grace had intended that she should.

'Would you mind extinguishing all the candles and lamps, Sir Malcolm? Before you go to bed?' Elouise asked.

'Of course. My pleasure.'

The three left Sir Malcolm alone and followed Elouise as she guided them to the bedrooms.

She paused with her hand on her bedroom door and turned to Lovelace and Grace. 'Good night. Let's hope we can get off this island tomorrow.'

They watched as Elouise turned the handle and disappeared into her bedroom. Grace took Lovelace's hand and pushed open her bedroom door. They disappeared inside, and the house grew ever quieter.

***

The ten o'clock sweep of A-Wing began precisely on time. The prisoners were herded unceremoniously from whatever they were doing and led back to their cells. It was an informal affair and conducted mainly in good

267

humour. Some of the men grumbled, and some complained vocally, but none ever refused. Even though they were expected back in their cells at ten, the lights weren't extinguished until midnight. For some, it was their quiet time—a time to watch TV or read a book.

Georgia took her usual side of the wing while other prison officers tended to theirs. She guided and cajoled her prisoners one by one into their cells.

'Good night, Rob.'

She closed the door firmly behind the gangland killer. The doors were open all day and programmed to lock automatically after ten once they were shut. Georgia watched as the green LED turned red.

Claus Fischer turned her stomach, and she breathed a sigh of relief as his door closed behind him, and the light went red.

'Come on, Jack, it's not like you to be one of the last to bed.' She said as she held the door to Jack Lovelace's cell.

'Evening, George,' Jack said, beaming at her. 'Sorry. My mind was elsewhere!'

'Somewhere warm, I hope?' Georgia joked.

'Oh, yes. Quite warm.'

He stepped inside, and the door closed behind him. Jack watched as the green light inside his door turned red. It was his only annoyance; they had forbidden him to cover the red LED while he slept. It was his constant reminder that he was a prisoner and his whole life was dictated by that ridiculous LED light.

Georgia finished her run and radioed that she had completed that evening's lockdown.

In the Citadel, the main screen in front of Gerry that showed the status of the cells in A-Wing had turned red. All the doors were locked. The same was true of the VP wing and the women's wing. Everything was just as it should be.

Twenty

Kellerman glanced at the digital clock above his head and sighed. It was approaching midnight, and there was still no sign that Gerry was any closer to working out the alien code that bothered him so much. He wasn't even sure he knew what it was about the system that bothered him, but he could sense the anxiety in his chest.

He stood away from his desk and walked over to the window that looked out on to the prison. Harsh lights shone down from the highest points of the prison and bathed everything in a crisp, white light. Here and there, shadows formed, and everything had a surreal, almost black-and-white existence.

'Looks like the storm's almost blown itself out,' he remarked to his reflection in the glass.

Gerry looked up. His eyes were reddened around the corners where the constant glare of his monitors had dried them out. He looked out of the window to where Kellerman was focused and smiled. The snow no longer drove in over the prison walls in a mad frenzy. It still fell, though less heavy than before, and it seemed to drift down from the sky in an almost leisurely fashion.

'Do you think we'll be able to get off the island tomorrow?' Gerry asked.

Kellerman looked back at Gerry and said, 'I hope so.' He looked back at the prison and said to himself, *I fucking hope so!*

Gerry felt it too. The prison was a claustrophobic place at the best of times, but knowing you couldn't get off the island had a jarring effect on the soul. He'd go stir-crazy if he had to stay on the island much longer.

***

Georgia Hope wrestled with a wave of tiredness that swept over her. She yawned and sat bolt upright in her chair.

The officer's room in the male wing of BlackRock was on the first floor, and they looked down over the cells. She glanced out over the view and then at her watch. It was just short of midnight, and the clock seemed to be ticking even slower than usual.

She also felt the claustrophobia of the prison, but it wasn't the case that their isolation had caused it. It was a feeling she could never shake, and she still had another three weeks of her rotation left to serve. She couldn't put her finger on it, but the prison had a bad vibe.

It had been a fantastic opportunity, to begin with. Her pay almost doubled, and it suited her lifestyle. She had no ties and commitments, and in the weeks she had off the island, she was able to satisfy her every whim. But still. She didn't like it, and on nights like these, her mind wandered to better places and better jobs.

Her eyes scanned the floor below. The lights had been dimmed, and everything seemed dark and unfamiliar. The little red LEDs on the doors of the cells winked back at her, like devil's eyes in the night. She shivered. And then she noticed something that didn't feel right, but she couldn't entirely focus on what it was. She concentrated even harder but gave it up as a bad job. It was too far away, and she couldn't tell what it was or even if it was anything at all. It was probably nothing. Just her mind playing tricks in the shadows.

She'd investigate it during her next floor walk in an hour. She'd have a coffee first.

***

Lovelace stood at the window in her bedroom and looked out at the landscape beyond. She had draped a robe over her shoulders and stood by the window, shivering in the darkness. Outside, the snow no longer fell as heavily, and it came down gently, almost casually. She heard Grace fidget behind her.

'Come back to bed. It's freezing.' She said.

'In a minute.' Lovelace replied. 'I think the storm's passed over.'

'Good. I want to get away from here now.'

Lovelace smiled. It had been a long few days. Too long. It was time it came to an end, she thought, reaching out into the darkness and closing the curtains. She turned back to Grace and let the robe drop from her shoulders. She climbed back into bed and snuggled in. Grace was still half asleep. She could sense it in the way her breathing was shallow and rhythmic.

Lovelace lay there in the darkness and let her mind wander. So much had happened in the last few days. She wasn't sure she knew where it was all leading or if there would be a happy ending for anyone. She felt sorry for Elouise and Johnathon, and she felt their pain. But would either of them survive the reckoning?

She didn't know Sir Malcolm very well and didn't much care for him. Would there be a reckoning for him? A wealthy, powerful old man? Maybe. Probably not. Justice was a fickle creature and often subject to the whims and fancies of other wealthy, powerful old men.

And what about her and Grace? What future was there?

She felt Grace snuggle in closer as if she had sensed her thoughts. She hadn't made her mind up about that, but she knew the time was nearly upon them.

She lay awake, holding Grace tightly to her. Time was ticking.

***

The mainland operations centre had gone deathly quiet. Outside, more TV crews had made the perilous journey across the snow-laden Scottish countryside and were setting up bases along the road that led up to the security fence.

Inside, DCI McBride poured himself another whiskey and relished the burn as he swallowed the amber liquid. He was getting bored now. He missed the comforts of home and his bed.

DS Sandhu had taken a small armchair that Liam Swift had brought over from his office, and she curled up in it and fell asleep.

Liam Swift had taken a seat near McBride and was working quietly on his laptop.

'This might please you,' he said abruptly, bringing McBride out of his own little world.

'What's that?' McBride asked gruffly.

'Weather forecast for the next twenty-four hours.' Swift said, smiling.

McBride sat up.

Swift went on, 'the worst of the storm has passed us. The winds will be considerably reduced in the next few hours, and the snow will slowly turn to rain. I've e-mailed our flight operations team, who agree that we should be able to get a flight out to the island in the morning.'

McBride beamed. Soon, he'd be able to get to the island and put this thing to bed. The list of suspects for Mackay's murder was small. Once off the island, he'd be able to set about them individually. The guests on BlackRock had quite a lot to answer for.

Excellent, he thought. It would all soon be over.

***

She sat in her car and watched as the TV crews arrived and set up along the approach road to BlackRock's mainland operations centre. The wind had reduced considerably since her arrival, and the snow no longer fell as it did.

They didn't know the right story, she thought to herself as she watched journalists to and fro. But they soon would.

She answered her phone on the second ring.

'This had better be good news,' she said, without waiting for the other person to speak.

There was a pause. 'Seb, tell me there's good news.'

'Good and bad.' Seb said slowly.

She sighed. Why did things have to be so complicated? 'Tell me.'

'People don't like to be woken on nights like these. Especially important people.'

'But?'

'I'm waiting on a call back from an old mate. I've had to play all my old favours for this one.'

'Thank you, Seb. You know I'm good for it.'

She hung up and dropped her phone on the seat next to her. It wouldn't be long now.

***

It played on Georgia's mind. It niggled at her and troubled her. At first, she didn't identify the cause of her unease, and it felt like a harmless touch of anxiety until she sat back down at her desk and her eyes were drawn back to the darkness on the floor of A-Wing.

What the fuck was it?

She placed her coffee on the table in front of her and stood up. She draped her jacket over her shoulders and walked over to the door of the office. A colleague sat at a desk nearby and looked up.

'Where you off?' He asked, glancing at his watch. 'It's almost an hour before your floor sweep.'

'Something's bugging me,' she said. 'I'll be back in a minute.'

She opened the door and stepped through it into a quiet corridor. Ahead of her, the steps to A-Wing's floor fell away, and she took the steps two at a time. Her feet made little sound as she walked across the floor to where she thought she had seen something odd. On either side of her, the cell doors were closed, and the red LEDs shone brightly—Devil's eyes. Behind the doors, she knew that some inmates would still be awake, watching TV or reading. Lights-out was due shortly.

She reached the edge of the floor and looked at the front door. At night, even the front entrance was locked. No one went outside after ten. And yet, the LED was green, not red. It had been that that had upset her mind. She was used to seeing the door glow red during the night shift and hadn't been used to it being green. It had confused her mind and given rise to her anxiety.

275

She reached for her radio and spoke into it. 'Six-One to control, receiving?'

The radio spat static at her for a moment before a voice came back. 'Control receiving. Go ahead, Six-One.'

'Evening Gerry,' Georgia said as she recognised the voice. 'It's probably nothing, but I've got a green light at the front door.'

'Stand by, Six-One.'

Gerry liked Georgia and would typically have called her by her first name, but he was painfully aware of Kellerman's presence. He looked up at his status monitor and found the offending door. Georgia was right. It was green.

'Is the door open?' He asked into the radio.

Georgia tried the handle, the door flew open, and a wave of cold air flew in. 'That's a yes-yes, control.'

Gerry could see. He had moved the camera overlooking the door to see it open.

'Okay. Stand by Six-One.'

Gerry felt Kellerman rise from his seat and take position over his left shoulder.

'What is it? What's going on?'

'Just a glitch,' Gerry said confidently. 'It's an easy fix.'

Kellerman watched as Gerry's fingers danced rapidly over the keys of his computer. It always amazed him how fast these people could type. It was unnatural.

'That's odd.' Gerry said.

'What? What's odd?' Kellerman asked, and Gerry couldn't help but sense the panic in his voice.

'I can't seem to get into my programme.'

'Why not? What's wrong? Have you forgotten your password?'

Gerry looked up at Kellerman like a schoolteacher at one of his students. 'It's not my password. I've been locked out.'

'How? Why? What do you mean?' He was about to go through a hundred more impossible questions when his eyes picked up another green light on Gerry's status monitor. 'Where's that one?'

Gerry turned and looked at the screen. 'Shit.' He spoke into his radio, and Kellerman picked up on the timbre of his voice. Gerry was scared. 'Er... Control to Six-One, could you do a status check on cell Thirty-Three.'

Georgia looked down the length of A-Wing to where Thirty-Three should be but couldn't see the door. 'Stand by Control. Going to take a closer look.'

She strolled through the wing and arrived at door Thirty-Three a little while later. She felt a lump in her throat. 'Six-One to Control. The door is green. I repeat the door is open.'

Kellerman reached down for his radio and tuned it into a different frequency. It was the frequency security was using that evening. He was about to speak into it when the words froze in his mouth. He watched in horror as all the A-Wing doors turned green on the status monitor.

'Fuck.' Kellerman said, 'fucking fix it. Now!' He screamed at Gerry. Gerry turned and desperately tapped away at his keyboard. Into his radio, Kellerman said, 'security to A-Wing. Code Five. I repeat, Security to A-Wing, Code Five.'

Gerry sat back in his chair and slowly turned to face Kellerman. His face had turned white.

'I can't... I can't get in. And...' The words failed him. Gerry turned and pointed to the status monitor.

'This can't be happening.' Kellerman said, dumbstruck. He watched the status monitor as every red LED in BlackRock turned green. Every door was opened, including the Citadel, the VP Wing and B-Wing.

Reluctantly, Kellerman pressed the emergency button on his radio which broadcast his voice across all frequencies. 'Code Ten. Code Ten. All staff, this is an emergency Code Ten.'

Gerry started to get up.

'Where the fuck are you going?' Kellerman demanded to know.

'Code Ten. That's an evacuation order. We should head to the Safe Room.'

There were several Safe Rooms on BlackRock, and Kellerman knew that all of the staff on duty were heading there for their safety.

'Not you!' Kellerman spat. 'I told you there was a problem, but you were too fucking arrogant to see it. So you can stay there and help me regain control of the prison.'

Gerry sat back in his seat. 'It's only a matter of time before they begin to realise the prison's not locked down,' Gerry cried. He pointed to the door of the Citadel. 'We're not safe here.'

'Then you don't have long, do you?' Kellerman said. Then, speaking into his radio, he said, 'Security to the Citadel. We're going to need some help here.'

Gerry felt a slight sense of relief. He turned and looked back at the security monitors in A-Wing. Shit. He'd forgotten about Georgia.

Georgia was standing outside door Thirty-Three when the Code Ten came down over the radio. She stepped back from the door and turned to walk away. She slowly realised that heading into the Wing to check on cell Thirty-Three had complicated matters for her. Had she been at the front door, she could have slipped out and been in one of the Safe Rooms by now. As it was, she was a long way from safety and in the middle of A-Wing. Her heart missed a beat as she realised that all the doors in the wing were now glowing green. Her heart damn near stopped as the cell doors began to open.

With panic slowly rising, she carefully walked towards the front door. It was unlikely that any prisoners were fully aware of what was happening. She still had time.

She was a hundred yards from the front entrance when a hand grabbed her from behind. Her attacker had grabbed her arms and pinned one of them down, but she struggled to free her other and slammed her elbow into his face with all her might. She turned to face him and watched as he went down, clutching a broken nose.

One by one, they started to come for her. Slowly, fearful of reprisals from other guards, they encircled her and drove towards her. Emboldened by the fact that no other guards were around, they attacked. They clawed at her and punched her. She felt the blows rain down furiously, and she was powerless to stop them. Some kicked and punched and spat at her, while some clawed at her clothes and started pulling them off.

And then they stopped.

She pulled herself up and dragged herself over to a wall. She could taste the blood dripping down her face and pooling in her mouth. Her body ached from the punches and the kicks, and her right eye was awash with blood. Through her good eye, she looked up to see what had happened.

Robert Askwith was standing in front of her, his arms by his side and his giant fists clenched. Two or three inmates were lying around his feet, and she guessed that he had pulled them off her and given them a slap for good measure. She had never been more grateful to see a man in her entire life.

'Now then,' Askwith said calmly, with his well-enunciated London accent. 'Anyone who wants the girl comes through me first.'

The gangland enforcer's reputation superseded him. The once emboldened mob hesitated. Askwith turned and looked at Georgia. 'If they change their minds, and they probably will, I may not be able to hold them for long. If I were you, I'd be somewhere else.'

He turned and faced the others. 'Right. Who's first?'

Georgia scrambled to her feet and began to walk away. The front door was tantalisingly close. As she approached it, Claus Fischer, the serial rapist, appeared at his cell door. He smiled at her through broken and yellowed teeth.

'Not going, are you?' He asked. 'What's the hurry?'

He reached up and ran his hand down her face, brushing her hair so it fell behind her ears.

'So pretty...'

She wasn't sure she had the breath in her body to fight him off, but she was damned if he was going to get her easily. She braced herself for the fight she knew would come. And then, for the second time in as many minutes, she was grateful for the intervention of another man. Jack Lovelace appeared from his cell and launched into the back of Fischer's head with a sock loaded with stones. It was an old-fashioned method, but it worked. Fischer crumbled at Georgia's feet.

She looked up at Jack's friendly face. 'Quickly, my dear,' Jack beckoned, 'before anyone sees you. You'll be safe in here.'

Georgia stepped through the door into Jack's cell and turned to her saviour. Jack Lovelace turned, grabbed Georgia's head, and slammed it into the wall. Georgia felt the pain streak across her eyes, and she fought the darkness for a second before falling to the floor.

'Stupid fucking girl,' Jack snarled and turned and closed his cell door.

In the Citadel, Kellerman and Gerry watched Georgia's fate play out in front of them. They were helpless to intervene, and even if they tried, they'd most likely be killed themselves. They were still watching when Jack Lovelace stepped out of his cell and rescued her. They were grateful for small mercies.

The door to the Citadel flew open, and Rupert and three fellow security officers raced in. They were armed with all manner of strange items, and to Gerry's eyes, they looked like a pleasingly tough bunch of characters.

'Come on. We have to go.' Rupert said, 'you can't stay here. It's not safe.'

They were words that brought joy to Gerry's expression. Kellerman didn't feel the same.

'We can't go. We need to regain control of the prison.'

'That's not happening.' Rupert said firmly. 'We've lost the island. All we can do now is get somewhere safe and wait for the mainland to come with force. We need to sit tight and wait it out.'

Kellerman faltered. 'Okay. But I need to call the Mansion House and tell Johnathon what's happening.'

'Okay. Be quick.'

Kellerman reached out for the telephone that joined the two halves of the island and pressed One. It rang for an age. No one answered.

Gerry was standing nearby, ready to leave. He had taken shelter between two guards and intended to stay there. 'Forget about them,' Gerry cried. 'They'll know soon enough. It's not our problem.'

Kellerman looked up at Gerry and regretted the day they had ever employed him. 'Get that man out of my sight before I do something I may regret.'

Rupert looked up at his two men and nodded. 'Get him out of here. Get him to a safe room.'

When they had gone, Rupert, looked down at Kellerman and said, 'what do you need to do?'

'They need to know what's happening. We can't leave them exposed.'

'I agree.' Rupert said. 'We can get a car and drive down.'

'No need.' Kellerman said, remembering a conversation he had been involved in as BlackRock was being built. 'Johnathon was pretty strict on security. He had Mackay install a World War Two type air raid warning system. If we set that off, they won't miss it.'

'Okay. Where do we set it off from? Is it computerised?'

'Fortunately not,' Kellerman said as he glanced at Gerry's monitor. 'There's a button in Johnathon's office in the prison.'

Rupert knew the office well. It wasn't far from where they were now, and it was on the way to the safe room. 'Okay. Let's go. Stay at my side at all times. Be aware.'

Kellerman grabbed his jacket, and the two left the room and descended the stairs until the front door was ahead of them.

Rupert turned and looked at Kellerman. 'Anything kicks off, make a run for Preece's office. Don't look back. Set off the alarm and get yourself into a safe room. Ready?'

Kellerman braced himself. 'Ready.'

***

When Kellerman had ordered Gerry to be sent away from the Citadel, Gerry practically leapt with joy. His two guards barely spoke. They communicated with each other through a series of looks and hand gestures. One of them turned Gerry around and physically shoved him out of the control room and down the stairs to the front door.

'Wait here.' One of the guards commanded. He drew a weapon from a pouch and nudged the door open. Cold air swept in, and the guard swept out. He returned a few seconds later. 'We need to go now. We're very exposed, and we'll be lit up all the way to the main building.'

Gerry thought about that for a moment. The Citadel was an isolated part of the prison far from the main block. To get to safety, they would have to cross several hundred yards of open ground, past the now unlocked security fences surrounding A-Wing, B-Wing and the VP Wing. With the security lights still ablaze, there would be no place to hide. It would be a mad dash across the yard, through the ice and snow, to the main building. Gerry regretted the diet that had left him so overweight. He wasn't built for speed.

'Ready?' The guard asked.

The second guard didn't wait for an answer and pushed Gerry through the open door and into the prison yard. Gerry dared not look up. He kept his head down and followed the guard in front. His feet fell heavily onto the snow-covered ground; on several occasions, he felt sure he was about to slip and fall over. They were halfway across the open yard when the worst happened. Gerry's foot caught a slither of ice beneath the snow, and he went down hard. He felt the pain as he held his arms out in front of him and his wrists snapped as he made contact with the floor.

The lead guard turned and swore. Gerry's scream pierced the night air and echoed around them. If they hadn't been noticed before, they had now. The guards watched in despair as the doors to the security fences swung open, and several inmates advanced on them. The guard following Gerry leant down and tried to pick him up, but his weight was excessive, and Gerry could not help himself. He turned and watched the progress as more inmates flooded out of A-Wing. Some had seen the three men come to a stop halfway across the yard and took advantage of Gerry's fall. They approached rapidly. Other inmates had crossed to B-Wing in the hunt for the women prisoners while others crossed to the VP Wing intent on killing.

'For fuck's sake, you need to get up!' One of the guards screamed at Gerry, but it was to no avail. Gerry rolled around in the snow and cried like a baby, his broken hands held out in front of him. He tried to get up but couldn't. He slipped with the effort and fell back into the snow.

'Fuck him,' the lead guard shouted to his colleague. 'Just leave him.' He turned without waiting for an answer and took off towards the main building.

The second guard reached down and clawed at Gerry's collar, trying desperately to help him to his feet, but Gerry couldn't find a grip on the ice and snow. The guard turned just as several prisoners approached. He drew his weapon, fired at one of them, and watched as several thousand volts shot through his body. He dropped to the snow, immobilised, but the others sped on. The guard released his truncheon from his waist and braced for the attack.

They came at them in a primal rage. The guard held them at bay for a few seconds before they descended en masse. He dropped to his knees as the blows kept coming, and he felt a numbing pain as something sharp pierced his back. He fell to the floor and struggled for breath before the darkness came for him.

***

Kellerman was hot on Rupert's heels as they exited the Citadel and made off across the prison yard. As they neared the point at which Gerry had fallen, Rupert stopped. He watched as four or five prisoners lay into a figure lying on the floor. One of the prisoners was holding a metal rod, about a foot in length and was using it to stab the figure lying motionless in the snow. When they had finished, they turned to another figure a few feet away. Rupert watched as Gerry sat in the snow, begging for his life, while the mob descended.

'We need to do something,' Kellerman cried as the prisoner with the metal rod fell on Gerry and plunged it deep into his body.

Rupert had already moved, even though he knew it was too late. He crossed the space between where he had been standing and where Gerry was being attacked in less than three seconds, and he launched himself at the prisoner. They both tumbled back into the snow, and Rupert was quickly back on his feet, slamming his fists into the prisoner. He grappled the metal rod from the prisoner's hands and used it to beat him across the side of the head. He went down like a rag-doll, and the blood gushed from the wound in his head. Rupert turned, faced the other prisoners, and braced himself for the attack he knew would come. They were within a couple of feet when the door to the main building flew open, and half a dozen heavily armed security officers descended on the prisoners. They ran into them with an intense fury, launching rubber bullets and electrified barbs from Tazers as they went. They fell into the prisoners as they dropped and beat them senseless with everything they had. No quarter was given, and Rupert couldn't have been prouder.

Kellerman made Gerry's side a few moments later and tried desperately to stem the blood flow from the several wounds he had endured. Rupert knelt by his side, and together they attempted to establish how severe his injuries were. Seconds later, Gerry's eyes rolled back into his head, and he was gone.

Rupert looked at Kellerman and shook his head. 'It's no use. He's dead.'

Kellerman looked at Gerry's lifeless body in disbelief. It had all been so quick. He hadn't stood a chance.

Rupert held his hand out and helped Kellerman to his feet. 'Come on. We need to get away from here. We won't be able to keep them at bay for long.'

Rupert led Kellerman to the main building, turned back to his men, and watched as they fought a fighting withdrawal. Their job was to save who they could, retire to a defensive position, and wait for backup from the mainland. The contingency plan for this situation had them holding the main entrance for as long as possible before seeking refuge in one of the safe rooms.

'Right,' Rupert declared as his men withdrew into the building. 'Hold this door. Don't let anyone through.' To Kellerman, he said, 'let's set this alarm off, shall we? Then perhaps we can get somewhere safe?'

Kellerman led the way through the unlocked corridors to Jonathon's office and let himself in. There was a locked glass box on the wall at the furthest end of the room that looked like a fire alarm. Beneath it, a small hammer hung from a chain. Kellerman smashed the glass and pulled the lever down.

***

'What the hell is that?' Grace asked, sitting bolt upright in bed.

Lovelace swung her legs out of bed and started to get dressed. 'That sounds like trouble,' she said. 'Get dressed.'

As they opened the bedroom door, they found Elouise and Johnathon leaving theirs.

'What is that?' Grace asked. 'It sounds like an air raid siren!'

'That's essentially what it is,' Johnathon admitted. 'There must be trouble at the prison. We need to get to the safe room.'

They knocked on Sir Malcolm's door as they passed it, but no reply came from within. Lovelace opened the door and shone a light inside. Sir Malcolm wasn't there.

'He must still be in the lounge,' Lovelace said. She took Grace's hand, 'we'll go and get him. Don't lock the safe room before we get there!'

The two groups parted ways at the top of the staircase. Elouise walked with her husband, and Lovelace and Grace disappeared into the lounge.

It was dark in the lounge. Several candles had long since gone out, and a single oil lamp was still alight next to the sleeping figure of Sir Malcolm.

It took almost two minutes to rouse the old man from his slumber. He sat up and coughed, 'what is it? What the bloody hell's the matter?' As the fog cleared from his head, he added, 'what's that bloody noise?'

'It's a siren, Sir Malcolm,' Grace said soothingly. 'We think something's wrong at the prison. We need to get to the safe room.'

They helped the old man to his feet and walked him, unsteadily, down the staircase and towards the safe room.

Elouise had already set up several oil lamps and candles, and Johnathon was lying across one of the sofas. Maeve stood at the door waiting. She helped the two young women get Sir Malcolm into a comfortable chair before Maeve turned to Elouise and said, 'I think I should go up to the prison and see what's going on.'

'Bloody good idea,' Sir Malcolm enthused, 'Probably a false alarm.'

'I can't let you do that,' Johnathon said weakly. 'It's not protocol. You have to stay here. Where it's safe.'

'Johnathon's right,' Elouise agreed. 'It's probably not safe.'

'I can't stay here, not if there's something I can do.'

'Then you should go,' Lovelace said firmly. 'But stay safe and come back if there's trouble. We'll let you in.'

Maeve smiled and looked to Elouise for her consent. Elouise nodded and said, 'don't do anything silly. The people in that prison are not worth your protection.'

Maeve turned and left the safe room, closing the door behind her.

Lovelace took a seat, and Grace sat next to her. Elouise poured wine for them all and sat across from them. Sir Malcolm closed his eyes and began to nod off.

After they had sat silently for some time, Elouise looked across at Lovelace and held her eyes. 'You know who killed Mackay, don't you?' She said firmly.

'Yes. I do.' Lovelace said.

'And Sampson and Esther. You know who killed them, don't you?'

'I do.' Lovelace admitted.

Sir Malcolm's eyes opened.

Elouise said, 'don't you think it's time you let us all in on the secret?'

'It's no secret,' Lovelace said slowly. 'I know as much as anyone else does. We've all been privy to the same information. We could all easily have come to the same conclusion.'

'And that conclusion is?'

'Okay,' Lovelace agreed. 'I'll tell you what I think....'

Twenty-One

Lovelace paced the floor of the safe room, gathering her thoughts. Sir Malcolm's interest had been piqued, and he powered through the lethargy that half a bottle of whiskey had wrought upon his body. Elouise sat upright in a nearby armchair, and Johnathon sat up on the sofa. Grace took a chair near Elouise, and the small crowd watched as Lovelace addressed them.

'Firstly,' she began, marshalling her thoughts, 'I think it's important to iterate that before we all came to BlackRock, I knew none of you, and none of you had ever met me. Being an outsider gave me considerable insight into you all, and I could view the events that followed with unbiased and dispassionate eyes.'

Elouise looked at Grace and smiled. How unbiased was she now, she wondered.

'I had heard of some of you, of course,' Lovelace added, 'there are few people in the world that haven't heard of Ethan Mackay. I knew of Sir Malcolm and heard of Esther Friedman, but I hadn't met any of you before we came to this island.

'I credit myself with being a good judge of character. I know people. I know how they tick, what makes them who they are, and, importantly, what people are capable of, given the right circumstances. When we came to BlackRock a few days ago, all those circumstances convened at the right time and place. My addition was entirely circumstantial. But I could see it. I saw it all.'

She paused for a long time and watched the faces of her audience, looking for some indication across their faces that told her that they knew that she knew. None came. They all wore their expressions like players at a poker game.

Lovelace went on. 'Ethan Mackay has to be one of the most unpleasant men I have ever met, and I've met a few. He was a powerful man, and he used that power to control and coerce people so that they fell in line with whatever it was he demanded of them. Ethan Mackay controlled most of the people that came to this island, and I suppose there was a certain inevitability to his murder. I wasn't expecting it, but it didn't surprise me when it happened.

'The trip to the island was carefully planned and choreographed by Mackay. Everything he did was carefully plotted to remind everyone that he was in charge and knew things that could destroy reputations. He started by insisting that all the guest rooms were named after people who had committed crimes similar to those committed by those who were to stay in them.'

Lovelace turned and looked directly at Sir Malcolm. 'He seemed to toy with you the most, Sir Malcolm. He took great pleasure in winding you up. During the meal we had on the night of Mackay's murder, he turned the conversation to some of the men held in the prison, particularly the number of serial killers. I believe you informed Mackay that five serial killers were held in BlackRock. Isn't that right, Johnathon?'

Johnathon looked up wearily. 'Yes. I believe I did.'

'He definitely said there were five.' Elouise added.

'Yes. He did.' Lovelace continued. '"*Possibly even six, on the island,*"' She added, looking directly at Sir Malcolm. 'What do you think he meant by that, Sir Malcolm?'

Sir Malcolm fidgeted in his chair. 'Couldn't say what the man meant.' He said solemnly.

'I think he meant you, Sir Malcolm. I'm sure Mackay had enough information on you to lay the deaths of several people at your door. That's why he named your bedroom after the infamous Dr Harold Shipman. When

Mr Kellerman said there were no doctors in BlackRock, Mackay said, *"Not yet, eh, Sir Malcolm."* I'm entirely convinced that Mackay had some serious dirt on you, and I'm equally sure that you are more than capable of exacting your revenge by plunging a knife into his back.'

Sir Malcolm puffed his chest out as if he were about to refute the allegation entirely before saying, 'yes, I suppose you could see it like that. But I didn't kill Mackay. Nor did I kill that security guard, and why would I want to harm Esther Friedman?'

Lovelace thought about that for a second. 'I'm sure Esther has been murdered, and I'm equally sure that her body has been thrown to the sea, and we may never know exactly what she knew, but she was a clever woman. She was an investigative journalist who had a keen eye for secrets. Unlike Mackay, she wouldn't have used those secrets against you, but she would have certainly made your life difficult. That's what she did for a living. She dug out dirty secrets and asked difficult questions. Questions like *"do you have any skeletons in your closet or have you had them all cremated?"'*

Sir Malcolm looked distinctly uncomfortable. Lamely, he said, 'well, I didn't kill anyone. I didn't do anything.'

'No. I don't think you killed anyone either, Sir Malcolm,' Lovelace said, 'at least, not on the island. I think the police may have some questions for you, however. I wouldn't count your chickens just yet.'

Lovelace watched as Sir Malcolm puffed out his chest and slid back into his chair. 'I'm not the only one he picked on. Esther came in for some stick too. And this lot,' he added, pointing at the others in the room.

'Yes, you're quite right.' Lovelace continued. 'In fact, the only person he didn't have any dirt on was me, and I suspect that was largely due to the fact he wasn't expecting me to stay here.'

'It did annoy him.' Grace said. 'He liked to control everything. Your being here really riled him.'

'I know.' Lovelace said. 'He tried his hand with me, but I'm afraid men like Mackay don't bother me in the slightest. I may have upset him a little bit.'

'You did tell him to go fuck himself,' Grace remarked.

'I did, and I'm sorry that you and Elouise had to deal with the fallout. That wasn't my intention.'

Elouise instinctively felt for the bruise that had long since faded. The memory lingered. Grace reached out and placed her hand on her arm.

'And you are right, Sir Malcolm.' Lovelace continued. 'Mackay's games weren't entirely directed at you. He knew that Esther Friedman had been married before and that her husband had died in mysterious circumstances. He likened her story to that of Florence Maybrick, who was jailed for poisoning her husband over a hundred years ago. But I'd have to say that Esther wasn't bothered by it much. *"He doesn't know what he thinks he knows."* And by that, she either meant that she played no part in her husband's death and was entirely innocent, or she was confident that no evidence could be found to do her any harm. Either way, she had no real reason to kill Mackay and the fact that she's no longer with us suggests that she's not the guilty party.'

'But why would anyone want to kill Esther?' Grace asked.

'She said something to me quite early on,' Lovelace explained, 'which goes a long way to answering that question. She said *"I'll find out your secrets, you know, I always do."*'

'You think she went digging?' Elouise asked.

'I do.' Lovelace admitted. 'Esther Friedman died because she found something out. Something that someone was prepared to kill for.' Lovelace turned and faced Johnathon. 'Like killing an innocent woman in a car crash and setting someone else up to take the blame. Someone who later committed suicide.'

Johnathon dropped his head into his hands and sobbed.

'That's unkind,' Elouise said as she got up and walked over to her husband. She sat next to him and pulled him closer to her.

'It may be unkind,' Lovelace said, 'but it's true. Your husband made the mistake of seeking Mackay's help to make the mess go away, which Mackay was pleased to do. But Mackay's help came at a considerable cost. It cost Johnathon a lifetime of servitude, and it cost you, too, didn't it, Elouise? It brought Mackay into your life, and it brought his focus onto your past, didn't it? He named Johnathon's room after a gay serial killer, and he named your room after Edith Thompson, an unfortunate woman hanged more for her morality than her crimes. What similarities were there between Edith Thompson's case and yours?'

Elouise glared at Lovelace. 'There were no similarities. Ethan was clutching at straws.'

'That's not entirely true,' Lovelace went on. 'Edith Thompson was married to a man a few years older than her and was engaged in an affair with a younger man. Not unlike you and Johnathon?'

'Yes, Johnathon and I were having an affair while I was still married. But Edith Thompson's lover murdered her husband. Johnathon never harmed a hair on my husband's head, and neither did I.'

'No, but when he fell ill, you did nothing to help, did you? You watched your husband die and did nothing to try and save him. You confessed as much to me.'

'It's true,' Elouise said softly. 'I watched my first husband die, and I have no regrets. I didn't commit any crimes. I'm not a murderer.'

'But you have the potential.' Lovelace pressed on. 'I think you're a capable woman, and you're more than up to stabbing Mackay in the back and getting rid of Esther Friedman. They were two very nosey people who had taken more than a keen interest in the lives and loves of the Preeces. I think you are just the sort of person who would kill to protect her family.'

'But what about the guard? Sampson? Why would I kill him?' Elouise asked, not for a second denying the truth in Lovelace's words.

Lovelace shrugged. 'It could have been that he witnessed something that sealed his fate.'

'All seems a bit tenuous to me,' Sir Malcolm said.

'I agree,' Lovelace said. 'It is all very tenuous, but I don't believe that either Elouise or Johnathon killed Ethan Mackay.'

Everyone turned and looked at Grace.

'But that just leaves me?' Grace said, and Lovelace felt the pain as it crossed her face.

'Yes, it does, Grace,' Lovelace said slowly. 'Because you murdered Ethan Mackay and Wayne Sampson.'

***

The room fell silent. Grace's eyes never left Lovelace's.

'What are you saying?' Grace asked, and her eyes welled with tears.

'I'm saying you murdered Mackay and the security guard, Wayne Sampson.' Lovelace said firmly. 'I didn't know at first, not until the guard was murdered and then it all sort of fell into place.'

'But why?' Elouise asked. 'Why would she kill Ethan? He's worth more to her alive than dead?'

'Because he underestimated you, Grace.' Lovelace explained. 'He didn't understand you, and he never saw you coming. That's why he named your bedroom "Lemon." It seemed odd at first, and then we had that conversation over dinner on the night of Mackay's murder which explained it. We talked about PG Wodehouse and Agatha Christie. I remember you saying that Poirot was your favourite. The ABC Murders, isn't it? Mackay was very dismissive of the books. He was dismissive of you, wasn't he? That was his mistake. He named your room after Poirot's secretary, Miss Lemon. It was a snide dig at you. You meant nothing to him—just an unforgettable secretary. But you were more than that, weren't you, Grace? You were about to become Mackay's nemesis.'

Grace looked at Lovelace and said nothing.

Lovelace kept watching Grace. 'I remember thinking on the helicopter flight to BlackRock that if the helicopter crashed, you and I would be the ones to survive. I recognised something in you, something I've later come to cherish and admire. You shouldn't fear me, Grace, but don't lie to me.

'As we were getting off the helicopter and seconds before you fell ill, you saw something, or rather someone, that restarted a process that began when you were a little girl. You saw Wayne Sampson. A man you hadn't laid eyes on for many years. The man that killed your brother while he was in prison serving life for murder.

'I began to put it together when Esther said "*he killed a man once, you know,*" and she told me of Sampson's dark history, particularly when he beat a young inmate in one of Mackay's earlier prisons. Then, during the interview after Mackay's murder, I discovered that your brother had died in prison when he was barely eighteen. You idolised your big brother, didn't you? His death hit you hard, didn't it?'

Slowly, Grace said 'yes. I adored him. I was heartbroken when he went to prison. I was inconsolable when he died. He didn't deserve that. He shouldn't have been in prison. He didn't kill anyone.'

'And there was no justice for your brother, was there? Mackay paid people off and made the problem disappear like he always did.'

Grace sniffed. 'Yes. It was buried so deep. No one cared.'

'But you did, Grace.' Lovelace said soothingly. 'You made it your life's work to bring the men responsible to justice, one way or another. You couldn't ever find the man who killed your brother, so you targeted the man who made it all disappear. You went for Ethan Mackay.'

'I did. It was my single focus in life. I worked hard to get myself into a position where I could get a job in Mackay's inner circle. It didn't take long before I was promoted to his PA. All you need to do with men like Mackay is work out how they tick and manipulate them to get what you want. They are not as complicated as they think.'

'What changed, Grace?' Lovelace asked. 'You've been in Mackay's employment for years. You could have moved on him a long time ago. But you didn't.'

'I changed my mind. I enjoyed my life. I lived an expensive life that I could only dream about. We dined at the best restaurants, stayed at the best hotels and flew

297

first class to the most exotic locations. What wasn't there to enjoy?'

'Mackay's company?' Lovelace suggested.

Grace smiled. 'He could be difficult. But you make sacrifices. And I truly believed we were doing good in the world. Like him or not, Mackay's money changed lives and helped people. We did good things.'

'And then you saw Wayne Sampson?'

Grace nodded. 'Yes, that was quite a shock. I hadn't expected that. He had been in Mackay's employment since he murdered my brother. Not only had Sampson not faced justice, but Mackay had also promoted him.'

'You knew Mackay's habits.' Lovelace continued. 'You knew he had a habit of going for midnight snacks, and you sought him out there. He laughed at you. He mocked you. Ignored you. Fatally, he turned his back on you.'

'It all came back to me at once. I was furious. Mackay had used and abused me, and I'd fallen into his web just as surely as anyone else in this room. He controlled me and everything I did. I felt like I had betrayed my brother's memory. I turned around and reached out for something to hit him with, and I picked up a knife from the knife block. It went in surprisingly easily. And then I went back to bed.'

'What happened with Sampson?' Lovelace asked.

'I couldn't let him live. I had to get to him somehow, but you got in the way.' Grace said, looking at Lovelace. 'We spent all our time together. But it didn't matter. I knew I'd get to him sooner or later. I left your room at around four in the morning and went downstairs to see who was guarding the kitchen. I thought there would be more than two at the door, but I found Sampson alone. He didn't take much persuading to leave his post. I offered to do things that would make a ten-dollar hooker blush, and he led me into the kitchen. I suggested that the cellar would be a fun place to go. The idea of doing it so close to Mackay's body seemed to excite him. Men can be weird. When he stepped into the cellar, I reached out with another knife from the knife block and slit his throat. He reached out and clawed at the wall and fell down the stairs. There was blood everywhere. I stood there and watched while he died.'

'Grace… I…' Elouise was shocked.

'They were evil men.' Grace added. 'I don't regret a thing.'

Lovelace walked over to where Grace sat and stroked her hair. 'Thank you, Grace. I'm glad you didn't lie to me.'

'But I don't understand,' Sir Malcolm declared. 'What happened to Esther?'

Grace looked up at Lovelace and said. 'I didn't kill Esther. I swear it.'

'I know you didn't, Grace.' Lovelace replied.

Grace shook her head. 'You can't *know* that,' she cried. 'You can't possibly know that for sure.'

'I can,' Lovelace said reassuringly, 'because I killed Esther Friedman.'

Twenty-Two

DS Sandhu came to with a sudden start. She took a moment while her eyes grew accustomed to the low light and the fog in her head cleared. McBride was still sitting where she had last seen him, and Swift had nodded off in his chair. She felt her mobile phone buzzing on the arm of her chair, and she reached out to answer it. It rang off just as she tried to answer and an alert popped on the screen saying she had six missed calls. She had always been a deep sleeper, but that was ridiculous. She was about to investigate who was so desperate to contact her when the phone lit up again. It was an unknown caller. She answered it on the second ring.

'Hello? DS Sandhu,' she croaked, still half asleep. She sat up in her chair, suddenly alert. 'Yes sir, he's right here next to me. Yes sir. One moment.'

McBride looked up as she came over. She held her phone out for him. 'He's not happy.' She said.

'Who is it?' McBride asked, taking the phone from his DS.

'The Chief Constable.'

McBride paused. The boss never got involved. Never. Especially not at this time of night.

'Sir?' He said cautiously.

Sandhu watched McBride's expression for clues, but her boss remained unflappable.

'Yes, sir. Of course. I'll get on it right away.'

McBride returned the phone to DS Sandhu and looked across at Swift, who had woken at the first sign of activity.

'What is it? What's going on?' Swift asked.

'There's a young woman at the front gate trying to get in to see us. Apparently, it's important. Get someone to bring her in.'

Swift made a quick call to the front gate and waited. The three of them sat in silence as the door to the office flew open, and a young woman in a thick coat and a head of hair that looked as though she had been sleeping rough swept in.

'About time.' She said with no sense of anger. 'Which one of you is in charge?'

'That would be me.' McBride said. 'Detective Chief Inspector McBride. This is my Sergeant DS Sandhu, and this is the head of mainland operations, Mr Swift.'

She held her hand out for McBride and smiled sweetly.

'And who might you be?' McBride asked, and his voice barely covered his annoyance.

'Lovelace.' The young woman said softly. 'My name is Lucy Lovelace, and you have a serious fucking problem.'

***

They looked at Lovelace like she had gone mad. Grace was the first to react. 'But why, Lucy? Why would you kill Esther?'

Lovelace smiled. 'Let's start there, shall we? You'll remember at the start I said that no one here had ever met me before. No one knew me. My name isn't Lucy Lovelace. My name is Zoe. I'm Zoe Lovelace.'

'But you said you were Lucy.' Grace replied, and her frown hinted at her confusion.

'Actually, I didn't,' Zoe said. 'I never once said my name was Lucy. It was assumed that that was my name, and I never corrected anyone.'

'But why?' Elouise asked. 'What's this all about?'

'Well, as we're in a period of revelation, I suppose now's as good a time as any to bring you all up to speed. You see, I'm not here by accident. We're not stuck on this island by accident. I've planned it all meticulously, right down to the last detail. I have to say I'm rather good at planning. And by the time this is over, I will have broken my father out of prison.'

'You're mad,' Johnathon exclaimed. 'It's impossible. No one can get off the island.'

Sir Malcolm agreed. 'Planned it all be damned. You couldn't have planned the storm and cut us off from the mainland. You couldn't have predicted that the helicopter would run into issues. It's all fanciful nonsense.'

Zoe smiled again. 'People have always underestimated me. And, in some ways, you are right about the storm. Well, you're right about this particular storm. I couldn't have made that happen. But storms occur with alarming frequency in this part of the world. All I had to do was wait.'

Zoe pulled up a chair and faced her audience. 'When my father was first jailed for the rest of his natural life, I made it my life's work to get him out. I grew up developing the skills to help me do that and relationships with people to facilitate that goal. I have become remarkably good at what I do.

'My biggest problem was that they sent my father to HMP Long Lartin in Worcestershire, a seriously heavily defended Super Max facility seemingly in the middle of nowhere. Unfortunately, it is a thirty-minute flight from Stirling Lines in Hereford, and the last thing I wanted was to face down some pissed-off-looking blokes from the SAS. As prisoners of the state, all prisoners are technically political prisoners. As detailed as my planning was, I couldn't avoid the oversight of the special forces.

'So when my father was sent here, I started a new train of thought.'

Everyone was watching Zoe with interest.

'I needed to get on the island and to be kept here for a few days. As I said, the storms are pretty predictable. All I had to do was wait. I have a few contacts in high places, and I managed to get a pass to travel here. I timed it so that I could get to the island as the storms were approaching. I never once lied to anyone or travelled under a false name. I had to use my own surname as it was the only way I could legitimately get here. At every step of the way, I used my own identity. I never lied.

'My first problem was at departures at the mainland when I bumped into Esther Friedman. Esther is a remarkable investigative journalist, and I knew very well that she knew all about me and my history. She has set the hounds on my trail a few times, but I have managed to avoid the worst of her scrutiny. The problem was that I knew that if I said I was Zoe, she would realise that something was afoot. That was her nature. She was not a stupid woman. I had half prepared myself to give her a false name, even knowing the issues that would throw up, but events came to pass that meant I didn't have to. One of the men on the mainland came into departures and introduced me as Lucy Lovelace. It seemed an ideal cover, so I didn't correct him.'

***

'Shit.' Swift said, sifting through the piles of paper that littered his desk. He found a typed sheet and read it in disbelief. 'Z. Lovelace.'

He handed the sheet to McBride.

'So why the fuck did we think that was Lucy Lovelace?' McBride asked. All eyes were turned to Swift.

Who the fuck is Sir Malcolm Zambert?

The memory came back to him instantly. A broken printer. A handwritten manifest.

That's an "L", not a "Z."

Swift looked at McBride and shook his head. He didn't know how to explain. He had seen the "Z" and assumed it was an "L". Lucy Lovelace. The famous daughter of the infamous Jack Lovelace. He wasn't even sure he *knew* there was a sister.

'I think that's my fault,' Swift said apologetically.

***

'Once my cover was established, I set my plan into motion.'

'Bloody nonsense,' Sir Malcolm sniffed. 'There was no way you could predict that the helicopter would run into issues or that you would be stuck here with us. It's impossible.'

'Not impossible,' Zoe corrected him. 'Difficult but not impossible. Once the helicopter landed on the island, I activated a small device disguised as a mobile phone. It was a very convincing phone. It worked just like any other and could withstand basic scrutiny. Most countries have similar devices or are at least developing them. I got mine from the Chinese, with whom I have a close relationship. It's a small Electro-Magnetic Pulse device which interrupts electrical equipment up to a hundred-meter radius. More than enough to disrupt the controls of a sophisticated machine like a helicopter. All I had to do was hope that engineers from the mainland couldn't be despatched in time to fix the problem. Even if they were, I had a plan for that.'

Zoe turned and looked at Grace. 'I'm afraid EMP devices can also interrupt frequencies used by the human body. It can make some people nauseous and give them a wicked headache.'

'That's why I felt so bad getting off the helicopter?' Grace said.

'I'm afraid so. The further away you got from the helicopter, the better you would have felt. It's why your illness was so short-lived.'

Zoe turned and faced the others.

'I shared a car with Esther to the prison. She was a shrewd woman, and I had to choose my words carefully. I knew she would try and pump me for information, and I had to be very careful with what I said to her. I had a feeling she was going to be troublesome.

'Once at the prison, I set the second part of my plan into action. Once I met my father, I passed him a USB device he could install on the computer in his cell.'

Jonathon scoffed. 'Even if that was possible, the computers in the cells are heavily monitored and have no direct access to BlackRock's mainframe computer.'

'True.' Zoe said. 'But people forget that my father was a specialist computer analyst in his day. Besides, all the USB had on it was a virus. A virus that we could manipulate to give us control of BlackRock. But first,' she continued, 'I needed to restart the island's computers to get the virus in.

'That first evening here was an enlightening one. I rather enjoyed myself. After telling Mackay to go fuck himself, I used the time to go to Johnathon's office and changed how the computers were backed up in the event of a power cut. It took a few seconds. Nothing more. I created a delay in the "Always on" power settings designed to step in and prevent the computers from completely shutting down. I needed a full restart. Once that happened, my virus could do its thing.'

'You couldn't have made the power cut happen,' Sir Malcolm interjected, finding a small hole in Zoe's story.

'By now, you should see that nothing has been left to chance.' Zoe said. 'This day has been years in the planning. Some associates of mine had a small incendiary device fitted to the electrical substation that feeds the island. It was very easy. I didn't need the power off for long, just a few seconds. The continued power cut has made everything so much easier.'

'That's why Sinclair had to die....' The realisation dawned on Grace as she spoke the words.

'Yes.' Zoe agreed. 'My planning had somehow failed to pick up that Adam Sinclair had been transferred to the prison. Once I had assumed Lucy's identity, it needed to remain hidden for as long as possible. My sister knew Adam Sinclair; he was the only person on the island who could safely testify that I wasn't her. My father realised the same thing. When I visited him, I casually remarked that Sinclair would likely get his throat cut in A-Wing. My father took the hint. Once the power cut had restarted the computers and we had access, he could open the doors to his own and Sinclair's cell and cut his throat. I had expected him to leave the knife there to make it look like suicide, but for whatever reason, he decided to take it with him. Intelligent men can be bloody stupid sometimes. Still, it muddied the waters and confused people.'

'But why Esther?' Elouise asked.

'Because she was too clever by half. She began to suspect that I may not be who I said I was. When she said to me *"I'll find out your secrets, you know, I always do,"* I believed her. It was only a matter of time before she started working it out, and I needed a bit more time. Then she started to bang on about the flight manifest, and I realised she knew and was on the hunt for the evidence. She collared Grace outside my room and declared loudly, for my benefit, that *"people aren't what you think. They are not at all who you think they are. People hide things. People hide their true selves. People are deceitful."*

'She was telling me clearly that she knew. It sealed her fate. On the night Grace left and sorted out her issue with Sampson, I stole across to Esther's room and sorted out mine. Once I had dealt with her, I threw her out of the window and into the night. I came down the stairs intending to avoid the guard outside the kitchen, but he wasn't there. I made my way outside, dragged Esther to the cliff edge, and tossed her into the sea. Problem sorted.'

'This is all mad.' Sir Malcolm declared.

'What now?' Elouise asked.

Zoe stood up. 'I'm going to the prison to get my father.'

'That could be very dangerous,' Johnathon said. 'If the prisoners are out of their cells, it could be very dangerous.'

Zoe walked over to the safe room door and placed her hand on it. She turned and looked back at the room. 'Thank you for your concern Johnathon, but they should be more afraid of me.' She looked at Grace, who looked lost and alone. 'Are you coming with me or what?' She asked.

Confusion ran across Grace's face.

'You have a choice, Grace. You can stay here and face your crimes and, most likely, end up in one of these institutions for the best part of your life, or you can come with me. You never lied to me, Grace. I can trust you. I could do with someone like you by my side.'

Elouise stood up. 'Stay here, Grace. Whatever happens, we'll take care of you. You can trust us.'

'As soon as the police start digging into their pasts, they'll throw you to the wolves to save their skins. I promised you I'd take care of you. I meant it.'

Zoe opened the door and waited. Grace stood up and looked at Elouise. 'I'm sorry, but she's right. I need to go.'

Grace walked up to Zoe and out through the safe room door. 'Make sure this door shuts firmly behind us,' Zoe said. 'Don't open it until you know it's safe.'

That said, she closed the door.

***

Lucy Lovelace stood for a long time waiting for someone to do something. No one moved.

''You need to get on the island now!' She declared firmly. 'You don't have long before she breaks my father out of prison.'

'The Civil Aviation Authority has grounded flights. We can't get on the island, and they can't get off.' Swift commented.

'You mustn't underestimate Zoe,' Lovelace said. 'She'll fly off that island, and once she's done that, you'll never see her again.'

Swift shook his head. 'She can't fly a broken helicopter.'

Lovelace looked at him in disbelief and then at McBride. 'Seriously? What the fuck do I have to do, spell it out for you? She would have planned everything. You need to act now.'

McBride hesitated. He would need to escalate to his superiors, who would escalate to the Home Office. Control would need to pass from his hands to the military, who could fly to the island and sort the problem out. But it would take time.

'Okay.' He said slowly, reaching for the telephone. 'I'll pass it up the chain.'

***

Zoe stepped into the flight seat of the Sikorsky 92 and started pressing buttons. She looked across at Grace, who had climbed into the passenger seat.

'Can you fly this?' She asked doubtfully.

'Of course,' Zoe said, smiling. 'She's a beautiful machine.' Then she said 'go to the back, would you? If you remember where I sat on the way over, you'll find my phone underneath the seat. Bring it to me.'

It took a few minutes before Grace climbed back into the front seat and handed Zoe what looked like an ordinary mobile phone. Zoe fiddled with it for a few seconds and then grinned. 'It did its job,' she said. 'It probably had enough juice for a day or so. Better safe than sorry, though. Don't want to lose instruments on a day like today.'

Grace folded the straps of her restraints over her shoulders and clicked them into place. It was dark outside, but the snow kept falling. It was breezy, too, but considerably less than it had been. She braced herself as the motors of the Sikorsky fired into life. Zoe steadily increased the power to the engines.

'No time to run through a safety check.' Zoe declared. 'Ready?'

Grace nodded nervously, and the huge machine climbed into the air. Zoe handled the machine expertly, and Grace began to relax as the ground fell away and the nose of the aircraft tilted towards the mountain. Even though it was dark, the white cliffs swam perilously close to them as they flew over. A few seconds later, the aircraft began to descend, and Zoe brought it close to the front entrance of HMP BlackRock. The snow was whipped up in a fury, and everywhere Grace looked was white. Zoe pulled back on the engines, and the rotors began to slow.

'What now?' Grace asked.

Zoe slipped off her restraints and looked at Grace. 'You should probably come with me. I can't protect you if you're not with me.'

Zoe opened her door and stepped out into the snow. Ahead, the prison was still lit up under the powerful lights that ran around its edge.

'Stay close.' Zoe said as Grace joined her. 'The only people out should be the prisoners. Everyone else should be safely inside the safe rooms. If anyone comes near, stay behind me and don't panic.'

Slowly, Zoe walked toward the prison.

***

'When? Shit.' McBride's face looked crestfallen. He had started informing the powers-that-be of what he believed was happening at BlackRock, but his

311

recommendations were lost in the melee of political improvement. The Scottish powers were keen to keep BlackRock's problems in-house and not transfer them to London. No one wanted a military solution to what they believed was a police issue. McBride's call changed the landscape, but now it was too late.

He looked across at the young woman with messy hair who had taken up a chair nearby and was drinking strong black coffee. It was her third cup.

Slowly, he said, 'Air Traffic control picked up a signal over the island ten minutes ago.'

Lovelace sat up.

'It was brief, but something flew over the mountain.'

Lovelace stood up. 'That's that, then.' She declared. 'By the time anything is arranged, they'll be long gone. It's over.'

'But where will they go?' Swift asked doubtfully.

Lovelace opened her phone and selected an app. It was called "Ship Tracking." 'There are almost a hundred ships out at sea, safely in international waters, waiting for the storm to pass. The helicopter has a huge range. She could be headed for any one of them. Probably a Chinese or Russian-owned one. We'll never find them.'

Lovelace picked her coat off the back of her chair and made as if to leave. She turned at the door and said, 'there's nothing left for me to do here. I tried. Goodnight.'

With that, she turned and left.

***

Jack Lovelace stood at his cell door. It was time.

George, the poor dear girl, had fought for her life, but it had been futile. He had taken her like he had taken so many young women, and he relished the taste. He had missed that. He had missed that so very much.

He looked back into his cell and at the bloodied, naked body. She was too good for the others, so he had cut her throat just like he had cut Sinclair's. He held her while the life left her. It had been a kindness that he'd shown so many young women, the memories of which were beginning to fade with time.

Still, the future beckoned—a bright, new future.

The floor of A-Wing had calmed since the initial frenzy that had overtaken the prisoners. Many inmates had gone off searching for the men in the VP Wing, looking to enact some odd kind of justice on their person. There was no doubt a handful of dead prisoners somewhere, Jack thought.

Some had headed to the B-Wing in search of women, and some had raided the dispensary looking for quietness amid the noise. As he walked from A-Wing, he went largely unnoticed. He was just another prisoner with nowhere to go.

Jack chuckled as the familiar thud of a helicopter's rotors cut through the night air and rippled through the yard. He saw its landing lights first as they cut through the snowy skies. He lost sight of it as it came to land beyond the front gate.

He was almost at the front door when a figure stepped in his way. It was a young woman in a security uniform, and he usually wouldn't have given her much thought, yet the darkness that filled her eyes gave him cause for concern. She looked like a very determined young woman, and Jack suddenly felt his age.

'You need to get out of my way,' he said unconvincingly.

She held a truncheon by her side and a Taser in her other hand.

'Not a fucking chance,' she said and gripped her weapons harder.

'What are you doing, Maeve?' Zoe asked as she stepped through the doors and into the building. She had seen Maeve step up before her father, but Maeve hadn't seen her.

Maeve turned cautiously towards the voice behind her. She was confused. What the fuck was going on?

'What are you doing here?' She pleaded. She looked behind Zoe as Grace stepped in close. 'What's going on?'

'I need you to stand down, Maeve. This isn't your fight. You should be in a safe room by now. Protocol dictates that you should not attempt to retake control, isn't that right?'

Zoe had read the security protocols for BlackRock and had used them in her favour. It was the opportunity she was exploiting to get her father off the island. Maeve was a problem she hadn't expected.

'I can't do that.' Maeve said carefully.

'Listen to me, Maeve,' Zoe said. 'Don't make me go through you, please. I don't want to hurt you.' Zoe approached Maeve slowly until she was within arm's reach. She opened her arms out in a non-aggressive fashion and smiled warmly. 'Please, Maeve. Put your weapons down and go away.'

Maeve looked into Zoe's eyes, looking for some indication of her next move, but she had shut off her soul. There was nothing there. For the first time in her life, Maeve felt fear grip her.

Maeve relaxed her shoulders, and Zoe reached out and took the Taser from her. 'Go and find somewhere safe to hide, Maeve. You didn't see a thing.'

Maeve looked at Jack Lovelace and then at Grace. To Zoe, she said, 'I hope you know what you are doing.'

'I do, Maeve. I do.'

Twenty-Three

Reckoning

Jack Lovelace stood on the upper deck of a massive container ship as it cut its way around Ireland and towards the open seas.

The Sikorsky had done its job and ferried the three of them to the ship that lay in wait, far out in international waters. Jack stood in the freezing wind with a blanket around his shoulders and watched as a tall metal derrick swung out from the side of the ship and dropped the multi-million-pound aircraft into the welcoming embrace of the North Atlantic. It sat and bobbed on the surface for a short time before the icy waters clawed at the cabin, and its icy fingers dragged her below the surface.

He sensed her behind him and turned to face her. His daughter. His beautiful, clever daughter.

Then his expression changed. The confusion swept over his eyes and dulled his senses. He couldn't make it out. It couldn't be, could it?

Zoe Lovelace stood ten feet from her father and held an automatic pistol in her hands. She was facing her father, and the gun barrel never drifted an inch from the centre of his forehead.

'Zoe? What are you doing?'

'What I've been planning to do since the day you murdered my mother.' She said calmly.

'I don't understand,' Jack stuttered. 'What do you mean? You're my daughter. My little girl. We're the same person.'

Zoe laughed. 'So everybody thought. Mum, Lucy. And you. And you were all wrong. We're nothing alike, you and I.'

Jack felt a wave surge beneath the ship, and he shifted his balance on his feet.

Zoe continued. 'When we were little, I was a daddy's girl, and Lucy was very much a mother's little girl. I was more tom-boy and active, while she was more girly and played with dolls. I don't know what you saw in me. Maybe we are alike a little bit. Maybe there's more of you in me than I'd like to think. But I also have my mother in me. But you wouldn't let me get close to her. You divided us. You kept me to yourself. All I wanted was to be more like Lucy, to be loved by our mother, and showered with her attention. But all I got was yours; sometimes, it felt as though mum hated me. She could barely look at me sometimes. She rarely hugged me like she hugged Lucy. I wanted that. I wanted my mother. I wanted *her* love, not yours.

'It began to change as we grew older. I became a young woman before Lucy, and she changed with me. It was like she saw me for the first time. We started to develop a beautiful relationship, and then you stood before us one day and took her away. You killed our mother before us, and I have never forgiven you.'

'But Zoe...' Jack began, but Zoe shut him down.

'No. No more. It ends here today. When you took Lucy and me upstairs that day and poured gasoline all over the house, I prayed you'd light it. I wanted you to die for what you did. If I had to die to ensure you did, too, then so be it. I was prepared to sacrifice myself to watch you burn.

'But you were gutless. You didn't have it in you. You could rape and kill defenceless young women and our mother, but you couldn't kill yourself. You're pathetic. So I lit the fire, laid back down with you and Lucy, and waited to watch you burn.

317

'Once we were rescued and the fire was extinguished, I vowed that one day I would finish the job, and I've waited a long time for this day. Lucy always blamed me, of course, but she didn't know any better. You made everyone think that we were kindred spirits. That you and I were somehow the same person. That was never further from the truth. Uncle Mike took us to Japan to escape your legacy, but you can't run away from that kind of thing. It comes with you. So over the years, I've developed a strategy to bring me whatever I want. It's got me respect and wealth and power. And with that, it's allowed me to do what has driven me for all these years.

'To watch you die and to know who killed you and why.'

Zoe squeezed the trigger, and a single shot rang out. The sound disappeared into the night.

Jack Lovelace stood for the briefest of seconds before collapsing to the deck. Zoe walked up to where his body lay and fired three more shots into him. She handed the gun to a young man who approached from behind her.

'Throw this into the sea. Then throw him in after it and clean up the blood.'

The young Chinese man said something in Cantonese, and three more men appeared behind him.

Zoe opened a door nearby, stepped through it, and never looked back.

**

Lucy Lovelace stood at her hotel's window and looked across the Thames. Behind her, on the bed, were the remnants of the day's papers.

Jack Lovelace's dramatic escape from BlackRock largely dominated the news, but they were beginning to pick up ripples of interest in Sir Malcolm Lambert, who had recently retired from public life. Lovelace could sense a story developing there.

She heard her phone vibrate gently on her bedside table and answered it quickly. It was a withheld number. She answered it anyway.

'Hello.'

Silence.

'Hello?'

'Hello, Lucy.'

Zoe. She knew that voice anywhere.

'Hello, Zoe.' Lucy said.

'I wanted you to know that he's dead.'

'Who?'

'Dad. Dad's dead. I killed him.'

'You don't expect me to believe that, do you?' Lucy said quietly.

'No. But I've sent evidence.'

Lucy felt her phone vibrate as a message came through. She held her phone away from her face and opened the message. It was a short video, and she watched and listened to it while Zoe waited. The video ended as her father was tipped overboard.

'I don't expect you to understand. Not right away. But you will.'

'I don't know what to say....'

'You don't have to say anything. I didn't want you to go looking for something that didn't exist.'

'You need to stop, Zoe. You can't keep doing this sort of thing.'

'I was afraid you would say something like that, Lucy. Always the goody-two-shoes. You can't help yourself, can you?'

'It's wrong, Zoe.'

There was a long pause. Lucy heard Zoe sigh. 'I'm going to tell you this only once, Lucy. Please don't come looking for me. Let's part here. Get on with your life and forget about me, and I'll do the same with you.'

'And if I don't?' Lucy asked. 'What will you do then, Zoe?'

'Well then, one of us dies, Lucy. One of us dies.'

Lightning Source UK Ltd.
Milton Keynes UK
UKHW020939160223
417123UK00007B/935